EXILE

BOOK 7 BEYOND THE THAW

TAMAR SLOAN
HEIDI CATHERINE

SEQUEL HOUSE

LUCA

There were two men who spearheaded the search for the Falcon. Their vile faces rise up in Luca's mind as he maintains his steady rowing.

Vitron made up for his bald head with a dreadlock beard that reminded Luca of twisted snakes.

Gunnar was pale haired and pale eyed.

They were both rich—well, rich in terms of the poverty-stricken Outlands. And they rose to the top by stealing, raping, and murdering anyone who got in their way.

Luca never meant to take them on. He never meant for the Falcon to even exist.

All he was doing was trying to find his mother.

Conscious that he's started rowing faster again, Luca slows down. With the Newlands almost an hour behind him, he needs a plan. There are two things he needs to do in the Outlands.

End the vengeful search for the Falcon.

And tell Aspen's parents their son died trying to keep the Falcon alive.

One will involve blood. The other, tears.

"I can't say either of those sounds appealing," he mutters to himself.

When the canvas on the other end of the boat rustles, Luca freezes, the oars sticking out mid-air. There's not enough breeze to be moving the heavy material…

Tarquin pops her head through, grinning at him. "Why are you peeling anything?"

The oars splash back into the water. "Tarquin! What the Terra are you doing?"

She settles on the bench seat across from him, her wild hair pressed at a funny angle from having hid under the canvas. She rolls her eyes. "Coming with you, obviously."

"Like hell, you are."

Luca jams one oar deeper into the water. There's no way he's taking Tarquin to the Outlands.

The boat tips crazily as it starts to turn and Tarquin grabs the side. "What are you doing?"

"Taking you back to Alyx," Luca says resolutely. "Of all the foolhardy things to do, Tarquin, this one's the worst."

The canvas flings back and Luca's rendered motionless again. Somehow, his heart soars and plummets all at once.

Not believing what he's seeing, he watches Mercy unfold herself from where she must've been tucked up with Tarquin. Dusting herself off, she sits down beside her.

"I thought the same thing." Her gaze connects with Luca's. "But sometimes, a girl's gotta do what a girl's gotta do."

"Yeah," agrees Tarquin. "We ain't gonna be hepless—"

"Helpless," Mercy corrects with a smile.

"That's what I said. Hepless, vunderable—"

"Vulnerable."

Tarquin scowls. "Vunderable females. We're strong women—"

"Who are going straight back to the Newlands," Luca interjects, jamming the oars into the water.

Mercy crosses her arms. "We'll just hop straight back into the boat, no matter how many times you try to run. We're going with you, Luca."

Luca snaps his mouth shut. "You've got to be kidding me."

Tarquin grins as she makes a show of settling in. "Nope. We're going to go help the Falcon."

"Worst. Idea. Ever." Luca snaps off each word, glaring at the two females in his boat, knowing he's throwing one of Mercy's favorite sayings back at her.

"We don't think so," Mercy says as she combs her fingers through her tangled hair. "The Falcon needs our help. He just hasn't realized it yet."

Tarquin nods so hard her wild hair starts a movement all of its own.

"So, we stowed away and"—Mercy waves her arms out wide as if to encompass the ocean around them—"here we are."

Luca tucks the oars back in the boat. He needs a moment to think. He needs to figure out how to convince Mercy and Tarquin they should be back in the Newlands.

"How did you know I was leaving?" he asks, rubbing his temples.

"You're actually more predictable than you realize. When Tarquin came and found me and told me what she learned, she'd already figured out what you'd do next."

Tarquin scowls. "You left without saying goodbye last time."

"And it totally made sense." Mercy's gaze slips away. "It seems you like to kiss and run."

Luca winces. Kissing Alyx was the lowest thing he's done so far. He hated doing it, but he didn't regret it...until now.

Because it seems it didn't work.

"But that's a conversation for another time," she tells him. Mercy leans forward. "So, why are *you* going to the Outlands, Luca?"

Luca feels like his brows are almost touching his nose. "To stop any more Outlanders from getting to the Newlands."

As he says the words, Luca realizes that's another way he can help the Seekers. Help Askala. If the Newlanders are planning an invasion, then the fewer people they recruit to their army, the better.

Mercy angles her head. "That's the only reason?"

"Yes." Luca grits out the lie through clenched teeth. Why does Mercy have to be so stubborn? So...so shrewd!

A sweet smile lights up her face. "Great. That's also why we're going, too."

"And you had to bring Tarquin?"

She might be tough, but she's still a child.

For the first time, Mercy looks sheepish. "I actually tried to convince her to stay."

"But I told her I'd scream when you got in the boat if she didn't let me come," Tarquin says proudly.

Mercy's eyes fill with certainty. "And I knew you couldn't do this alone."

Luca doesn't know whether he should grab her and shake her. Or finally tell her how much he respects her courage and determination.

Even kissing the woman who sold him out didn't keep Mercy away.

Luca's head drops into his hands with a groan. He can't go back to the Newlands. If they cause a ruckus when he hits land, he could be taking these two straight into a bloodbath.

His own.

From the corner of his eye, he sees Tarquin lean over toward Mercy. "He's realizing, isn't he?"

"He's a smart guy," Mercy murmurs back. "It was only a matter of time."

Yes, Luca's realizing he has no choice but to take them with him.

He picks up the oars and angles the boat in the direction of the Outlands.

He glares at Mercy and Tarquin. "Under one condition."

They look at him, waiting.

"There's no talk of helping the Falcon. Too many people want him dead."

The whole idea of leaving on his own was so no one could be associated with his alter ego—the Outlands' most wanted guy.

They glance at each other, then nod in unison. But even as they agree, Luca knows he's looking at two females who have never blindly followed orders.

Sweet Terra, how is he going to keep them safe?

With a sigh, he starts rowing again.

At least Luca now has a plan. There's no way he can go after Vitron and Gunnar. Not yet.

First things first.

They're going to Fairbanks.

HAWK

The world has a gaping Sam-sized hole in it everywhere Hawk looks. She doesn't love him. Well, not in the way Hawk wants her to. Not in the way he loves her.

How could that kiss have meant nothing to her? He'd been so sure she'd felt the same tsunami of emotions he had. Fireworks. Magic. Bliss.

But it seems not.

That kiss made her realize they're no more than *best friends.*

He's never wanted to be anyone's best friend less in his life.

"Hawk!" hisses Gust from the other side of the shelter. "You're doing it again."

"What?" Hawk tries to shift position, but his ribs won't allow it.

"You're talking in your sleep." Gust huffs in the darkness.

Hawk manages to turn over just a little bit. "But I wasn't asleep."

"Then you were talking to yourself," says Gust. "Unless you were asking me to be your best friend."

"You actually are my best friend on this island right now."

Hawk shakes his head. If that statement weren't so sad it might even be funny.

It's just Hawk and Gust left in the Newlands now. The last two Seekers standing.

Luca and Mercy left him without even saying goodbye. Well, that's only half true. Mercy had tried her best to say goodbye without using those actual words. It's so obvious now that she'd been up to something the last time he'd seen her, but he'd been too caught up in thinking about Sam to pay much attention. The way she'd fussed over him, making sure he had everything he needed within reach. The words she'd said, letting him know that she loves him. The instructions she'd given Gust about exactly what care he needs to heal properly.

Not that Gust had been listening. Although, Hawk has to admit he's done a good enough job since they'd been left alone. Bringing him water and any food scraps he's been able to scavenge. Helping him to walk to the tree line when biology demands. Putting up with him groan and moan and talk in his sleep as he's tried to process what's happened here.

Sam left with Ekon for Askala.

Siena and Nikita are dead.

Mercy and Luca have vanished into thin air. He can only assume they've gone after Sam. But why wouldn't Mercy have told him that? It's not like he would've tried to stop her.

Whatever the case, he's happy for Mercy. She's with the guy she loves. And he must love her back if they've run off together. They're no longer cousins. Or *best friends*.

Hawk grits his teeth.

"Can you stop that?" asks Gust. "It sounds like you're breathing out of your ears."

"Sorry." Hawk rolls his eyes in the dark. "I'll try not to breathe."

"Gee! Defensive much?" There's the sound of Gust rolling

over on the pile of leaves that make up his mattress. "You know there's still one more boat left on the beach, don't you?"

"Are you suggesting I leave?" Hawk props himself up on his elbows, pleased to see this is a movement he can manage at last. It seems he's getting some of his mobility back.

"I'm suggesting we both leave," Gust hisses back in a failed whisper. "Let's get the sweet Terra out of here before we get killed."

"You can go if you like," says Hawk. "But I'm staying here. I'm going to finish what we came here to do."

"I'll never make it back on my own," sighs Gust. "What if a leatherskin tries to get me?"

"Don't worry. I'm sure it would spit you right out again the moment it tasted you." Hawk smiles at his own joke.

Gust lets out a strangled moan. "I know you all hate me. Don't think I don't realize it."

"We don't hate you," says Hawk, a wave of shame washing over him. "We just don't always see eye-to-eye."

"It wasn't easy for me in the Proving," Gust continues. "None of you were going to give me any tokens. That's why I had to take them. I wasn't trying to upset you. It's just that...well, I have dreams of my own, too. And sometimes you have to do whatever it takes to reach those dreams."

Thoughts of Hawk's mom filter into his mind. She'd told him she felt much the same in her own Proving. That nobody liked her. That everyone thought of her as Felicia, the annoying pest. It had been a really difficult time for her. Maybe he's been too hard on Gust? But then he remembers the way Gust abandoned his own brother when he was bitten by the snake, and his sympathy for him quickly vanishes.

"I know what you're thinking," says Gust. "You're thinking about Bryan."

"Sprung," says Hawk, seeing no reason to deny it. "I don't

understand how you could be more interested in stealing tokens than your own brother's death. It was so callous."

"Things aren't always how they look." Gust crawls closer as the first rays of morning light filter through the trees. "I was devastated by Bryan's death. But we had a pact."

Hawk stays perfectly still, waiting for Gust to explain the impossible. Nothing can excuse the way he behaved.

"Bryan and I knew there was a chance one of us wouldn't make it as a Seeker. Either by not getting enough tokens or... worse. We agreed we'd do whatever it took to make sure one of us got through. You're not the only one with ambition, you know. We wanted to make our parents proud. Put our family on the map by adding something to this world. To our future."

Hawk has to admit he's a little surprised by this. He'd never really stopped to think about why Gust wanted to be a Seeker, having just assumed it was for some selfish reason. But to even be in the running to be a Seeker, Gust had to have passed his original Proving—a process that judged him to be both smart *and* kind. Could he have this guy all wrong?

"When Bryan got bitten by the snake, I knew I had to act," says Gust. "I didn't have much time. I took Mercy's tokens from her pocket. It was the only way I was going to get through. How could I have gone home and looked my parents in the face knowing Bryan's death was for nothing? I did it for them. I did it for Bryan."

"I'm sorry, Gust." Hawk tries to sit up, finding he can manage it without too much pain. "You're right. I did judge you. And not in a good way. We all did. I wish you'd told the other Seekers what you just told me."

"I'm annoying," says Gust. "I know that. I can't help it. I just have a different sense of humor to the rest of you. But I'm not a bad person."

Hawk's thoughts return to his mom, and he misses her with

a sharp pang. This is exactly what she's said about herself. He needs to start giving Gust more of a chance.

"I really am sorry." Hawk squints at Gust in the dim light. "And I'm grateful for everything you've been doing for me since the others left. How about we start fresh?"

"I'd like that," says Gust. "And I appreciate your apology."

"I'd give you a brug if my ribs didn't hurt so much."

"What's a brug?" asks Gust.

"A bro hug," Hawk smiles. "It's what my uncle Dex calls the hugs Kian gives him."

"You sure it's not Dex hugging Kian?" asks Gust. "Kian's pretty good looking for an old dude."

Hawk's smile morphs into a laugh. "Maybe it's a bit of both."

"In any case, I think I'll say no thanks to the brug." Gust holds up his palms. "I wouldn't have said no to one from Mercy, though, if she hadn't been so busy chasing after Luca."

"It wouldn't be a brug if Mercy gave it to you." Hawk tries to stop himself from rolling his eyes again. "It would just be a hug."

"Oh yeah!" Gust slaps himself on his forehead. "Wonder where she is? Mercy, I mean. And Luca. It's pretty poor form for them to skip out on us like that."

"Not really," says Hawk. "You just said it yourself… things aren't always how they look. We don't know what their reasons were but I'm sure they had our best interests in mind."

"Glad you're so confident." Gust pulls himself to his feet. "Nature calls. You need to go, too?"

"I'm okay," says Hawk. "I think I might try walking on my own today. I'm feeling a little better."

"Thank goodness." Gust steps out of the hut. "I need someone to help me finish putting up the walls on this thing. I've practically had to build the whole thing myself."

Hawk shakes his head as he watches Gust walk away. He might understand him a whole lot better after that talk, but he still can't say Gust would be his number one choice of companion out here.

Still, he's all he has right now.

Pushing away thoughts of Sam, Hawk sees the familiar shape of Grace walking toward him. He's managed to avoid her since their last chat. The one where she made it abundantly clear what she wants from him. Which is everything he doesn't want to give.

Using the early morning light as his shield, he shuffles back to lean on one of the posts in the hut, placing his hands over his chest and pulling his face into an expression of pain.

"Hawk." Grace slips into the hut and sits down beside him. "When are you going to finish the walls on this thing?"

"I'm still recovering," he tells her, wincing for effect. It's only half an act, really. He is still very sore. "The walls will have to wait."

"I was thinking you might like to go for a walk with me." Her voice is soft. Seductive. Made worse when she shuffles over closer to Hawk. Her hair's been pulled back and she tilts her head, biting down on her lip. He's not sure if her beauty makes this situation better or worse.

"I'd love to go for a walk," says Hawk, hating the way these words bring light to Grace's eyes. "But I can barely sit up, let alone walk."

"I'm sorry," she says, taking his hand. "I'm making you uncomfortable. It's just that—"

"I remind you of someone," he finishes. "You told me. The guy you were in love with when you were my age."

Grace's eyes well with tears. "I miss him so much. He was so brave, always looking out for the people he cared about. Just like I've seen you do with Sam. And Mercy. He was the best person I ever met."

"Where is he now?" Hawk asks, not sure if he should delve into this.

Grace shrugs. "He could be anywhere. Dead, most likely. But when I'm with you, I can almost pretend it's him. That he's here with me, keeping me safe."

"But I'm not him," says Hawk. "Nobody can replace the one your heart truly belongs to."

"You know, I thought Sam was the clever one." Grace pulls back her shoulders. "But she's not so clever to leave you behind. I bet she's not moping around Askala thinking about you. Not with a handsome guy like Ekon to distract her."

A sick feeling punches Hawk in the gut. Surely, not Sam and Ekon? But there's no denying Ekon was the one Sam chose to take her home.

"I thought we could help each other mend our broken hearts." Grace smiles at him. "But I can see you're not ready."

"I just need time," he says, wondering how long he can hold her off. He knows at some stage he's going to have to make a decision here. There's no way he can string her along forever. "Please, just give me some time to get better."

Grace gets to her feet and smiles down at him. "Okay. But not too much time."

"Stay and talk to me." He reaches up a hand. She'd said there are secrets to tell him. Maybe it's possible she'll let some of them slip before he has to do what he's somehow promised.

And maybe the sky will turn green.

"I have things to do." Grace steps from the hut. "I'll see you later on."

Strangely she didn't seem to have any urgent things to do when she'd thought there was the possibility he'd go for a walk with her.

Hawk withdraws his hand and nods. "See you later."

Gust appears out of nowhere and flops back down on his bed of leaves. "What's your secret?"

Hawk's brows spike. "I don't have any secrets from you. It's her secrets we need to get."

"I mean what's your secret with the women." Gust sighs. "They all trip over themselves to get to you. Grace. Nikita... well, before, you know... And Sam."

"Not Sam," says Hawk. "We're *best friends.*"

Gust chokes on something. "Best friends, my ass. You'd have to be blind not to notice the way she started looking at you after we came here."

"You've got it all wrong," says Hawk. "She told me herself that she doesn't feel that way."

Gust springs to his knees and bats his eyelashes dramatically. "Oh Hawk," he says in an unnaturally high voice. "You're so big and strong. Protect me, Hawk!"

"Okay, for one thing, that sounds nothing like Sam." Hawk glares at Gust. "And she never said that."

"She didn't have to." Gust slumps back down on his bed. "We could all see it."

"Yeah, well a wise man once told me that things aren't always how they look." Hawk crosses his arms, then uncrosses them when it puts too much strain on his bruised chest. "Sam told me she doesn't feel that way just before she left."

Gust makes a noise that Hawk can't interpret.

"Just say it," Hawk demands. "Whatever it is, I can take it."

"I know you don't think I'm very smart," says Gust. "But Sam didn't tell you that because it's the truth. She said that so you didn't try to follow her."

Hawk shakes his head. Sam wouldn't lie to him. She doesn't even know how to lie. It's not in her DNA. Gust has got it all wrong.

Or has he?

Hawk lies back down and turns his back to Gust. Talking never works out for him. He really should go back to being silent.

It's not just this hut that needs some walls. Hawk has to start

13

building a few of his own. Starting with one that goes all the way around his heart.

SAM

*S*am's only been back one night, but just like she remembered it, Askala is every shade of life. A pulsing, breathing kaleidoscope that draws her into its bosom.

As she makes her way back through the forest, Sam brushes her hand over the trunk of a *Pinus rhizophores*. So much bigger and older than the ones that have found a home in the Newlands.

Probably far bigger than those trees will ever get to grow to.

She stops at the tree line, taking in the sprawling community that raised her. The sun has just inched over the horizon, its warm light bathing the huts as people start to come out. They breathe in deeply, their smiles drawn up from the bottom of their grateful hearts.

Sam already knew her people did this. She used to make a conscious effort to do it herself. But since returning from the Newlands two days ago, she's noticed it so much more. The smiles. The love.

The peace.

And yet, she no longer feels a part of it. Almost like...an outsider.

Shoving away the thought that almost feels like a betrayal, Sam tucks the basket of herbs she's carrying further up her arm as she makes her way to the path. She wanted to get all this together before Seb was up. He barely has any appetite as it is. Maybe if she gets to him first thing, he'll be more likely to drink the tea she'll make from these immune boosting leaves and roots.

Her parents didn't exaggerate. Seb's far sicker than she could've imagined. He's always been pale, but now, it's like color has never inhabited his body. He's always been weak, but now, he hasn't been out of bed in weeks.

People greet her as she walks past. Avis and Thea as they pick chamomile from their front garden. Aarov as he carves intricate vines into his walking stick. Little Dove as she waves frantically from her window.

Sam tucks her head down as if she didn't notice her. Hawk's family had been the hardest to see again. Phoenix with his copper hair that hurts to look at. Flick and her curls that are so achingly familiar. His brood of sisters all asking after him.

And if it wasn't hard enough to hear his name, it was being unable to tell them what they needed to hear. How she wanted to tell them Hawk's doing great. That being a Seeker is everything he thought it would be. That he's happy.

Sam winces, walking a little faster like she can escape the bad taste in her mouth. Right now, Hawk has a broken body and a broken heart. And she caused both.

Because she mistook her naivety for optimism. And her foolishness for bravery.

Their hut is quiet as Sam stops just inside the door. Her mother is sitting at the table in the center of the room, her father leaning over as they scan the book in front of them. "Anything?" he asks.

Sam already knows the answer before her mother responds.

It's in the heaviness of her shoulders, the downturn of her mouth. "Nothing."

They've been reviewing any medical or health texts they can get hold of. Looking for answers. Looking for a solution that will save Seb.

Her mother clasps her father's hand as it rests on her shoulder. "But we'll find something."

Sam looks away, knowing that's exactly what she would've said only a few days ago.

Her parents look up, the movement alerting them she's here. Her mother's face fills with a smile. "Good morning, Sam."

Sam will never forget their joy when they'd seen her walking up the path. Her mother had cried. Her father had choked her name out over and over again as he'd held her. She didn't have the heart to tell them that she didn't choose to be here.

"Hey, Mom." Sam lifts the basket to show her parents. "I've brought these for Seb."

Gratitude floods her face. "He's been having elderberry tincture along with as much echinacea tea as we could get into him."

Sam nods. Both great immune stimulating herbs. "I found some *Astragalus*. It's more of an immunomodulator, which has a balancing effect on the immune system." For some reason Sam can't hold their gaze. "They're more appropriate in autoimmune conditions."

Her mother frowns. "You think that's what this is?"

"I have no idea what this is," Sam says quietly, refusing to give her parents false hope.

"Either way, we're glad you're back," her father says warmly. "We knew you'd have something else we could try."

"Well, it seems I wasn't cut out to be a Seeker."

Her mother rises so she can embrace her. "You wanted to help, and that's admirable."

Sam pulls away, trying not to wince. Everyone saw that she

didn't have what it takes. How could she have been so blind? All she ended up doing was hurting those she loves most.

Passing her mother the basket of herbs, Sam heads to the bedroom, stopping when she hears the sound of voices drifting out.

Seb's awake and chatting? Sam rushes forward with excitement. He must be feeling better!

But Sam comes to a halt in the doorway. Seb's lying in bed, his face as pale as the sheets, his eyes closed. Charity is sitting beside him, chattering away quietly.

"Charity?" Sam asks in surprise.

The girl looks up, a smile already alive on her face. "Oh, hey Sam."

Seb's eyes fly open as he turns his head toward the door. "Sam?" he rasps out, his chalk-colored lips tipping up.

Sam's by his side in a blink, crouching down beside the bed. "Hey, Seb. I went and got you some herbs."

"Thanks, sis." He pauses to catch his breath. "I'll have them later. I've already...had breakfast."

That's when Sam notices the bowl of broth Charity's holding in her lap. She smiles apologetically. "I bring it to him every morning." She turns to Seb. "I'm still waiting to win back my title in rocks."

Rocks. The game Seb loves to play, mostly because he could actually win. There's no running, no feats of strength needed. Just his sharp mind and quick hands.

Seb's lips twitch as his eyes flutter closed. "I'm faking it...so you can't win."

Sam's heart aches as his fragile body relaxes and he falls asleep again. Seb wouldn't have been awake for very long. And yet he already looks exhausted.

Charity stands, placing the bowl on a nearby table. "He's eating less and less. That's why I try to get in as early as I can."

"Thank you, Charity." Sam tries to keep the strange resentment that's bubbling up out of her voice. "You're taking wonderful care of him."

Charity flushes. "Seb was the one who showed me around Askala. He's the smartest person I've ever met! He took me into the forest and showed me where to find plants we can eat, all about how everything is dependent on everything else to survive." She looks warmly at Sam. "He told me you taught him everything he knows."

Sam strokes Seb's hair back from his forehead, noting his skin is cool and clammy despite the warm air. "My father said we were both sponges when it came to knowledge."

Sam thought her role was to share it. She was wrong. She should've been here, using it to help those who valued knowledge.

Charity comes to stand behind Sam. "Your parents have tried anything they can think of to make him better. In the Outlands, Seb would've…"

Sam doesn't look up. She already knows what Charity was going to say. Seb would've been left for dead.

She lifts her hand away as it tightens into a fist. "Well, I'm glad you got to see there's another way to live."

"Askala has welcomed me with open arms."

There's a hitch in Charity's voice but suddenly Sam pushes to her feet as an idea strikes her. "Gentian! That's what we need. Its active ingredients increase appetite by stimulating the production of saliva, gastric acids and bile."

Charity draws back in surprise. "That sounds like a great idea."

Sam's about to say she'll go find some now when her mother appears in the doorway. "It's almost time."

Her whole body stilling, Sam nods curtly. "Okay."

She's deliberately not letting herself think about what's been scheduled for this morning. A meeting of the leaders. So she can report on the Newlands.

Where she'll have to relive all her failures.

Her mother turns to Charity. "Do you mind staying with Seb?"

"Of course, Nova." Charity smiles warmly. "I'll try and get more broth into him if he wakes."

Seb's slack face doesn't look like he'll be waking anytime soon. Sam presses a kiss to his forehead. "I won't be long and then I think we get you out for some sunshine," she whispers.

Seb doesn't stir as Sam walks out, her heart heavy in her chest. If she can't make him better, then she's failed all over again.

Her parents are waiting by the door and they all make their way to the table that's waiting for them under the canopy. Birds sing in the sunshine, the scent of green and earth is everywhere.

Sam trails behind her parents, trying to find the comfort and serenity she always did. If something troubled Sam, all she had to do was wander the paths of Askala. Within minutes, she'd reconnect with the beauty unity can create. She'd remember that her ancestors built this. She'd realize that she was walking through undeniable proof she was part of something bigger.

For a little while, she thought her role was to take this and let it touch others. Sam scuffs her foot on the path only to find herself pitching forward. Her father quickly catches her, the movement almost as instinctive as Hawk's used to be. Her mouth twists. The evidence was there all along. She's as uncoordinated as she is naïve—she should never have become a Seeker.

And yet the peace that Askala always sparked seems out of reach, too...

Her parents take their usual seats at the large, timber table and her mother taps the space beside her, eyes shining with pride. Sam imagined herself sitting next to them around the leaders' table countless times. It was a dream she couldn't wait to come true.

But as she sits, Sam finds there's no joy. No sense of... belonging.

Hushed voices filter into her consciousness, and as Sam looks up, she realizes she was so caught up in her thoughts that she hadn't noticed how full the space around them is. It seems everyone turned out for this leaders' meeting. The leaders are all there, but so are the other people of Askala. Sam swallows when she sees Phoenix and Flick with their daughters. How much of the truth are they going to find out?

Her father stands, lifting his hands although the place falls silent without the prompt. "Thank you for coming, my friends. As you all know, our daughter, Sam, returned home yesterday." Her father beams at her and Sam can feel every smiling face turn in her direction. "Seeing her walking toward me was one of the most wonderful sights I've ever seen." He turns back to his peers. "But she also brings us news."

Sam nods as her father sits down, knowing this is her cue to speak. She stands on shaky legs, holding onto the table for support. "The Seekers' visit started well. The Newlanders didn't welcome us, but they allowed us to stay not far from the village. We helped them by digging wells and starting a garden with the seeds you sent. We began showing them how to breed hares and pods for food."

Several of the leaders nod, satisfaction stamped across their faces. Except for Wren. She's watching Sam with an intensity that says she knows there's more.

And it's not good.

"It was just what the Newlanders wanted." Sam scans the faces around her. "Because their plan is to make themselves strong."

"What for?" Wren asks quietly.

Sam can't hold her gaze. "We're not sure. They told us they want to expand."

"Of course, they do." Wren grips Dex's hand, her face filled with inevitability.

Dex squeezes reassuringly. "We don't know for sure they're a threat."

Sam looks up again. "Outlanders arrived not long after we did and killed Siena...with a flamethrower." A collective gasp circles the table. "Hawk and Luca were injured trying to save her. The day I left, the Commander's son, Raiden, demanded I marry him to unite Askala and the Newlands. Nikita was killed as a warning if I refused."

Her mother gasps. "Of course, you refused."

Sam looks away. It's why she came back. So she didn't make things worse.

Nikita's mother, one of the leaders, is staring straight ahead, glassy-eyed. She and Siena's parents were both told of the news not long after Sam's boat scraped across Askala's sand. Sam glances around, registering that Siena's parents aren't here.

It seems they couldn't face hearing about her death again.

Drawing in a shaky breath, she continues. "Hawk had barely recovered when he was tricked into fighting in one of their Tournaments. He was beaten quite badly."

Flick's cry is muffled as she buries her head in Phoenix's chest. His powerful arms come around her as he whispers into her hair.

Sam snaps her gaze away, unable to look at the pain that's too similar to her own. "Violence is entrenched in the Newlands. Whatever they plan, they will do it with brutality and bloodshed."

Sam sits, her knees finally giving out. Somehow, each of those tragedies feels like they were her fault. As a Seeker, she was supposed to bring peace, not death.

Zali shoots to her feet. "Askala is in danger! They're going to attack us!"

Sam's father raises a placating hand. "We don't know that for sure, and we've made the message clear that anyone is welcome to share in what Askala has."

Sam stares down at her hands. That's what she told Raiden…

Just before he impaled Nikita with his spear.

Dex nods. "And the construction of the boat is further along than we expected."

Sam's startled gaze shoots to her uncle. Boat? What boat?

He must notice because he watches Sam as he explains. "After the Seekers left, we realized we needed to be able to ensure the safety of our vulnerable if an attack should happen. We commenced building a boat—more of a ship, really—that will allow anyone who cannot defend Askala to escape."

Sam nods slowly, trying to absorb what she just heard. Askala is building a boat. A ship.

So they can flee.

Jagger's hands are fists on the table. "We cannot sit here and wait. We need to stop this before it starts."

"What are you suggesting, Jagger?" Sam's father asks tersely.

Jagger scans every face around the table. "Askala must be ready for war. We must fight, not wait and defend."

The people of Askala shift and mutter. As Flick tucks herself further into Phoenix's arms, Sam sees a sharp movement behind her. Charity slips behind the trunk of a *Picea* tree and doesn't come back out.

Sam frowns. Charity was supposed to be with Seb. It seems she wanted to hear the outcome of this meeting more than she admitted.

"Why?" Zali demands. "What do you know that we don't?"

"That everyone here will be killed if we don't fight this," states Jagger flatly.

Zali draws back, her eyes wide with fear. "Because that's what they've told you?"

Wren shoots to her feet, planting her hands on the table as she glares at Zali. "Jagger doesn't even have a necklace with the pendant to be able to communicate with the Outlands." She jerks her own pale disc out of the neckline of her shirt. "I do, though. Did you want to accuse me of being a traitor, too?"

Zali visibly withdraws. "I wasn't suggesting he's a traitor." Her gaze slides away. "Just that he seems very sure an attack is imminent."

"Because he's one of the few people here who know what the Outlanders are capable of," Wren snaps.

Silence reigns again, broken only by shuffling of feet as people move closer to their loved ones. A sense of threat hangs heavy in the air.

"Unless Sam marries Raiden…" It's Avis's soft voice that feels like a whip cracking through the air, making Sam wince.

"No!" Sam's father's denial is instantaneous. "We do not use women as collateral here in Askala."

Avis nods, compassion stamped across her features. She was once the wife of the Commander. The same man who brutally and callously scarred her. "Of course."

Sam's father stands. "Askala is a peaceful society. We will not meet violence with violence. Construction of the ship will be hastened so we can care for our most vulnerable. Everyone must stay vigilant. Meeting adjourned."

The people around Sam disperse quietly, gazes averted. She wonders if they're as confused as she is. Everyone here believes in the power of kindness and compassion. The paradise they live in is a testament to what it can achieve.

But Sam tried to be kind and compassionate in the Newlands.

And people died.

As several people make their way toward Sam and her parents, she quietly slips away. She doesn't have the right to be part of this decision making. Thinking she had all the answers is what got her in trouble in the first place.

And yet the people of Askala are looking to her father for

leadership... And her father is carrying the responsibility... Sam shakes her head, realizing her naivety ran deeper than even she was aware.

As she makes her way back to their hut, Sam finds herself detouring toward the beach. She's been drawn to the edge of the ocean since the moment she arrived. It's like even those few feet mean she's closer to Hawk.

Here, on the west end, though, is where they're building the ship. Sam stops as she takes in the timber skeleton. Dex was right, it's far more a ship than a boat. Curved lengths of wood spear high like the ribs of some massive beast. Planks of timber are piled beside it, waiting to encase them like skin. Like a giant hand, this vessel will cup the people of Askala and carry them to safety.

Sam turns around, knowing she needs to get back to Seb. Making him better is her only goal right now. It's all she'll allow herself to think about.

Because, the truth is, she no longer feels like she belongs in Askala.

Her heart is with Hawk. Tied to the dream of being a Seeker.

And yet, Sam can never go back.

MERCY

"When are we going to get there?" Tarquin asks for what feels like the hundredth time in the space of as many minutes.

"You wanted to come," Mercy reminds her.

Tarquin shoots Mercy a smile from her position on Luca's back. "I didn't know it was going to take so long."

"Should we take you back?" asks Luca, jiggling Tarquin into a more comfortable position.

Tarquin shakes her head furiously. "I'm fine, thank you."

Mercy laughs. She can't really blame Tarquin for being impatient. It's been a long journey. Made worse by the fact that Tarquin's ankle is sore from when she twisted it in the Newlands doing a somersault.

Back in a time when Mercy had thought life was complicated, but it was actually extremely simple.

Because when she decided to hide on the boat Luca was taking to the Outlands, life stepped up to a whole new level of messy. She hadn't even really stopped to think the whole thing through, which was foolish. All she'd known was that there was no way in this world that she was going to let Luca run away from her *again.*

In an ideal world, she wouldn't have brought Tarquin with her but that small determined girl hadn't exactly given her much choice. She'd threatened to scream, and Mercy knows her well enough by now to believe her.

It was either the both of them go, or neither of them.

Tarquin rests her head on Luca's shoulder and closes her eyes.

"Would you like me to carry her for a bit?" asks Mercy.

Luca shakes his head. "She's not heavy."

Mercy shifts the bag of supplies on her shoulders. They've been walking since sunrise, heading for Fairbanks. It's hard to believe after hearing her grandmother talk about Fairbanks so often that Mercy's finally going to see it with her own eyes. She'd always imagined if she ever made it there, Avis would be the one to show her.

Not Luca and his annoyingly handsome face.

"Do you think Alyx will be worried about Tarquin?" Mercy asks, almost certain Tarquin's fallen asleep given how unusually quiet she's gone.

"Of course." Luca rolls his eyes. "Alyx is her sister."

"But she must've figured out that Tarquin's with us." Mercy rolls her eyes straight back at him.

Luca ignores her. "All the more reason for her to worry."

"Why? Because you're the Falcon?" Mercy asks, letting Luca know she's very aware of exactly who he is.

"Did Tarquin tell you that?" He lets out a long sigh.

Mercy nods. "She was pretty upset about it."

"I thought she'd be happy the Falcon's alive."

"You lied to me," comes Tarquin's sleepy reply. "Alyx said we could trust you. But you lied."

"Go to sleep," Luca says gently. "You can trust me. I promise."

Tarquin nestles in closer, wrapping her arms around Luca's neck in a way that makes Mercy's ovaries hurt.

Damn that Luca! Finding out he's the Falcon hasn't helped at all in distancing her heart from him. Because now he has that face *and* he fights off bullies to protect the weak.

Which goes way beyond just being heroic.

It's…hot!

Mercy fans her face, trying to push down the blush that's creeping up her neck. Luca's treated her so poorly, yet she just can't seem to move on. It's no wonder why.

They walk on and the sound of Tarquin's gentle snore soon becomes the background noise to this barren land. There are no birds singing. No leaves moving in the breeze. No sound of twigs snapping under their feet.

It's just mile after mile of nothingness. Actually, that's not true. There's dirt. A few rocks. Some flies. And plenty of sun. Way too much sun. Mercy hadn't realized how much protection the trees in Askala give them from the elements. It seems impossible that anybody could actually survive out here. It's no wonder they're so desperate for a better life. One that could be given to them if only they considered another way.

"Is it like what you imagined?" Luca asks, noticing the unimpressed look on Mercy's face.

"It's worse." She stumbles on a rock, which makes her think of Sam. Her cousin who didn't tell her she was returning home. Although, she was staring down the barrel of having to marry Raiden, Mercy supposes. Not exactly an appealing thought…

"We're almost there," Luca says.

"How can you tell? Everything looks the same."

"Look at the horizon." He points ahead. "See the tops of the buildings starting to appear? And notice how the dirt is more compacted? This used to be a road."

Mercy squints, pleased to see he's right. She's not sure how much longer she can walk. Her feet are swollen and pinching in her shoes, her back aching from carrying the supplies, and her skin is smarting from sunburn.

"Are you sure we'll be safe in Fairbanks?" she asks.

Luca shakes his head. "Nobody can be sure of anything in the Outlands. But you'll be safer there than any of the villages."

They'd passed a few villages, although not close enough for Mercy to get a good look. Which is fine with her. From what she could see, they hadn't exactly looked inviting with their falling down huts that screamed of hunger and misery.

"I think I'm going to sleep for three days when I finally get a chance to lie down," she says. "So, you'd better not be lying to me."

"Don't tell me you don't trust me either." Luca twists his head to try to see Tarquin on his back. "It's bad enough with the serve this one gave me."

"She trusts you," says Mercy. "It was just a shock for her to find out that her idol and her hero were the same person."

"Doesn't mean she shouldn't trust me." Luca lowers his voice, and Mercy can only hope that Tarquin really is asleep. "It's her sister who can't be trusted."

Mercy's brows hike to the sky. "It didn't look like that when you had your tongue down her throat. You looked like you were trusting her just fine."

Luca stops walking to turn to Mercy. "You don't get it, do you?"

"Get what?" Mercy frowns as she tries to work out what she missed.

"I was trying to scare you away." His dark eyes zone in on Mercy and she feels the familiar tightening of her belly whenever she looks at him.

"Now *that* I didn't miss," she says. "You've been trying to scare me away ever since I could walk."

"Mercy." He says her name like he really wants her to listen, not realizing she already pays attention to every word he says. "I was trying to protect you. Alyx sold me out. She took a reward in exchange for telling the Commander that I'm the Falcon. A big reward."

Mercy's jaw falls slack and her hand flies to her lips. "She didn't."

"She did." Luca scowls deeply. "That's why I had to run. Before they came looking for me. And anyone who means anything to me."

Now Mercy's shocked for a whole new reason. Is it really possible that Luca is telling the truth? That he kissed Alyx to protect Mercy?

"Well, I hate to be the one to have to point out the obvious," she says. "But your plan sucked. It also failed. Quite abysmally, in fact, because here I am."

"And that's why we have to make this right." Luca starts walking again and Mercy shuffles to catch up to him.

The shapes on the horizon grow with each step they take and soon the skyline is filled with the jagged forms of crumbling buildings. Not one of them seems to have survived the hardship of time. Some have collapsed onto the buildings beside it. Others seem to be held together by the tangle of vines climbing up their sides as nature tries its best to reclaim the city.

"What's that?" asks Mercy, pointing at a large rusted object by the side of the road.

"It's a car," says Luca.

"Oh." Mercy's heard of cars, of course. But this is the first one she's seen. It's hard to piece together that rusted skeleton with the shiny photos she's seen. She wonders what it must've felt like to ride in one of them. Sam says they could cover a hundred miles in an hour. It seems impossible to believe that heavy hunk of junk could ever have moved faster than a slug.

Scanning the buildings as they walk deeper into the city, Mercy knows what she's looking for...The building Avis described to her so many times she almost feels like she's already been there.

"It's right there." Luca points ahead, knowing exactly what her eyes are seeking.

She follows his finger.

And she sees it.

Her grandmother's former home. The place Avis established as a refuge for all the imperfectly perfect people the Outlands rejected.

There's no mistaking the towering mangrove pine that's growing right out the top of the fallen slabs of concrete. So many branches have found their way out that it almost looks like the building is growing out of the tree instead of the other way around.

Mercy knows this whole city is called Fairbanks, but to her it's all about this building. This is Fairbanks. And she can't wait to get inside.

"Wake up, Tarquin." Luca slides Tarquin to his front and sets her down on her feet. "We're here."

"Why didn't you wake me?" she complains, rubbing her eyes.

"I did wake you." Luca ruffles her hair. "You're awake, aren't you?"

"Is that the beam that used to be the entrance?" Mercy asks, pointing at a large piece of steel lying across the ground.

Luca nods. "It used to stretch right up into the sky. I loved running up it as a boy and diving off."

Mercy's extremely glad to have been told earlier that this isn't the way they gain access to the underground colony now. She might have conquered her fear of heights when it comes to climbing a tree, but diving off the end of a tall beam with nothing but blind faith to catch her is a whole new level. There's no way she could do that.

A boy appears out of the rubble, almost like he'd risen from it. Mercy blinks at him, taking in his torn clothes and skinny frame. His hair is so blond, it's white. A stark contrast to his dirty face.

Tarquin's eyes light up at the sight of someone her own age and Mercy's heart breaks to think how lonely she must've been in the Newlands.

"Luca!" The boy smiles as he picks his way across the rubble toward them.

"Hey, Relic." Luca holds out a hand and the boy slams his palm on Luca's, smiling at the loud sound it makes.

"Mom and Dad have been waiting for you to return." Relic pulls at his tangled hair. "Have you got news?"

"Let me talk to your parents about that," says Luca with a strained look sweeping across his face.

Tarquin steps forward and smiles at the boy. "Hello."

"Who are you?" Relic's eyes are wide as he stares at Tarquin. "I've never seen you before."

"These are friends of mine," says Luca. "This is Mercy, and this is Tarquin. Why don't you two run ahead and let the others know I'm back?"

Tarquin nods her head wildly and Relic reaches for her hand, takes it and they disappear into the rubble.

"Her ankle looks magically better," says Luca, shaking his head. "Little scamp."

"Where did they go?" Mercy cranes her neck. "I can't see them."

"It wouldn't be much of a secret entrance if you could see it." Luca reaches for the bag of supplies and takes it from Mercy now that he's free of the small human he'd been carrying on his back. He tucks the straps over his shoulders and adjusts them.

"Thanks." Mercy has no intention of complaining about being relieved of that weight. They can discuss women's rights when her shoulders aren't so sore.

"Before we go in…" Luca puts a hand on Mercy's arm and

draws her in close. "I still wish you didn't come. But I *am* glad you're here."

Mercy fights the urge to push up on her toes and kiss him. If her lips weren't so cracked and her throat so dry, she probably would. But she wants him to be the one to kiss her the next time. She's chased after him enough already. A girl has to have some self-respect.

"Let's get out of this sun," she says, using all her inner-strength to step away.

Luca leads her across the rubble. She still can't see where Tarquin and Relic disappeared.

"After you." Luca points to a slab of concrete that's leaning against a crumbling pillar.

Mercy squats down and brushes away a cockroach that comes rushing out. Peering into the darkness, she wonders if this is a joke. The only thing in there is a few square feet of nothingness.

Luca puts an encouraging hand on her back and urges her forward.

"You're sending me into a cockroach nest, aren't you?" She turns to look at him.

"Just get in there," he laughs.

She crawls into the blackness only to find that instead of hitting her head on the remains of the pillar, she continues to edge forward. She's in some kind of tunnel.

"Keep going!" calls Luca from behind her. "You're safe."

Drawing in a deep breath, Mercy moves on, wondering if she needs to add enclosed spaces to her list of fears.

The ground is smooth under her hands, well-worn from the passage of time. But the air is hot and suffocating. Keen to get this over with, she picks up her pace, pleased to find the temperature falling the deeper into the tunnel she moves.

Her hands land on a sudden drop where it seems the ground

falls away with a sharp slope. She stops and tries to figure out if there's a way around this.

"I can't go any further," she calls back to Luca.

"You can," he says. "Keep going. Trust me."

This puts Mercy in a difficult position. After the way Tarquin questioned Luca's trustworthiness, she doesn't want him to think she's also doubting him. But…if she edges ahead, she's going to fall.

The drop feels like it's made out of some kind of metal. Not rusted like the car door but slippery. Oh, great Terra! This is some kind of slide.

Drawing in a deep breath of stale air, Mercy decides there's only one way to get this over and done with. Because she *has not* come this far only to turn around again.

She scrambles forward and throws herself down the slide headfirst, letting gravity do the rest of the work. Quickly realizing that was a mistake, she tries to turn herself around, but it's too late. She has no choice but to hurtle down on her stomach with her feet flying up in the air behind her.

Aware she's screaming, although not sure she cares, she squeezes her eyes closed as she gathers speed and waits for the nightmare to be over.

She's going to be okay. She knows it. Because as terrifying as this is, she *does* trust Luca. He wouldn't let her do anything that was going to put her in danger. Everything he's done so far has been to protect her.

The slide bends to the right like its wrapping itself around something and the constant turning makes Mercy dizzy. Just when she thinks she can't stand it another moment, it levels out and she comes to a slow stop. Instinctively curling herself into a ball, she tries to get a hold of her breathing. Her heart is pounding so loudly, it's surprising it isn't beating the metal surface of the slide like a drum.

"Watch out!" calls Tarquin.

Mercy's eyes spring open and she sees Luca flying down the slide behind her. Leaping up, she scrambles out of the way, only to find a group of around a dozen people staring at her. Tarquin and Relic are at the front, grinning.

They're in an underground room that Mercy knows was once used for people to park their cars below the earth. It's cool down here, with flickering light that's just enough to illuminate her surroundings. Looking back to the slide, she sees that it's wrapped around the trunk of the giant mangrove pine. The tree is far bigger than Avis described. It seems it's spent the past sixteen years growing. And Avis never said anything about a slide. That must be new, too.

Smoothing down her clothes as she composes herself, Mercy gives the group a smile. "Hello. I'm Mercy. Pleased to meet you."

"I already told them you were coming," says Tarquin proudly.

"She looks like her," whispers a woman with red hair to the man beside her.

He nods. "She does."

"Who does she look like?" Tarquin asks.

"Like Avis," the woman says. "She looks like her grandmother. The woman we owe our lives to."

Mercy's smile takes on a whole new level of genuine. Half her grandmother's face was disfigured by Ronan, the man whose statue resides in the Round House back in the Newlands. A man who makes Mercy ill to think of as her grandfather. But the other half of Avis's face tells a completely different story. One of a woman who was born with both physical beauty as well as kindness in her heart. Mercy's flattered at the idea of looking like her. It's a feeling that makes her miss home.

"I'm Dharma," the woman says. "And this is my husband, Finn. I'm told that you already met our son."

Relic grins at Mercy.

"You grew up in Askala, didn't you?" Mercy asks Finn. "I've heard your name."

Finn nods, pleased to have been remembered.

"We have a stone for your brother, Jay, in the ballroom garden," says Mercy. "It's how we honor our fallen now. My parents did their Proving with Jay."

Finn gives Mercy a sad smile, then turns to Luca who's climbing off the slide. "Luca, you never told me there's a stone for Jay!"

Luca shrugs as he straightens himself out. "Sorry. I never thought to mention it."

Dharma smiles kindly. "Welcome to Fairbanks, Mercy. I won't introduce you to everyone all at once as there are way too many of us for you to remember just now."

"Except me." A middle-aged woman giggles as she throws herself at Mercy and wraps her in a hug. "I'm Annabel."

"Oh, I've heard all about you," says Mercy returning the hug. "Avis says you're the person she misses most."

Annabel hugs her harder at this news.

"Clint died," says Annabel, letting go of her almost as suddenly as she'd taken hold. "But Finn cooks for us now. He's a great cook!"

Mercy scans the sunken cheeks of the people watching her, wondering what exactly Finn's cooking for them. It doesn't look like any of them have had a good meal in years. Possibly ever. They make the starving people in the Newlands look positively obese.

"Is there any news on Aspen?" Dharma asks Luca, her face filling with lines and Mercy remembers Relic had said his parents were waiting for some kind of news.

Luca flinches at the question, then recovers himself. Mercy has no idea who Aspen is but it's obvious that Luca has news they're seeking.

And it's not good.

"What is it?" asks Dharma, going to Luca and planting herself right in front of him.

"We need to know," says Finn. "Please."

"Let's talk in private," says Luca, placing a hand on Dharma's arm and giving her what Mercy knows is his best attempt at a reassuring smile.

Luca leads Dharma and Finn away, and Mercy reaches for Tarquin, needing the comfort of the small girl close by. Anxiety is heavy in the air. It seems these people have all been waiting for some kind of news from Luca. This is just another reason why he had to come back here. A reason that has nothing to do with Mercy. She really has been self-centered assuming that his every move has had something to do with her.

Because it's obvious now that Luca hasn't been running away from her.

He's just been running.

Spending his life trying to look after everyone with little thought for himself.

Mercy pulls back her shoulders deciding that's going to change.

Right here. Right now.

She remembers a book that Sam read to her as a child. The fastest animal in the world is the peregrine falcon. Mercy was always drawn to that name and now she knows why.

Because that's exactly who she's going to become.

The Falcon no longer flies alone.

LUCA

*F*airbanks has always had the feeling of home. The cracked concrete, the twisted roots winding their way through as Mother Nature reclaims what was always hers. This was Luca's playground when he was growing up. He thought it was the safest, most beautiful place he'd ever seen... until he went to Askala.

Luca leads Finn and Dharma up to ground level, knowing they're going to need privacy. He stops as they reach the wide, old trunk of the mangrove pine that's just as much a part of this building as the rest of it. Turning around, he sees Finn and Dharma are holding hands like they're expecting a storm to hit any moment.

Luca's shoulders sag. His words won't tear them apart, but they'll certainly shred their hearts.

He clears his throat. "I have news of Aspen."

They nod, silent and pale. They know their suspicions are about to become reality.

"He was killed in one of the villages."

Dharma gasps, her knees giving out. But Finn's already

holding her. He draws her against him, his face stoic. He swallows. Then nods. His throat works as if he's trying to find words.

Neither of them says anything.

Giving the grieving parents a moment, Luca moves closer to the trunk. Three steps west. One to the left. He squats down, brushing away the layer of pine needles by his feet. The wooden lid of the box he buried there is just inches below, easily found if you know where you're looking. Aspen must've followed him one day.

He opens the box, finding it empty as he thought he would. He looks up at Finn and Dharma. "He took the mask." These two are some of the only people who knew about the Falcon. Luca's chest feels hollow and crowded all at once. "Aspen died a hero, trying to keep the legacy of the Falcon alive. He was captured and killed."

Luca omits the grizzly details of Aspen being hung from the spear impaled through his gut and burned. Finn and Dharma don't need to live with those images.

"We suspected," whispers Dharma.

Finn nods. "Aspen would never leave for this long without getting a message to us."

"I'm so sorry," Luca chokes as he pushes to his feet.

Their grief feels like it's eating him from the inside out. The guilt is multiplying so fast he feels like he's choking. Aspen died because of the Falcon.

For some reason, Dharma shakes her head, her eyes moist but gentle. "Aspen died fighting for something good, Luca."

Finn nods, his mouth tipping up in a sad smile. "That's more than what most people can say here in the Outlands."

Dharma releases Finn and walks over to Luca, wrapping her arms around him. "The world needs more Falcons. Aspen knew that."

Humbled that these people are comforting him right now, Luca can only nod. This is what so many people fail to see in the Outlands. The compassion and grace that refuses to die.

Dharma releases him and turns back to Finn. "We need to tell Relic."

Finn opens his arms and Dharma folds back into them. They lean against each other, heartbroken but obviously finding comfort in each other. In their love. They nod as they gaze at each other, already resolute about what they have to do next.

Luca doesn't move for a long time after they're gone. If he'd never created the Falcon, Aspen could still be alive.

But without the Falcon, so many others would've starved or lived a life of slavery...

Huffing out a sigh, Luca glances at the trunk beside him. Brushing his hand over the rough bark, he cranes his neck as he tries to see the top. This was his favorite place to be as a child. He used to perch on the highest branches, eyes scanning the horizon, wondering where his mother was.

Whether she was looking for him, too.

Without conscious thought, Luca finds himself climbing, his feet easily slipping into all his old footholds. Branches scrape past as the scent of pine fills his lungs. He leaps and hauls his way up, liking the sensation of leaving the world behind for just a few moments.

Luca's just reached the top, the bright sunlight blinding him for a moment, when the shuffling sounds of footsteps reaches him from below. Luca freezes, even holding his breath.

He needs time to think. To decide what to do next.

"Finn and Dharma said this is where he was."

Luca's heart jolts at the sound of Mercy's voice.

"You don't think he's run again, do you?"

The hitch in her voice is unmistakable. Luca winces, knowing how much he's hurt the one girl he never wanted to.

He's about to call out when another voice carries up to the top of the tree.

"He's up there," Tarquin stage whispers.

"How do you know?" Mercy asks.

"Because we didn't pass him coming up here," Tarquin responds, sounding like she's rolling her eyes.

Mercy doesn't answer and Luca holds his breath, hoping they're realizing he'll come down when he's ready. At least Mercy is afraid of heights. She's one of the decisions he has to make.

There's some whispering that Luca can't make out and it has him frowning. Those two conspiring will always make him nervous.

"You're right," Tarquin says, almost too loudly. "Let's head back. He obliously doesn't want to talk."

Knowing he's being a coward, Luca lets out a breath as there's the sound of retreating footsteps. Just a few minutes up in the untouchable heights of the tree and he'll head back down.

"Ouch."

Luca's eyes widen. He shuffles forward, gripping a branch as he peers down. Way below, the frowning, determined face of Mercy is making its way up the tree. "Mercy! You're afraid of heights!"

"Only if I look down," she retorts.

Clambering down, he reaches out to help her but she slaps his hands away. "I'm going to the top," she mutters.

His lips twitching, Luca moves out of the way. She climbs past, her chin set at a familiar angle. Staying close behind, he follows her slow but steady ascent. She places her feet carefully, checks each branch before she puts too much weight on it, but never stops.

Memories of finding Mercy wedged in the dare tree, her top acting as a pouch for the raven eggs, has his blood heating. That was their first kiss. The beginning of an inevitability that he fought every step of the way.

Mercy reaches the top and the Outlands spread out before her. Her gasp is almost a whimper. "It's destruction from horizon to horizon."

"Yeah, it really is," Luca sighs. The desolation in her voice is as total as the desolation they're gazing at.

Mercy reaches out to him, almost as if it's unconscious, but Luca's already there. He lifts her to sit in the juncture of a branch and the trunk and pulls her close as he stands on a lower limb. Trying to stay away from Mercy was one battle he was never going to win. One a traitorous part of him never wanted to.

Mercy tucks her head in under his chin. "Tell me about the Falcon, Luca."

Luca stares out over the gray wasteland. "He was never part of the plan," he says resignedly. Mercy deserves to know the truth. "I was going from village to village, trying to find out anything I could about my mother. I started with the one closest to Fairbanks and worked my way further and further afield."

He feels Mercy nod. "It's the question that's always haunted you."

The one unknown in Luca's life that demanded an answer. A faceless woman, a decision to abandon him amongst the rubble.

Did she want to leave him? Has she ever regretted it?

"I visited the leaders of one of the nearby villages. Vitron's village."

"The man who killed Aspen," Mercy breathes and Luca's not surprised she remembers. Tarquin's story of his death isn't one anyone would forget easily.

His eyes close with the painful memory. "A girl, a child no older than Tarquin, had just been sold to him. Her father was desperate for food. Her mother was begging him not to do it. Vitron was practically salivating."

Mercy shudders, drawing closer to Luca.

"I didn't say anything at the time. I couldn't. His men would've killed me." Even if they didn't, if they knew anything about Luca's mother, they never would've told him. Luca's muscles harden as he remembers the little girl's confused, frightened face. "I came back that night. They'd plucked a raven. Their feast before their...feast. I needed to hide my face so I glued some of the feathers on with sap." He shrugs. "The short of it is, I got the girl out. The family now live in Fairbanks."

Mercy squeezes his arm. "There were others, weren't there?"

"I didn't mean for there to be. But every village had someone enslaved, traded, or abused. All girls or women. All collateral damage in a world that can't afford to have a heart. I helped those I could. After a while, I needed the mask. It's the only way I could keep my identity a secret." Luca shrugs. "Each one promised if they heard anything about a woman abandoning a baby all those years ago, they'd get a message to me."

"Did you find anything out?"

"No," Luca huffs. "I'm starting to realize she's probably dead." Or some man's property somewhere, with no capacity to get a word out even if she wanted to.

Mercy pulls back so she can look at him. "I wish you'd just told me, rather than..." Her eyes flicker with pain.

She's thinking of how he promised they'd build a hut, then ran.

Of how he told her to stay away from him, despite not being able to stay away from her.

Of when he kissed Alyx, knowing full well she was there.

"I was doing what I could to protect you."

"Why?"

"Why what?"

"Why are you so determined to protect me, Luca? I may not know everything about the Outlands, but I'm not some fragile flower. I'm stronger than you think."

"I know that," Luca grinds out. Mercy is smart, brave, and tough. And darned persistent. All this would've been much easier if she wasn't.

"Then, why?" Mercy demands angrily. "Why did you do all of that?"

Luca grips her arms. "Because I've fallen in love with you!"

Mercy's mouth pops open, but the surprise only lasts a second. A sweet, beautiful smile blooms across her face. "Say it again," she breathes.

Luca sighs. "I tried to stop it, I really did. But it was like trying to stop an avalanche. I'm in love with you, Mercy." He holds his gaze steady, letting the truth shine through. "I love you."

"Thank Terra," Mercy murmurs before pressing her lips against his.

Raw passion detonates, no longer hampered by lies or circumstance. Mercy's lips are soft and sweet, her moan touching him somewhere deep. Luca cups her face as the world dissolves.

There's no Outlands waiting to attack.

No Askala needing to be saved.

No questions without answers, no need to keep moving, even though there's no clear way forward.

It's just Mercy and Luca. Finally reveling in their love.

Mercy pulls back an inch. "Do you know falcons mate for life?"

Luca's heart thuds in his chest. "I can see the advantages."

"I know," she smiles against his lips. "I love you, too, Luca."

He already knew. Everything Mercy's done has shown him. But hearing it still has his soul soaring for the stratosphere.

He kisses her again, knowing he's clinging to this moment. "Never change, Mercy."

That has her grinning. "I'm going to remind you of that, someday." She pulls back. "So, what next?"

Luca's jaw tenses. He's no hero, and Mercy has to realize that. "I need to kill Gunnar and Vitron. They won't rest until the Falcon's dead, he took too much from them."

Mercy nods. "Exactly what I was going to suggest."

Surprise spears through Luca. "You were?"

She shrugs. "Well, I can't see them wanting to change. And they don't just want the Falcon. They want anyone who's connected to him."

Luca's hands tighten around Mercy's shoulders. "Which is why you can't come with me."

"These men have hurt a lot of people." Her gaze narrows. "And they want you dead."

"Exactly my point." He tries to let her see how important this is to him. "You'll be safe in Fairbanks. I promise I'll come back."

Mercy shakes her head. "You still haven't figured it out, have you?" She cups his face. "You're. Not. Doing. This. Alone."

Luca doesn't know whether he should shake her or kiss her. He goes for the latter, pressing his lips quickly against hers. "We'll see."

She smiles as if she just won. "Yes, we will."

Turning around before he can answer, she starts the slow climb back down. Luca slips around the other side of the trunk, quickly shimmying down so he's just below her. Mercy glances down in surprise.

He grins. "I'll always keep you safe, Mercy."

She smiles back. "I know." Glad she understands, Luca holds out a hand, but she ignores it as she continues down. "And I'll always do the same for you."

Snapping his mouth shut, Luca clambers down so he can catch her if he needs to, trying not to frown. Mercy believes there's nothing she can't conquer, which is quite possibly true. The world is learning that she's a force to be reckoned with.

But if she's wrong, that assumption will cost her life.

His chest loosens a little as her feet touch solid ground. With a quick happy kiss, Mercy takes his hand as they head back down to the parking lot. Sweet joy wars with tense uneasiness.

The truth is out about how he feels about her. But one thing hasn't changed. One question still waits for an answer.

How does he love Mercy *and* keep her safe?

HAWK

*H*awk stretches outside his hut as he admires the new walls. They're not as sturdy as if Luca had built them, but they're holding. It seems Gust had paid attention to Luca and learned some of his basic building techniques.

It feels good to be standing on his two feet again without having to lean on Gust. His ribs are still sore but nothing like when the injuries first happened. Not that he wants Grace to know this. He's really going to need to come up with a more long-term excuse if he wants to get out of coming good on the promise he made her.

One of Corbin's goons sees him and comes ambling over. That's not going to be good. Messages from Corbin are never good. Especially right now.

"The Commander wants to talk to you," the goon grunts. "In the Round House."

Hawk nods to show he heard but makes no move.

"Now." The goon looks at Hawk like he's daft.

Hawk nods again, his feet still planted to the ground. He really isn't keen on talking to Corbin. Especially if the chat has anything to do with Grace... Could someone have told the

Commander what Grace has been proposing? Surely not. Corbin would be more likely to kill Hawk in his sleep than call him in for a chat if that were the case.

The goon shrugs and walks off. "Your funeral," he mutters.

"What was that about?" Gust sticks his head out of the hut.

"Corbin wants to talk to me in the Round House." Deciding he may as well get this over with, Hawk takes a step away, but Gust is right behind him. "What are you doing?"

"We stick together," says Gust. "Safety in numbers."

"You'd be far safer to stay here," Hawk points out.

Gust joins Hawk at his side. "I was talking about you. I've got your back."

Hawk nods his thanks as he walks toward the Round House. Gust really has changed since arriving in the Newlands. Even more so since the other Seekers left, and it's just been the two of them. Over the last few days there have even been instances where Hawk's wondered if he actually might like the guy.

"I fixed the boat," says Gust. "Took me all morning while your lazy ass was in bed but if you change your mind, we're good to get the sweet Terra out of this place. Just say the word."

"We can't." Hawk stops outside the Round House and faces Gust. "We have to finish what we started here."

"All our work's been undone." Gust throws out his hands. "The vegetable patch is gone. The breeding program is useless. More trees are being cut down than before. Even the wells are drying up from overuse."

Hawk opens his mouth to tell Gust he's wrong but quickly closes it again. He's more right than Hawk's prepared to admit.

Corbin appears at the door to the Round House. "Are you going to get in here, or not? I haven't got all day to wait for you two to have a chat like a couple of old women."

Hawk braces himself for the intense heat as he steps inside the round structure. There really isn't any need to burn this fire every minute of the day. Grace is seated near the statue of

Ronan and nods at Hawk as he arrives. A couple of men are strategically placed nearby. Another appears at the door once Hawk and Gust are inside.

"Nice of you to bring your girlfriend with you," says Corbin.

For a moment Hawk thinks he means Grace and his spine stiffens. Then he realizes he's talking about Gust.

"Seekers stick together." Gust glues himself to Hawk's side. "Anything you want to say to him, can be said in front of me."

Corbin scratches his chin. "Does that mean anything he agrees to that you agree as well?"

Gust glances at Hawk. This is clearly a trick question. But what's the trick?

"What do you want, Corbin?" Hawk asks, instinctively positioning himself in front of Gust.

"That was some fight you put up in the Tournament." Corbin paces in front of Ronan's statue, stopping to look up at it. "A chip off the old block, eh?"

"I never met my grandfather," says Hawk.

"But his blood runs thick in your veins." Corbin fixes his gaze on them. "You have it in you. I can see it. You have his potential."

"I lost the fight," Hawk points out. "Your son beat me."

"Only because you were already injured." Corbin takes a step to him. "And you didn't strike when you had the opportunity. With a bit of training you could be the best fighter we've ever seen."

"No, thanks." Hawk crosses his arms.

Corbin tips back his head and laughs. "Did you see that, Grace? He actually thinks I was asking him a question."

"Give him time to heal," says Grace hiding a smile. "We want him in his physical peak so he can perform."

Hawk coughs, glad he wasn't eating anything, or he'd have been sure to have choked. Grace needs to be more careful with what she says or Corbin will take another swing at her. And sweet Terra only knows what he'll do to Hawk. She's not being as subtle as she might think she is.

"We have a Tournament coming up soon," says Corbin, focusing back on Hawk. "I can hold it off for a few days but no longer than that. Is that enough time for you to man up?"

Hawk shakes his head. "I won't fight."

"Raggid," Corbin snaps at one of his men. "The fire is getting low. Fetch me that timber we spoke about earlier."

Raggid smiles broadly at his Commander before scurrying from the Round House.

"Don't you think it's hot enough already in here?" asks Gust. "I mean, you don't even really need a fire in here."

"The fire keeps the spirit of our fallen Commander alive," says Grace, leaving her seat to approach them.

"I'm not sure you need a fire to do that." Gust shakes his head. "Pretty hard to forget about a guy who has a statue the size of a polar grizzly."

Hawk puts a steadying hand on Gust's back, trying to urge him to keep quiet, but it seems the damage has already been done. Corbin practically has steam coming out his ears, and it's not due to the intense heat in the room.

"This one will do just fine as a warmup at the Tournament." He jabs a finger into Gust's chest. "An early kill will get the crowd excited."

Gust trembles underneath Hawk's palm. "I won't fight, either."

This sends Corbin into more fits of laughter as he takes a few steps back.

Anger boils deep in Hawk's gut as he realizes if he and Gust don't get out of the Newlands, they're both going to die. It was wrong of him to deny Gust's request to leave on the boat. The first chance they have, they need to go. Gust had said all Hawk needs to do is say the word. They're no good as Seekers if they're dead. They should have left this morning.

"I'm saying the word," he whispers to Gust. "Do you understand?"

Gust nods and relief slides through Hawk. This is the right decision. It's the *only* decision. Staying here is suicide.

"I'd like to talk to Hawk alone," says Grace. "Do you think you could all give us a moment?"

The anger in Hawk's gut morphs to shock. Does Grace have a death wish? For both herself and him!

"What are you on about, wife?" snaps Corbin, seeming unimpressed with the suggestion.

"I think I can convince him to fight," she says, running her index finger down Corbin's bare chest. "It will be a better Tournament if he's a willing participant."

Corbin spears his hands into her hair and pulls her to his chest. "A woman like you could convince a man of anything." He presses his lips to hers in a kiss that contains far too much tongue and not enough respect. "Just don't be too convincing, okay?"

Grace smiles at Corbin with a look that for anyone who didn't know any better would fool them that she actually loves this creep.

"Everyone out." Corbin claps his hands.

"I'm not leaving." Gust plants his feet. "I'm with Hawk."

"Not right now, you're not." Corbin grabs Gust by one arm, as one of his men lifts him off the ground by the other.

They drag Gust from the room. Hawk doesn't try to stop them knowing it will only do more damage if he does.

"It's okay, Gust!" Hawk calls. "I'll be out in a moment."

The Round House falls silent as Hawk's left alone with Grace, and the heat from the fire crawls around his neck. The fire has gotten a little low, which only means there's more smoke than flame, adding to his feeling of suffocation.

He sits down on one of the benches and stares up at the statue of his grandfather—a man whose likeness he shares in

51

appearance alone. For what's contained in their hearts couldn't be more different. It's important he remembers that.

Grace moves toward him, but instead of sitting beside him like he'd expected, she slides onto his lap.

"What are you doing?" he asks, trying to shift back on the seat to regain some of his personal space.

"You know what I'm doing." She dips her head to place a kiss on his cheek, trailing her soft lips across his jawline until she reaches his mouth. "I'm mending our broken hearts."

"No, Grace." Thoughts of Sam swirl through his mind. He can't even close his eyes and pretend it's Sam here before him, because Sam would never be this...direct.

Grace kisses him. Hard. With the kind of lust he knew must exist in this world but had been yet to experience himself. His kiss with Sam had been all about love and connection, never given the real chance for the spark to ignite into this scorching flame.

But he's not kissing Grace back.

Because...he can't. It's not right. His body might be starting to respond to her against his will, but it doesn't belong to her. Every part of him belongs to Sam, even if she's made it clear she doesn't feel the same.

It's crunch time and Hawk knows it. He either gives her what she wants, or he angers her by pushing her away. Who knows what story she'll tell Corbin! He's never going to take Hawk's side against his own wife. And what use is he to anyone if he's dead?

Giving in, he slides his hands to Grace's back, parts his lips and gives her the kiss she's been searching for. But each tiny movement of mouth against mouth kills a little part of himself inside. Thinking of Alyx and how she manages to do this every day for her survival, he tries harder to inject more enthusiasm into his actions. He can do this. He *has to* do this. Then as soon as he can get away, he and Gust will be on their way back to Askala.

Back to Sam.

Back to the life he couldn't wait to leave but now can't wait to return to. Because he knows so much more now than he did back then.

"What's going on in here?" Corbin roars from the doorway.

Grace groans before sliding off Hawk's lap and turning to face her husband.

"I was just inspecting his injuries," she says, smiling innocently.

"Like hell you were!" Corbin grabs Grace roughly by the arm and drags her several feet away from Hawk, throwing her to the floor.

Hawk stands, raising his palms to show he means no harm. "It wasn't what it looked like."

Corbin lunges at Hawk, taking him by the shoulders and shoving him backward. Fresh agony screams through Hawk's ribs and two of Corbin's men step between them, hissing something in his ear.

He looks at his men, draws in a breath and shakes his head, his disgust clear. "If I ever see you near my woman again, I won't wait for the Tournament to kill you."

"You're going to kill me in the Tournament that I refuse to fight in?" Hawk asks, straightening his back.

"I'm going to kill you, period," Corbin sneers. "Understand?"

"Whatever you say," Hawk spits back.

Corbin rolls his eyes and turns to the door. "Raggid! Bring it in!"

Raggid appears at the door, his solid arms laden with timber planks. Gust is dragged in behind him, his face pale and stained with tears.

Hawk watches as Raggid throws the planks on the fire, one

by one. It's only then that he recognizes them. Trees don't grow in plank shapes...

"You destroyed our boat!" Hawk shouts, tearing at his hair. "Those are from our boat!"

The fire catches the fresh fuel and sparks leap into the air, sending all Hawk's hopes for escape up in flames.

He falls to his knees, understanding why Gust looks so upset.

They're stuck here now. Without that boat they have no way of getting back home.

Which means that even though Hawk will never willingly participate in one of Corbin's Tournaments, he's right about one thing.

Hawk no longer has a choice.

It's time to fight.

SAM

The infirmary is quiet, as it usually is. Sam tidies the herbs lined on the shelves in clay jars for the fifth time that day. Each is clearly labeled, and she silently lists their uses.

Goldenseal, used to treat stomach upsets and skin irritations. Turmeric, useful for inflammation. Echinacea, the herb her mother hoped would help Seb.

But hasn't.

Somewhere beside one of the cots, her mother is murmuring something to a patient. She has such a way with them. People come in tense and in pain. A cut hand. An upset stomach. But within minutes, they're sitting or lying comfortably, their faces relaxed and relieved as their beloved Nova calmly fusses over them.

Sam watched closely over the past two days she's spent here, trying to emulate the compassionate efficiency. But it seems the patients don't find the knowledge that meadowsweet is one of the best digestive remedies because it contains salicin, as soothing as the smiles and vague reassurances her mother gives them. The people always thank Sam, but they don't call for her to come back once she's moved away. They always ask for her mother.

Sam never thought she'd fit in here in the infirmary. She has her mother's knowledge of herbs, but not her unconscious, natural way with people. She always expected she'd work with her father and the pods.

But she tried that.

And she's never been more bored in her life.

From the first day she returned from the Newlands, Sam went there with her father whenever she wasn't with Seb. The barrels with pods were as beautiful as they've always been. The pteropods swimming below the surface, their glowing bodies forming shifting constellations in the dark water.

But the intricate system that's kept them alive for years runs as smoothly as everything else in Askala. Her father checks the water quality every morning—temperature, oxygen, nitrates. He monitors the islands of phytoplankton floating on the surface to ensure the pods have an adequate food source.

Then he sighs with satisfaction and smiles at Sam, secure in the knowledge their people are being well cared for.

Sam always smiles back, but inside, she's working hard not to frown.

She's not feeling what her father is. She thought she would. He assumes she does.

But she doesn't. There's no challenge. No variables to identify and adjust for. No people desperately depending on the successful outcome.

Sam turns from the shelves, pushing the thoughts away. Going down that path always ends up at one painful destination.

Thoughts of Hawk.

Memories of Hawk.

Desperately wishing for Hawk.

"Just rest," her mother murmurs to a woman as her eyes drift closed.

Sam watches as her mother approaches, noting she looks a little pale. She's always given so much of herself to Askala, but maybe she's been overdoing it? Pulling out a chair, Sam indicates for her to sit down, and she's surprised when her mother actually sinks down onto it.

She's more tired than Sam realized.

"We'll need more willow bark?" Sam asks. Another plant that contains salicin, willow bark is great to treat pain.

Her mother nods, glancing at the sleeping woman. "Her headache seems to be the thing bothering her the most."

"I'll get some this afternoon."

"Thanks, Sam. It's wonderful having you here."

Sam looks away, wishing she could say the same. She needs to find her niche in Askala. This is her home now.

She's about to ask her mother if she's okay when there's a sound at the door.

Aarov stumbles through, gripping his head. "Nova? Are you there?"

Her mother is on her feet in an instant, rushing over to slip beside him. "I'm here. What's going on?"

He leans against her, pressing his hand harder into his temple. "I'm just..." He glances around, like he's surprised to find himself in the infirmary.

Sam's mother leads him to the nearest cot and he collapses onto it, panting a little. Sam goes to her mother's side, wanting to help. She presses her hand to Aarov's forehead, checking if he has a fever.

Aarov looks at Sam, clearly confused. "Who are you? And why are you touching me?"

Sam draws her hand back. "It's Sam. Nova's daughter."

Aarov grips his head. "Could you speak a little quieter?" He squints as he looks around the hut. "And why is the sun so bright?"

Confusion. Sensitivity to light and sound.

Sam sees the flash of a frown on her mother's face, telling her she's probably trying to figure it out, too. As far as Sam knows, this isn't something they've seen in the infirmary before.

"Just close your eyes, Aarov. We'll get you something to help with that."

Aarov does as he's told, his head sinking into the pillow.

"Any ideas?" Sam asks quietly.

Her mother chews her lip. "Not yet. He looks a little dehydrated, though. We'll start with that."

Sam nods, already turning away. She quickly fills up a cup from a nearby pitcher as her mother wanders over to the herb jars to see what may help.

Sam leans over Aarov, noting his sunken cheeks. Dehydration is definitely an issue. "Would you like some water?" she asks gently.

His eyes shoot open in alarm and he pushes himself upright so fast Sam stumbles a little as she yanks back. "No! No water!" he turns to Sam and recoils. "Stay away from me!"

Her mother is instantly in front of her, blocking Aarov's view of Sam. "Shh, it's okay, Aarov. It's me, Nova."

He instantly relaxes, collapsing back onto the cot. "I just need peace and quiet."

"Of course," her mother soothes. She strokes his forehead in slow, smooth strokes Sam's seen many times before. It's her signature move.

The fight drains from Aarov's body as his eyes close. He looks exhausted after his short outburst.

Sam creeps backward, not wanting to disturb him. Once it's clear Aarov is asleep, her mother joins her on the other side of the room.

She smiles apologetically. "It must be because you were gone for a little while."

Sam's gut twists. "Maybe I should go run some errands or something."

Her mother squeezes Sam's hand. "Why don't you go check up on Seb? Rose is arriving shortly, anyway."

Sam turns away before her mother can see her wince. Just like the Newlands, the infirmary's better off if she's somewhere else.

Out in the sunshine, Sam hesitates. She only left Seb a couple of hours ago, and Charity was with him. She's needed there about as much as she's needed in the infirmary or with the pods.

Like she always is, Sam's drawn to the beach. It's like even over those few yards, she's closer to Hawk. Her feet move her unconsciously forward as she follows her heart.

She had to leave him with the biggest lie she's ever told. That her feelings didn't extend past friendship.

Which is as far from the truth as they are from each other.

Her heart aches for Hawk. Her skin misses his touch. Her soul mourns everything they were never able to discover together. It's a constant pain that no amount of willow bark will ever be able to numb.

But she had no choice. It was the only way she could ensure no one else died.

The closer Sam gets to the beach, the louder the sounds of hammering and shouts grow. She leaves the tree line to find the ship still looks much the same as it did yesterday and the day before that. The giant ribs pointing to the sky, a few more boards creeping up the side. More skeleton than ship.

Jagger is standing, bulging arms crossed, only a few feet away. Sam stops beside him to watch the men work.

"It's a slow process," she observes.

Jagger grunts. "Too slow."

"You're worried, aren't you?"

"You've been there." He turns his sharp gaze to Sam. "What do you think?"

Sam looks away, turning to look at the barely-built ship. How odd to think it was only weeks ago that Jagger oversaw her second Proving.

At the time the tests seemed cruel and harsh.

Now, she knows they were little more than a gentle introduction to what they were going to face.

Sam squints against the sun, which suddenly feels too bright. "The tests were your idea, weren't they?"

"We needed to find out whether there was anyone strong enough to go over there."

Sam wasn't. She was weak and naïve. It's a good thing she's back. But she pushes that knowledge away. "Because you want to keep Askala safe."

Jagger nods, his gaze firmly on the ship. "They're coming."

Corbin's dirty face rises in Sam's mind. His hard eyes. His thirst for...more. The Commander has been working toward this for a long time. Jagger's hypothesis has merit.

"The Seekers will show them there's another way," Sam says quietly.

Despite her own failure, she still believes in them. Hawk, Luca, Mercy, even Gust, all showed they have what it takes. They're smarter in ways Sam will never be.

"I hope so," mutters Jagger. "But we need to be ready if they don't."

Hence, the ship.

Except, if anyone arrives on Askala's shores, intent on taking it by force, they wouldn't be ready.

Sam's eyes widen. "We need to build faster."

"Yes, we do." Jagger's arms unwind as he strides down to the beach.

Sam's about to follow him when she hears her name being called out.

"Sam!"

There's an urgency that has her spinning around, her frantic gaze spotting Charity running toward her.

"Sam! Quick! It's Seb."

Sam's already running before she's finished speaking. She rushes past Charity, her heart thumping against her ribs. Seb was pale when she left, his pulse thin and reedy, but he'd been like that the day before. And the day before that. He'd promised that he'd be fine in a breathless whisper.

Sam trips and stumbles twice as she navigates the paths to her house. But each time, she pushes herself upright, barely losing momentum. There was panic in Charity's voice.

Fear.

Sam darts through the door of their hut, drawing herself to a stop. Trying to get her breathing under control, she hurries to Seb's room, pasting a smile on her face. No matter how bad Seb looks, she always greets him with joy.

But she stops in the doorway, sucking in a startled breath. Seb's eyes are closed so he doesn't see her smile dropping faster than a stone. Her stricken face loses all color.

Seb has wasted away in the few hours she's been gone. His skin is so pale and thin, it's almost transparent. His breathing is barely visible. He looks…smaller. Less.

Her parents rise, stepping away when they see Sam standing there, rooted with grief.

Her father's eyes are moist. "He was asking for you."

Dropping to her knees beside his bed, Sam takes Seb's hand, noting how cold it is. "Seb. I'm here."

For a moment he doesn't respond. His hand remains limp in hers. Sam's chest constricts. She can't have been too late.

Seb's eyelids flutter, as if lifting them takes a herculean effort. They crack a fraction, seeking her out.

"Sam?" he croaks.

"Yes, it's me. I'm here. Just rest, everything's going to be okay."

Her mother told her never to make empty promises to patients, but Seb isn't a patient. He's her brother.

His mouth works, the edges tipping up ever so slightly. "Make…me…a promise."

"Anything," Sam vows, her throat tight.

She should've come back as soon as she left the infirmary. No matter how sick Seb got, it never occurred to her that he was so close to…this.

"Do what I couldn't."

Sam blinks. "There's still time, Seb. We just need to find the right herb."

Right now, it's like Seb's being paralyzed from the inside out. Maybe asparagus leaves! They haven't tried asparagus leaves!

"No." Seb's hand twitches in hers, as if he's trying to give the word strength. "You need to…"

Behind her, Sam can hear her mother's quiet sobbing. It seems to fill the room and Sam leans closer to Seb.

She needs to hear his breath. To hear proof that this isn't happening.

His eyes widen, a flash of triumph sparking in them at the small victory. "You need…to live."

Heavy tears are tracking their way down Sam's cheeks as she nods. Seb's gaze holds hers as if he's waiting for something.

"I promise," she whispers.

Seb lets out a wheezy breath.

Suddenly, his hand goes slack.

His shallow breathing stops.

Her little brother goes still. Silent. Lifeless.

The only movement is the thin trickle of blood that seeps from the corner of his mouth, bright and garish against his pale skin.

"No," Sam moans. She presses her ear to his chest. "Please, no."

But there's nothing.

Seb's gone.

Not Seb. He can't be. His final words showed he knew it, too —he died without really getting a chance to live.

Sam feels her parents move in close, contracting around her. A harsh sob escapes her mother's lips, her father collapses to his knees. A little stunned, Sam shifts back, knowing they need to be close to their son.

A deep, piercing sadness spears through her, making her wrap her arms around her middle. She folds over, streams of saltwater coursing down her face. She wants Hawk.

She needs him to hold her. To keep her from falling apart.

But she's alone. In a place she no longer belongs.

And she couldn't stop her little brother from dying.

A movement from the corner of her eye has Sam turning, blinking away the tears that blur her vision.

Charity is standing in the door, her hand clamped to her mouth. She looks…horrified.

Before Sam can say anything, her mother's pushing herself upright. "I need a cloth. I want to clean him up."

Her father nods, probably recognizing that the healer in Nova needs to do this. That this is the last thing she can do for her son.

But her mother's taken two steps when her hand comes to her temple.

"Nova?" her father asks, concerned.

She doesn't get a chance to answer. Her eyes flutter closed. Her hand drops away.

In a graceful pirouette, her mother's knees give out.

And she crumples to the floor, unconscious.

MERCY

*M*ercy stirs. It's early morning, although she can't really be sure in the dim light of Fairbanks. All she knows is that the space next to her in the flattened-out root of the mangrove pine is missing the warmth of two humans.

Luca and Tarquin had said they were going to hunt rabbits today, but she hadn't realized they'd leave so early. Mercy would've gone with them, but she'd promised Annabel she'd look at her treasures today, which seems to be an assortment of colorful objects she's collected over the years. Annabel had been so excited that she'd given Mercy one of her special feathers to look after, whispering that it was an actual feather from the Falcon's mask. Mercy had tucked it in her pocket and promised to take good care of it.

She stretches out, deciding that staying behind isn't such a bad thing. She's still tired from the walk here, not having bounced back as quickly as someone as young as Tarquin or fit as Luca. The opportunity to have a quiet day isn't entirely unappealing. Every day has been pumped full of adrenaline since she left Askala. She can only hope their time in Fairbanks will be more peaceful than life in the Newlands had been.

Her stomach growls, reminding her it's empty. With any luck, Luca and Tarquin will catch something today. Because it became obvious very quickly soon after their arrival why the people here are so thin. Despite the two overflowing buckets of roasted cockroaches in the kitchen, only a small handful had been offered to the people last night, leaving Mercy to draw the conclusion that they're saving them for leaner times. Something that's pretty hard to imagine right now.

Mercy and Luca had glanced at each other as they'd gratefully accepted their portion of roaches, trying to eat them slowly to make them last. Mercy had thought of Hawk and his intense hatred for eating these crunchy insects and had to fight back tears. She left him in the Newlands with only Gust for company. But they have a boat that shouldn't be too difficult to fix. Surely, they'll have headed back to Askala by now if they needed to?

Swinging her legs out of the makeshift bed, Mercy stands and rubs her stomach.

A few rabbits are just what this colony needs to lift their spirits. The news of Aspen's death hadn't gone down well. Mercy had always imagined the feeling of closure to be like a door gently sliding over a person's grief, allowing them to move on. But for Finn and Dharma it was more like a gaping portal of misery had been slammed wide open, swallowing up the unknown and replacing it with a certain hell.

There's the sound of heavy breathing as the people of Fairbanks sleep in the maze of roots their magnificent tree has spread far and wide. Flat and tangled, they're a complex system that provides sustenance to the tree and shelter to the people. After their dinner, Luca had led Mercy and Tarquin to the space he used to call his own as a young boy—one that's kept free for him whenever he returns.

The three of them had crawled in and fallen almost immediately to sleep.

Avis's bed is still there, unoccupied, waiting for her to lie down once more in the familiar hollow. Although, Mercy doubts she'll ever return. Her life with her family in Askala was all she ever dreamed of and more. Her work here was finished long ago. Establishing this colony has proved to be a lasting legacy.

A loud bang has Mercy spinning around. She blinks in the darkness, trying to figure out what's happening. The sound comes again. Mercy freezes and listens, having learned in the Newlands it's better to know what danger you're facing before you go running at it headfirst.

Besides, this may not even be a danger.

Shadows move across the room, accompanied by frantic whispers and the banging comes again.

"Quickly!" someone hisses. "We don't want to make them angry."

"I'm scared," someone whispers back.

"Stay where you are, Dharma!"

"No! We stick together."

Mercy waits. Whatever's happening, they don't need her input. But that doesn't mean she's not going to find out what's going on.

Creeping forward, she feels her way over the tangle of tree roots. Avis had told Mercy about the old cook called Clint who could move around this place at lightning speed despite being blind. It's a shame he's no longer alive. Mercy would've liked to have met him.

Following the sounds and shadows, Mercy stays out of sight in the dim light, tucking herself behind a concrete pillar. She sees Dharma run to the kitchen while Finn is on his way to the door that leads to a staircase that goes all the way up to ground level. It's a staircase that Mercy could have used when she arrived, rather than almost breaking her neck flying headfirst down the slipperiest piece of metal she's ever encountered.

Luca had found that funny when he'd told her about it. Mercy, not so much.

Ensuring that she can't be seen, Mercy peers out as two more men join Finn at the door while a woman meets Dharma in the kitchen. They each lift a bucket of roasted cockroaches from the benchtop.

Finn nods at the men by his side and they open the door, positioning themselves to try to prevent access to whoever's on the other side.

It's a shame Luca isn't here because Mercy's got a bad feeling about this. Although, at least Tarquin's out of harm's way.

Finn heaves back the door, which looks to be made out of some kind of heavy steel, and two of the ugliest men Mercy has ever seen burst through, pushing Finn back. She's not sure if it's the scowls on their faces or the patchiness of their matted beards that make them so unattractive, but whatever the case, she remains firmly planted behind the pillar. Why would Finn let these men in? Although, by the way they were banging on the door she doesn't suppose he had a whole lot of choice.

"What have you got for us today?" the taller of the men sneers, brandishing a flamethrower. "Better be more than that skinny rabbit you gave us last time. Didn't even touch the sides of my belly."

Dharma and the other woman emerge from the kitchen with the two wooden buckets of cockroaches. Mercy notices the way they keep their eyes downcast as the two men helping Finn race over and take the buckets.

"Stop right there," the taller man shouts. "Let the women bring them. Food always tastes better when it's served by a wench."

The other man sniggers, putting his hands on his hips and thrusting out his pelvis like anybody cares what he keeps down there.

Dharma and her friend take back the cockroaches. Keeping their gaze to the floor, they approach.

The men peer into the buckets, screwing up their faces to see what's inside.

"Roaches!" The tall man spits on the floor. "You're giving us roaches?"

"They've been cleaned and roasted," says Dharma. "Please. It's the only food we have."

"If you don't want them, we'll gladly keep them," says Finn, stepping up to stand beside Dharma.

Mercy's eyes are wide as she tries to process what she's watching. Is this some kind of bribe? What exactly have these two creeps threatened if they don't hand over the only food they have? It has to be something fairly drastic.

The men move their flamethrowers to their backs and snatch the buckets, smiling proudly like they've earned the right to hold them. The taller man licks his lips, although it's not the roaches he's staring at.

It's Dharma.

"Give me an hour alone with this one and you can have one of the buckets back," he says, not even having the decency to look at Dharma's face while he speaks. Although, this isn't surprising given the indecency of his proposal.

Finn steps in front of Dharma, the strain on his face is clear. He has a crazed look in his eyes like the toll of the last couple of days has finally made him crack. And Mercy can't blame him. She's frozen to the spot behind the pillar, weighing up whether jumping out right now would make the situation better or worse. She might be able to deflect attention away from Dharma, but it will likely result in an all-out brawl.

No. She learned a few lessons in her time in the Newlands. And one of them is that sometimes it pays to wait. Look what happened when Siena fought against her captors. Maybe if they'd let the Outlanders take her, they'd have been able to rescue her and bring her back alive. Mercy's not going to make that mistake again.

Finn shoves the bucket of roaches firmly at the tall man's chest. "You got what you came for, Vitron. Now get out of here."

Vitron? Mercy frowns, realizing he was one of the men who killed Aspen. Luca had told her he'd kept the details of Aspen's death brief when he'd talked to Finn and Dharma. This must have included omitting the names of his killers. Because there's no way Finn would be holding onto his clenched fists if he knew he was staring directly at the man who killed his son.

Maybe it's better he doesn't know for now.

Vitron takes a step back. "Don't think we'll let you get away with a couple of buckets of roasted insects next time. Men like us need meat."

"Or women," the other man laughs. "Your choice."

Finn's hands clench at his side and Dharma puts a steadying hand on his back.

Vitron and his companion leave, and the door is secured in place. The immediate ease in tension in the air is obvious.

Mercy steps out from behind the pillar. "You're giving them your food? You don't even have enough for yourselves!"

Finn shakes his head sadly at Mercy. "What other choice do we have? If we refuse, they'll torch our home and take our women."

"We have to go after them!" Mercy smooths down the fabric on her trousers and pulls back her shoulders, preparing herself for what she knows she has to do. Luca may not be here right now, but she is. And she's ready to do whatever it takes.

"No!" Dharma rushes to Mercy and grabs hold of her arm. "Aspen went after them and look what happened to him. It's too dangerous."

"But we can't just stand here and do nothing." Mercy pulls her arm free. "You heard what they said. Next time they'll want more from you. And the time after that they'll want even more.

It's never going to stop if you don't stand up to them. Don't you see that? Eventually they'll take your home and you'll be too weak to stop them."

"That's what people say about Askala," says Annabel, stepping from the shadows.

Mercy spins to look at her. "What do you mean?"

"That the men are going to take Askala and you'll be too weak to stop them."

"We're not weak in Askala," snaps Mercy, wondering how accurate this is. Her home is filled with peace-loving people. If Ronan hadn't made so many mistakes in the last attempt at an invasion, Askala would be overrun with Outlanders right now. They owe their lives to their intelligence and a whole lot of luck.

"I didn't mean to upset you." Annabel blinks as she wraps her arms across her chest. "I'm sorry."

"You didn't upset me," says Mercy, more gently. "Those men who came here did."

Annabel smiles with relief.

"Finn," says Mercy. "Would you open the door for me please?"

He shakes his head. "It's not safe yet. They've only just gone."

"That's kind of the point," she says. "It's a bit hard to follow them if they get too much of a head start."

"That's dangerous!" Annabel gasps. "No, Mercy."

"Step aside, Finn." Mercy tries her best to smile encouragingly. "I know what I'm doing. You forget that I'm a Seeker."

"I don't even know what a Seeker is," he scowls. "But I do know that I can't let you follow them."

Knowing that every minute counts and that as capable as Mercy is, she can't overpower a whole group of people, no matter how frail and hungry they are.

She spins and heads toward the slide, kicking off her hemp

shoes as she gets there. Using the bare soles of her feet to grip the metal she scrambles upward. So much for a quiet day…

"Stop!" cries Dharma. "Mercy, don't do this!"

"Go, Mercy!" cries a voice that sounds like Relic's.

Smiling, Mercy grabs the edges of the slide to help haul herself up, deciding that as difficult as this is, she still prefers it to sliding down.

There's a thump behind her and she realizes someone is following her. Please let that not be Relic. It was hard enough having Tarquin tag along on the journey here. What she's doing is dangerous. She can't risk the life of Finn and Dharma's only remaining child.

A glance over her shoulder confirms her fears. Relic is indeed scrambling up the slide behind her.

"Relic!" cries Dharma. "Get back here."

"Listen to her!" Mercy pleads with him. "Don't follow me."

"We need to stop them!" Relic shouts. "Just like the Falcon!"

What is it with kids idolizing the Falcon? Mercy continues to climb, losing her footing for a moment and sliding back before catching herself and regaining the distance she lost. Who's she kidding? *She* idolizes the Falcon. With perhaps a bit of fantasizing thrown in. The idea of Luca in a mask rescuing damsels in distress is more than a little bit appealing.

Shaking her head of such thoughts, she continues her scramble upward, hoping the fact her legs are longer than Relic's means she can outpace him.

The metal of the slide gets warmer the closer she gets to the top. But it also gets darker and she remembers the tunnel she'd had to crawl through to get to the slide. Relic is closer to her now and she knows what she has to do even though it's not something that sits entirely well with her.

Feeling the very top of the slide, she pulls herself up to the horizontal platform and spins around. Lying down on her back with her knees and head raised, she listens and waits.

"Mercy!" Relic calls. "Where are you?"

She doesn't reply. He's close and she needs to catch him by surprise.

Focusing all her energy on the soles of her feet, she waits until she feels the slightest brush of Relic's hair. Then dropping her feet until she connects with his shoulders, she kicks out.

Hard.

"Argh," comes the strangled noise from the surprised boy as he's sent hurtling back down to safety. His momentum is sure to take him all the way to the bottom before he's able to stop himself, where Mercy can only hope his parents will pounce on him and prevent him from following again.

"Sorry!" Mercy calls down the slide before crawling through the tunnel as fast as she can and popping out into the bright sunlight. This isn't a mission for a child. It's most likely not a mission for an unarmed woman either, but she's going to stick to the plan she knows works best.

Watch.

Wait.

Act.

Blinking as her eyes adjust, she feels the sweat break out on her forehead. The heat hasn't gotten any less intense out here.

Moving quietly across the rubble, she scans for Vitron and his unwashed friend.

They're not hard to find, swearing and swatting at flies as they amble away with their haul clutched to their chests and their flamethrowers strapped to their backs.

Mercy's blood boils as she watches them. How dare they take from these people who mean no harm and have so little!

She creeps along behind them, although she probably need not even bother being so quiet as these two thugs don't seem like the brightest specimens the Outlands has to offer.

They reach the edge of Fairbanks, both men panting from

the effort of carrying their haul. Walking out into the desert, they strike east and head into the nothingness.

Mercy squats down behind the rusted remains of the car she'd asked Luca about on their way in. She can't follow too closely with landscape this barren. She'll have to wait until they near the horizon, then make her move. With nothing to carry, she should be able to move faster than them.

She watches the men grow smaller and smaller in the distance, tapping her foot on the ground. This action reminds her of her mother, always the impatient one. She wishes she was with her now. Her mom would know exactly how to handle this situation. Nobody walks over her. Just like from now on nobody is going to walk over Mercy. Which is exactly why she's not backing out of this.

Just before the men disappear from view, she takes off after them, stopping only once to tear a branch off a shrub that's struggling to grow by the roadside. Using it to shield her from the sun as she hurries forward, she hopes the sparse leaves will be enough to camouflage her if the men decide to look back.

But the men never turn around. They walk on in the stifling heat until they reach what has to be the only tree for miles.

Mercy squats down to make herself small and holds the branch in front of her, counting on the fact these men aren't smart enough to realize they didn't pass any shrubs over the last half mile.

The men lie down in the shade and Mercy dares to continue to creep forward. She keeps herself low and moves slowly, hoping these men intend to nap rather than just rest. By her calculations they must've been up well before the sun to have arrived at Fairbanks so early. They possibly hadn't gone to bed at all. They must be exhausted. Stealing food from the poor is tiring work.

But stealing it back is…exhilarating.

Mercy continues moving forward. When she's only a few

yards away, she stops and listens, hearing the sounds of snoring floating in the still air.

Perfect.

Leaving the branch on the ground, she creeps up to the men, keeping her footsteps silent in just the way her mom taught her back in the forest of Askala. Her heart is thumping and for a moment she wonders if the men can hear it. Telling herself not to be foolish, she moves forward until she's standing right in front of them, unable to tell if the sweat beading on her forehead is from the sun or pure terror.

Vitron and his friend are both lying on their backs with their arms shielding their faces from the bright sunlight. Their snores are the only reassurance Mercy has right now that she's in any way safe.

A glint of metal catches her eye. A flamethrower is leaning against the trunk of the tree. Unable to resist the opportunity, Mercy weighs up her options, deciding that stepping over Vitron is the cleanest way to retrieve the weapon.

Holding her breath, she raises her foot and carefully places it on the other side of this snoring beast of a man. She reaches out, only just able to make contact with the strap of the weapon and raises it into the air so that now both she and the weapon are hovering above Vitron.

His snoring halts and Mercy freezes, praying to whatever god might be out there that this man is not about to wake. His breathing seems to have stopped altogether and Mercy finds herself holding her own breath as she waits.

Then making a loud snorting noise, Vitron hauls in a deep breath and his snoring resumes.

Mercy steps back quickly and quietly, her heart racing so fast now she feels like it's going to burst out from her ribs. She loops the weapon over her shoulders and goes to the closest bucket of roaches, not surprised to find it's now only three quarters full. Those greedy pigs have been having a feast while they walked. Clearly, they hadn't stolen this food to share with their families.

Lifting the timber bucket, Mercy winces as a splinter of wood catches on the pocket of her trousers, almost sending an avalanche of roaches over Vitron. She fiddles with the fabric and gets the bucket free, hoisting it to her chest. It's heavy but she should be able to manage. Maybe it's just as well it's no longer full.

Vitron continues to snore, unaware of what's just been taken from him.

Deciding she needs just one more thing, Mercy picks up Vitron's water flask and holds it to her lips, letting the cool liquid slide down her throat. She feels instantly better.

She moves away as silently as she'd arrived, only this time with her arms full. The flamethrower is heavier than she'd anticipated but at least she has some way of protecting herself now if either of these men choose this moment to wake up. Not that she has any idea how to use it. Does it have a safety catch? What would a safety catch even look like?

Once she has some distance between herself and the men, she picks up her pace, having the confidence to step with less caution and more speed. Her stomach groans at the sight of all this food in front of her, but never once does she treat herself to any. Not even one roach. This is for the people of Fairbanks. It's up to them if they decide to share it with her. Eating any of these roaches would make her as bad as Vitron.

The flamethrower on the other hand... Well, that's all hers. Not even Luca's going to get his hands on that weapon. She's going to figure out how to use it and she's going to keep the people safe. Vitron won't know what hit him the next time he bangs on that door.

With her arms aching and her feet blistering on the hot dirt, Mercy continues on until Fairbanks comes back into sight.

She did it! She put things right. Those thugs will never

suspect who stole from them. There's no way they'll believe anyone from Fairbanks would have been brave enough to have followed them.

But Mercy was and it's filled her with such exhilaration. Now she knows how Luca must have felt as the Falcon. She's never felt this amazing in her entire life. Her parents would be so proud.

Damn, she's proud of herself! She can't wait to tell Luca.

Then she sees someone moving toward her from Fairbanks. At first she thinks it's Relic, having broken free to follow her at last.

But as he gets closer, she sees it's someone taller than Relic. Someone with darker hair and a far more annoyingly handsome face.

It's Luca.

And he looks anything but proud.

LUCA

*A*ny relief at seeing Mercy walking toward him is quickly replaced. By a burning flood of anger.

Luca strides over the barren ground, dust kicking up with each step. He considers running, but stops himself. There's a possibility he'd pick Mercy up and not stop until he found somewhere safe.

On the other side of the planet.

The smile she had fades and something twinges in Luca's chest. But then Mercy places down the bucket she was carrying and crosses her arms, waiting for him to reach her.

The defiant gesture, so typically Mercy, has the anger dissolving and detonating all at once.

Luca stops with a few feet between them. Although he only walked, it takes a few seconds to get his breathing under control. "Dharma said you went after Vitron and Gunnar. You know Vitron is the one who murdered Aspen!"

Mercy nods as she tightens her arms. "Did you know the people of Fairbanks are buying their safety?"

Surprise jerks through Luca. No, he didn't know that. "That's beside the point right now. Did you go after them?"

Although the evidence is clear that Mercy did, there's a part of Luca that's hoping there's some other explanation. That she didn't willingly put herself in that sort of danger.

That she wasn't that naïve.

Mercy lifts her chin a notch. "I got some of the food back. What they did isn't right."

Luca's at a loss for words. He's desperately hoping he's still asleep, tucked up in the tree roots with Mercy and Tarquin. That this is all some bad dream. "You what?"

"I followed them, at a distance. They never knew I was there." Mercy shrugs like none of this is a big deal. "The idiots stopped for a siesta, so I took a couple of things while they were having a nap."

A couple? It's then that Luca sees it. A strap is slung over Mercy's shoulder, the tip of a flamethrower sticking up behind her.

"You took one of their flamethrowers?" he chokes.

Mercy smiles victoriously. "Pretty cool, huh?"

"No. Not the least bit cool. It's as far removed from cool as you can get." He holds out his hand. "Here. I'll take it."

But Mercy jerks her shoulder back, pulling the flamethrower out of reach. "No. She's mine."

"She?" Luca asks incredulously.

"Her name's Fleur. And she stays with me," Mercy says stubbornly.

Luca wipes his hand down his face. The image of Mercy creeping around and stealing the bucket and flamethrower when the men could've woken at any moment, makes him nauseous.

She steps in closer, her gaze seeking his. "I told you I could do this."

Luca's arms explode out wide with the frustration that's building inside him. "You were lucky, Mercy! What would you have done if one of them had seen you?"

Mercy clamps her mouth shut.

"What if they woke up? How would you have fought them off?"

Her gaze slides away. "That's why I got Fleur."

"A flamethrower you don't even know how to use?"

Mercy kicks at the dust by her feet. "If someone as stupid as those two men can figure it out, I sure as hell can."

Although she says the words obstinately, she keeps her gaze down.

His brave, stubborn Mercy.

"You can't do that again." The fear that sliced through Luca when he learned Mercy had gone after Gunnar and Vitron shreds him anew. "I just aged fifty years in the last twenty minutes."

Mercy's face softens and steps in close. "You were worried."

"Of course I was worried! I love you, remember?"

"I hadn't forgotten," she murmurs, her voice sending ripples down his spine. "I love you, too, by the way."

The air whooshes out of Luca's lungs. His head is tipping down before he can stop himself, the movement almost instinctive. He doesn't bother fighting it—his heart was drawn to Mercy from the beginning—and he presses his lips to hers.

Her mouth is warm and willing, her body molding to his. He groans, wishing this is where he could keep her forever. The thought of losing Mercy is just too painful.

He pulls back, his gaze pleading. "Please. Don't run off on your own like that again."

Mercy's hands come up to cup his cheeks. Her eyes are soft with love, her lips still moist from their kiss. "You can't ask me not to, Luca. I can't just sit back and watch that sort of stuff happen."

His eyes drift shut. "I had a feeling you'd say that."

He opens them to find Mercy grinning. She presses another quick kiss on his lips. "But I love you for asking."

Glancing around as defeat sinks heavy in his gut, Luca knows they can't stay out in the open like this. He pulls away, bending down to pick up the bucket as he shakes his head. "Come on, we need to get back to the others."

Underground. Where it's safe.

Maybe he can tie her to a pillar or something.

Taking Mercy's hand, they make their way back to the parking lot. Luca glances over his shoulder continuously, like Gunnar and Vitron are about to creep up on them any second.

Mercy rolls her eyes as he does it for the fifth time. "They wouldn't be expecting anyone from Fairbanks to have followed them." She bites her lip. "They're all really scared of them."

"That's because they're smart," mutters Luca. But he knows what Mercy's getting at. "We need to find out what's going on."

Luca left Fairbanks a while before he returned to Askala. He stopped off at as many villages as he could, seeing if he could uncover any tiny shred of information on his mother. When he left, the people of Fairbanks didn't know Gunnar and Vitron existed.

Luca leads Mercy to the large metal doors, deep in thought. The irony that his friends are buying protection from those who are most likely to hurt them isn't lost on him.

Mercy throws a glare his way as she passes through. "It would've been nice to know about these doors when we arrived."

Luca's lips twitch with the ghost of a smile. "It's important to know all entry and exit points."

Her only response is to hoist the flamethrower further up her shoulder. Luca's not sure how he feels about...Fleur. A weapon means Mercy can protect herself.

It also means Mercy's more likely to put herself in a position where she'll need to use it.

The moment they've stepped through, Luca and Mercy are

surrounded by concerned faces. Finn claps him on the shoulder. "Thank goodness. We were worried."

So was Luca.

There's a flurry of movement and a rocket-child slams into Luca's stomach, drawing out an "oomph."

Tarquin grins up at him. "I've already skinned the rabbits."

Luca ruffles her tangled hair. "Good job. I got Mercy back like you told me to."

Tarquin launches herself at Mercy, hugging her as well. "Next time, take me with you," she scolds with a cheeky grin.

"I tried," comes another voice. "You'll get a foot in your face if you do."

Luca looks up to find Relic standing not far away, arms crossed and his face scrunched in a scowl.

Mercy rolls her eyes. "I pushed your shoulders, Relic. And it wasn't safe to come with me."

Luca's about to say it wasn't safe for anyone to go but Mercy shoots him a glare. She turns a smiling face to Relic as she lifts up the bucket. "Plus, I brought these back."

Relic's face blooms with amazement as gasps carry through the crowd. Dharma steps forward. "You got some of them back?"

"The bucket's almost full, too," says Mercy proudly.

Murmurs of excitement ripple through the parking lot and Luca has to work not to frown. This isn't the response Mercy needs to be seeing. Don't they realize it will only encourage her?

"Those bullies won't think you came after them, but we'd better eat the cockroaches so there's no evidence." Mercy grins. "Just in case."

When a round of applause almost lifts the cement roof, Luca wants to bury his head in his hands. Mercy lifts the bucket higher, like some sort of trophy, and the clapping only gets louder.

Finn steps forward. "I'll make sure they're divided equally between us all."

"Maybe give Relic a couple extra." Mercy winks at the little boy. "That's one brave boy you've got there."

Relic looks like he grows two inches under the warmth of Mercy's gaze. Finn passes him the bucket. "Here, take these to the kitchen."

Relic takes the bucket like it's the holy grail, struggling a little under its weight. Tarquin is by his side in an instant to help him, and the two disappear further into the parking lot.

Luca turns to Finn. "What's been going on?"

Finn shifts his weight, his gaze sliding away. "They came not long after you left. Said they'd heard rumors the Falcon was gone."

Dharma slips under Finn's arm in a silent show of support. "They said they'd protect us from any attacks in return for payment."

Luca's gut clenches. "And when you refused?"

Dharma's eyes well with sadness. "They killed Clint. They said that it was only the beginning. That we needed their protection."

"Bastards," Luca growls.

Mercy called Gunnar and Vitron bullies. But they're more than that. They're dangerous. Greedy. Deadly.

"They come each month," says Finn. "We give them what we can."

Mercy grips Luca's hand. "It's wrong. They're starving them to death."

She's right. Gunnar and Vitron need to be stopped. Luca nods resolutely. "I'll take care of it."

"We both will." Mercy's hand tightens around his.

Luca sets his jaw. "No."

"It wasn't a question."

Dharma and Finn glance at each other. Keeping his arm

around her shoulder, Finn leads her away. "We'll go divide the cockroaches."

Luca watches them leave, focusing on his breath. In. Out. In. Out.

Mercy steps in front of him, that blasted flamethrower still slung over her shoulder. "I'm coming."

"You aren't. You retrieved that bucket with nothing but luck. Next time, they won't be asleep."

Mercy's eyes narrow and he knows her determined mind is ticking over. "Then train me."

"What?"

"Train me. Teach me how to fight, so I can defend myself."

Not in this lifetime!

But Luca weighs up his answer. Butting heads with Mercy isn't getting him anywhere but frustrated. "I really don't think—"

Her hands come up to settle on her hips. "I'm coming, with fighting skills or without."

Luca steps back, energy buzzing through his body. He paces a few feet away before turning and striding back. Mercy's still there, hands on hips, eyebrows raised.

Telling him those are his only two choices.

Spinning around, Luca paces again. Mercy's already shown him she'll follow him, no matter what. No matter where. He glances at her as he returns, noting the way she lifts her chin.

He's never experienced wanting to kiss someone and strangle them at the same time as much as he does now. The feeling is almost overwhelming.

Luca frowns. Tying her to a pillar is looking more and more like the only solution.

After his next restless lap, he stops in front of Mercy. "If we train, we train hard."

"Is there any other way to train?"

"We have a month before Gunnar and Vitron come back. In that time we'll get you fit and strong."

Mercy grins. "After a month, you'll be struggling to keep up."

Luca snorts. "I can barely keep up with you right now." The only thing that's predictable about Mercy is her unpredictability.

Mercy's eyes warm as she realizes she's won. She steps in close, pressing her lips to his. Luca braces himself, knowing he's lost.

But it's not a kiss of victory.

It's a kiss of gratitude. For giving Mercy the opportunity to fight for what she believes in.

Luca's knees almost buckle at the tsunami of emotion that envelops him. If he could, he'd give Mercy everything.

Of course, she had to ask for him to give up the hardest thing of all.

Her guarantee of safety.

Mercy pulls back, her eyes shining with so much love it humbles him. He presses his forehead against hers. "You have no idea what you've just agreed to."

If the only way to keep Mercy safe is to train her, they're going to train as never before. As if her life depends on it. Luca straightens as another thought strikes him. Mercy might give up after the first few days!

Her eyes narrow and it looks like she's about to ask what he's thinking when her name rings through the parking lot.

"Mercy!" Annabel is bowling at them with the same enthusiasm Tarquin did earlier. Mercy steps away, opening her arms as if she's trying to capture all that happiness.

Annabel engulfs her in a hug. "I heard you're a hero! Just like the Falcon."

Mercy slides a glance at Luca. "I'll never be as amazing as him."

Luca's glad her attention returns to Annabel because it

means Mercy doesn't see the flush that creeps up his cheeks. What is this girl doing to him?

Annabel pulls back. "Can I have my feather back now?" She grins. "It looks like it was a good luck charm."

Mercy smiles. "Of course." She tucks a hand into her pocket only to frown. A quick wriggle of her fingers and she frowns deeper. She digs down then checks her other pocket before returning to the first.

Mercy pulls her hand out, except there's no feather. Her hand is empty.

Luca's stomach sinks. "What feather?"

Annabel clasps her hands, her face alight. "A black one. From the Falcon's mask."

"I'm so sorry, Annabel," Mercy says, her face and voice full of apology. "It must've fallen out."

Annabel's face crumples. "Oh." Only to quickly brighten again. "That's okay. I have plenty more. I've been making a new Falcon mask!"

Her sunny smile back, Annabel skips away.

Mercy looks at Luca, chewing her lip. The uneasiness shifting across her beautiful features tells him the troubled feeling in the pit of his stomach is justified.

When she doesn't say anything, he narrows his eyes. "You lost a black feather."

"Uh huh."

"What happened, Mercy?"

Her gaze slides away as she scuffs at the concrete floor with her toe. "I don't know for sure, but when I picked up the bucket, it got caught on my pocket and some of the cockroaches almost tipped out."

Part of Luca doesn't want to ask the next question. He just agreed to train Mercy. She's going to expect to fight by his side.

But he needs to know. "Where?"

Mercy's gaze lifts to meet his. Her eyes are full of apprehension. Or is that apology?

"I was standing over Vitron at the time."

Luca pushes the image away of how close Mercy came to getting caught. He reminds himself she's here, safe. That she'll be sleeping in his arms tonight.

It's tomorrow and every day after that they need to worry about.

Because Luca has no doubt the black feather landed on Vitron.

Which means he knows the Falcon is back.

HAWK

"*W*e're going to die on this island," says Gust, his back pressed against the wall on his side of the hut he shares with Hawk.

"We're not going to die," Hawk replies. But his words seem to be made of sawdust as they sit on his tongue, dry and without form. "We'll just have to find another way back to Askala."

"Catch a ride on the back of a leatherskin?" Gust suggests. "Learn how to walk on water?"

"I could try to send a raven." Hawk's hand flies to his throat. "Except Grace took my pendant."

"Then you have to get it back." Gust's eyes light up as he leans forward. "We can send a message for Ekon to come and get us!"

"Not sure Ekon would be too keen to come back here," says Hawk.

"Well, whoever then. Someone. *Anyone.*" Gust throws out his hands. "Honestly, I'd hitch a ride back with Wren right now, that's how desperate I am."

"What's wrong with Wren?" Hawk narrows his eyes.

"Way too scary for me."

"She's half your size and twice your age!" Hawk laughs.

"And three times as intimidating." Gust shakes his head. "I was worried when I met Mercy that she was going to be like her."

"She's more like her mom than you think. Besides, you never seemed too worried." Hawk remembers how hard Mercy had to work to keep away from Gust.

Gust makes a strangled sound. "What does it feel like?"

Hawk frowns. "What does *what* feel like?"

"Being in love." Gust sighs as he flops down on his makeshift bed. "Having girls want you. What does it feel like? I hoped to fall in love before I die. Or rather, for someone to fall in love with me back. But now…"

Gust's words spear Hawk in the chest. That's all he wants, too.

For Sam to love him back.

"We're not going to die," he tells Gust instead. "Stop talking like we are."

"Then we need the pendant back," Gust says. "It's our only hope. We need Mercy's scary mom to come and get us."

"It's in Grace's hut somewhere." Hawk rakes his hands through his hair. "And Raiden hasn't left that hut since the Tournament."

"That would be because you broke his ankle," says Gust. "Remind me never to get on your bad side."

Hawk shakes his head. "The guy tried to kill me!"

"I wish you killed him when you had the chance." Gust sits back up and stares at Hawk. "Maybe then Nikita would be alive."

"Or maybe the rest of us would be dead," says Hawk. "I'm not sure Corbin would have been too pleased if I killed his son."

"Still wish you did," Gust grumbles.

Hawk sits up, wincing as his ribs remind him they're not fully healed. If he doesn't do something drastic then Gust's prophecy of doom is going to come true. They're already starving to death. It wouldn't take all that much to finish them off.

"Where are you going?" Gust asks when he pushes to his feet.

"To get the pendant back." Hawk rolls his eyes. "I have nothing to lose by trying."

"You mean *we*." Gust heads for the door. "*We* have nothing to lose by trying."

"Gust, since when did my *me* become a *we*?" Hawk raises his eyebrows.

"Since everyone else left us." Gust puts a hand on his arm. "Since I became all you've got."

Hawk lets out a sigh. "Just so you know, I'm done with the brugging, okay?"

Gust's hand flies back. "Hey, me, too. Don't go getting any ideas in that meaty head of yours in the middle of the night."

Hawk chuckles as they walk out into the center of the clearing. They need to figure out where everyone is before they're bold enough to go to the hut Grace shares with Corbin and Raiden. With any luck Raiden will be there alone, passed out on Grace's special herbs.

Trying to look casual, they cross their arms and point at the trees, muttering nonsense to each other as they watch what's going on.

Corbin exits the Round House and strides across the clearing, making an abrupt turn when he sees Hawk, and lifting his hand to his face. But he's not fast enough for Hawk not to notice what he's hiding.

"Corbin has a black eye," Gust whispers.

"Shh," Hawk warns. They can talk about this later. It's far too risky out here to try to have a private conversation.

Three of Corbin's men walk out of the Round House, following him into the tree line.

They wait, but nobody else emerges.

Hawk heads over to the Round House, needing to see if Grace is inside. If Corbin's in such bad shape, what must she be like?

Grace may be making Hawk uncomfortable with her advances, but he still doesn't think she's a bad person. She's just a product of what her environment has turned her into. A lonely soul desperate to be loved. The sooner she realizes he's not the soul to love her back, the better. Because if she doesn't push him too far, he could still be her friend.

"Grace?" Hawk calls as he steps into the Round House and looks around.

"There's nobody in here," says Gust. "She must've left before Corbin."

"Hawk!"

It's only faint but that was definitely Grace calling his name.

"Where are you?" He scans the rows of empty benches.

"She's there!" Gust runs toward the statue of Ronan.

Squinting in the dim light, Hawk sees Grace crumpled in a ball, tucked behind his grandfather's oversized silver feet.

"This could be a trick," says Gust, turning to Hawk. "Be careful."

Hawk shakes his head as he goes to the statue, certain he's not in danger. "What happened? Did he hurt you?"

"I'm okay," says Grace, in such a weak voice that it's obvious she's anything but okay.

Hawk puts a gentle hand on her back. "How can I help you?"

"Can you get me back to my hut?" Her dark eyes blink up at him as she clutches at her sides.

Hawk scoops his hands underneath her light frame, hesitating before he lifts her into the air.

"This might hurt," he warns. If she has broken ribs, then he knows full well just how much.

Grace winces as she reaches up to put her hands around his neck.

He lifts her as gently as he can until she's nestled against his chest. Closing his eyes for a moment, he draws in the comfort of her familiarity. He'd rather be holding Sam, or his mom, or one of his little sisters right now, but in the absence of them, he has to admit that it feels good to have this human contact. And it sure as sweet Terra beats brugging Gust.

"What happened?" he asks.

"Corbin wasn't happy," she whispers. "About what he saw. He laid into me. I managed to get in one kick to his face, but that only made him madder."

Hawk can't see any bruises on her face. Corbin must have focused on her core. What is it with Corbin and his son's passion for breaking ribs?

"Gust, make sure he's not coming back," says Hawk, motioning to the door. The last thing Grace needs is Corbin finding his wife back in Hawk's arms, no matter how innocent it is this time.

When they get the all clear from Gust, Hawk hurries to the door, trying to keep his steps as even as he can. Grace makes a soft whimpering noise as she keeps her face pressed against his chest. That bastard Corbin! Nothing gives a man the right to put his hands, or his feet, to a woman like this! It doesn't matter what he thought she'd done wrong.

They walk over to Grace's hut. At least he has a reason for going inside now. He might even be able to ask Grace about the pendant and save himself a whole lot of trouble with Raiden.

Gust leads the way, pulling back the door without so much as a knock.

"Hey!" comes Raiden's surprised gasp from within.

"Your mom's injured," says Gust, putting up his hands as Hawk enters.

"Mom?" Raiden uses a double-ended spear as a cane to

hobble over to them. "What did you do to her?" He glares at Hawk, raising his spear off the ground.

Grace lifts her head from his chest. "Hawk didn't hurt me. He helped me. It was your father."

Hawk studies Raiden's face as he processes this, searching for a hint of incredulity or anger. But instead he shrugs, stepping aside so that Hawk can go to the small room off the side of the hut where Grace sleeps. He places her on the very same bed where he'd been taken when he was nursed back to health.

"Let me see the injuries," he says gently, trying to delicately lift Grace's shirt.

But she pulls it back down and pushes him away, reaching for a blanket and covering herself as she curls into the same ball he'd found her in.

"I can take care of her," says Raiden, tapping his spear at the doorway.

Hawk goes out into the main section of the hut where Gust isn't doing a very subtle job of searching for the pendant.

"How's your foot?" Hawk asks Raiden, trying to deflect the attention away from Gust.

"It's my ankle," says Raiden. "And it hurts."

"Yeah, I'm still sore, too." Hawk pats his middle theatrically, trying to catch Gust's eye to get him to keep still.

"What are you looking for?" Raiden snaps, poking Gust in the arm with the tip of his spear. "We don't keep food in here."

Hawk notices the dark red stain on the end of the spear. Sam hadn't said how Nikita died. Surely it wasn't at the mercy of that sharp point?

"He's looking for my pendant," says Hawk, deciding maybe it's best just to come straight out with it. "It has sentimental value."

"You think I'm a fool?" asks Raiden, letting the spear drop. "You want to send a raven, don't you?"

Hawk considers pointing out that even a fool could figure that much out, but he holds his tongue.

"It's mine now." Raiden pulls back his shirt and Hawk's eyes bulge to see he's wearing the pendant around his neck. "I've grown attached to it."

The disappointment emanating from Gust is so thick it almost chokes the air. That pendant was their only ticket out of here.

"Looks good on you." Hawk turns toward the door, not wanting this fight. Not right now, anyway.

"You know there's another boat, don't you?" asks Raiden.

These words have both Hawk and Gust halting.

They wait for him to continue.

"We wouldn't be stupid enough to live here without a boat, would we?" Raiden shakes his head.

"I wondered if you had one," says Hawk. "But I've never seen it. Where do you keep it? And why would you tell us about it?"

"I want you to take me to Sam." Raiden lowers his voice, although Hawk is certain Grace must be able to hear. "Take me to Askala. I need to talk to her. We have unfinished business."

Hawk looks at Gust, whose eyes are shining with hope. But Hawk isn't so sure. It's true they're desperate to get back, but would saying yes to this put Sam in danger? Although, at least over there Raiden would be outnumbered. And he's injured. They could overpower him easily. He can keep Sam safe. They might even be able to tip Raiden overboard on the way there if he gives them any trouble. He'd make a nice snack for a leatherskin.

"It's a deal," says Gust. "We can leave right away."

"Not so fast." Hawk holds up a hand. "If we're going to do this, we need to be careful. We'll leave tonight."

Raiden nods. "Meet me at the well at midnight. The first well you dug, not the one in the clearing."

"I haven't seen a boat there," says Hawk.

Raiden rolls his eyes. "I'll take you from there. You don't think I'm going to tell you the location now, do you? An untrustworthy bastard like you will leave without me. I know your sort."

Hawk considers this for a moment like they really have any other option than to say yes.

"Okay." He puts out his hand for Raiden to shake. "We have a deal."

Raiden slips his clammy hand into Hawk's. "I'll see you then."

When Raiden lets go, Gust sticks out his hand, keen to be part of the deal, but Raiden only laughs.

Wiping his hand on his trousers, Gust leaves.

"Look after your mom." Hawk throws a glance toward Grace's room. He hates the idea of leaving her all alone in the Newlands with Corbin, without anyone to protect her. "See if you can convince her to come with us."

"You'd like that, wouldn't you?" Raiden scowls. "I've seen the way you look at her. And I don't like it."

Hawk opens his mouth to protest but closes it again. There's no point trying to correct him. Raiden thinks whatever Raiden wants to think. The truth isn't going to get in the way of that.

"See you tonight," he says. "Don't let us down."

Raiden nods and Hawk steps out in the sunlight, blinking as his eyes adjust. Gust is waiting for him outside. Poor guy. Not only do the girls refuse to give him the attention he craves, but even a slimeball like Raiden refused to shake his hand.

Hawk puts a hand on Gust's shoulder as they walk back to their hut.

"You're a good guy," he says, meaning it.

"You don't have to say that." Gust shrugs off his hand.

"We're going home," says Hawk, trying to get a smile out of his depressed friend. "That couldn't have worked out any better. We went looking for a pendant, and instead we got a boat."

"And Raiden." Gust steps into their hut and slumps down

onto the floor, leaning against a wall and pulling his knees up to his chest.

Hawk lies down on his bed. "Yeah, and Raiden."

"What if it's a trick?" Gust asks.

"You think everything's a trick," Hawk laughs. "You thought going into the Round House was a trick and if we hadn't gone in then Grace would still be lying there under that statue."

"Are you sure she was injured?" Gust asks. "I couldn't see anything wrong with her."

Hawk frowns, wondering where that came from. "Of course, I'm sure. She was in agony when I picked her up."

"Well, I don't trust her." Gust lets out a long sigh. "And I don't trust her son. But I guess we don't have a lot of choice right now."

"I'm having a nap." Hawk yawns. "I suggest you do, too if we're going to be rowing all night."

"Where do you think the boat is?" Gust asks. "I've been all over this island and never seen one."

"Hidden in the bushes somewhere." Hawk folds his arms over his face to cover his eyes. "Buried in the sand perhaps."

"What if the boat doesn't exist? What if Raiden made it up?" Gust really isn't giving up on this.

"You know when I said you're a good guy?" Hawk asks. "I meant to add that you're even more of a good guy when you're quiet."

Gust mumbles something that Hawk doesn't hear, mainly because he's stuffed his fingers in his ears.

Sleep beckons him in the same desperate way it has ever since he was injured in the Tournament. It's like his body is crying out for time to heal. And who's he to fight it? When he gets to Askala he can sleep as much as he likes. Nova will give him something to help with his pain and he'll be back to his old self.

With Sam.

Her beautiful face fills his mind and he's glad Gust can't see him because he knows he's smiling. The yearning to be with Sam grows with each day they're apart. It's no wonder Raiden wants to see her again, too. If that's even the true reason for him wanting to go to Askala. But for once in Raiden's life things aren't going to go the way he's planned. He's not going to go anywhere near Sam ever again. If he's lucky enough to make it to Askala alive then Hawk will make it his life's mission to keep them apart.

It's these thoughts that carry him to sleep and when he wakes several hours later with Gust's face hovering over his own, he has to work hard to shake himself back to full consciousness.

"The moon's up," Gust hisses. "We should head down to the well."

"Let me just pack up all our belongings." Hawk sits up and stretches.

"We don't own anything," says Gust.

"Shouldn't take long, then." Hawk grins in the darkness as he looks around the hut. The only thing on this whole island that in any way belongs to them is this structure.

And he's not going to miss it one bit.

"Come on." Gust is at the doorway. "I let you sleep as long as you could."

"What have you been doing?" Hawk gets up and rubs at his eyes, wondering how a nap could possibly leave him feeling even more tired than before. Perhaps his body is more broken than he realized.

"I went looking for the boat," says Gust. "Couldn't find it. I don't know, Hawk. Do you really think there's one here?"

"Only one way to find out." They step out of the hut into the warm night air and Hawk is hit with a wave of apprehension. What if Gust is right and this is a trick? But try as he might, he just can't figure out what would be behind something like that.

The moon is indeed high in the sky like Gust had said and it lights their path through the trees as they walk toward the well. The island is quiet with barely a breath of wind in the air. Hawk can only hope that wherever this boat is that it's already in the water. With his injuries, Raiden's broken ankle and Gust's distinct lack of strength it will be a challenge otherwise. But still, it's a challenge he'll gladly accept if it's one that leads him back to Sam, no matter how awkward their reunion might be.

"He's already there," whispers Gust. "I can see him."

Hope lights Hawk's soul. Hope that he hadn't dared to allow itself to ignite until he felt certain this was really going to happen. Is it possible that tomorrow he'll be home with all the people he loves most?

"You came," says Raiden, not bothering to lower his voice to a whisper.

This puts Hawk on edge. People don't rendezvous in the middle of the night with raised voices.

"Of course," Hawk replies in a hushed tone, his senses on high alert. "Where's the boat?"

"Down on the beach," says Raiden, his voice still far too loud. "It's all ready to go."

"Keep it down," hisses Gust. "Voices carry out here."

"After you," Raiden whispers, sweeping out his hand. "You two go ahead. I'm still a little slow."

Hawk looks at Gust. If they're fast enough, this could be their chance to leave without Raiden. But surely that's too obvious? Raiden might not be especially smart, but he'd be able to figure that out. Hawk's got a bad feeling about this. But what other choice do they have?

"I'm not *that* slow," he says. "Just start heading to the beach. Same place where you Seekers first landed. I'll be right behind you."

"We can walk together," says Hawk. He's not sure what Raiden's planning. But whatever it is, he's determined to ruin it.

"Fine." Raiden smiles, his teeth glinting in the moonlight.

They walk through the trees, Raiden using his spear as his cane, the pace painfully slow.

"I don't like this," Gust whispers in Hawk's ear when they break out onto the sand.

"Me, neither," says Hawk.

But it's too late. Whatever Raiden's up to, they're now firmly in his trap. They can only hope they're wrong and this boat actually exists.

"Over there." Raiden points to a dark shape on the water's edge. "I covered it in branches."

Hawk squints, surprised that what Raiden's saying seems to be true. The shape and size are right for a boat.

Breaking away, Gust and Hawk pick up their pace and head down to the water.

"Be alert," says Hawk as they approach the pile of leaves. "He's up to something."

Gust nods and is about to reply when a branch flings back to reveal one of Corbin's men. More branches go flying in all directions to reveal half a dozen men, all crouched over, doing their best impersonation of the shape of a boat.

The sound of Raiden's howling laughter filters down the beach, as does the scent of smoke.

Spinning around Hawk sees flames leaping into the sky from the other side of the tree line and he knows it's their hut. The last thing to belong to the Seekers on this island is gone, reminding him of everything else they've lost.

Hawk's not sure what emotion is dominant right now.

Disappointment? Fear? Humiliation? Desperation? His entire body is a boiling soup of pain.

He's *not* going home. Gust was right. This was a trick.

And Gust was right about something else as well.

They're going to die on this island.

And they're going to die tonight.

SAM

*S*am can't remember a time she's ever seen her mother sick. Her mom has always been the one caring for everyone else when *they're* sick. Always calm. Always smiling.

She tells herself that's why it's so hard to see her in bed, pale and weak. Like Seb was.

Sam hesitates in the doorway, the cup of herbal tea clutched in her hands. The shadows of her mother's eyelashes are lost in the dark circles under her eyes. She needs sleep, but she also needs help getting better. Does she wake her?

Her mother stirs as if she can sense her daughter is nearby, her eyes fluttering open. "Sam," she croaks with a smile.

Sam's instantly by her side, sitting on the chair she has no doubt her father only recently vacated. "Hey, Mom. I finally found some reishi mushrooms." It had taken three hours of trekking in the forest and scraped knees after a fall, but seeing the fleshy bronze caps had tears stinging Sam's eyes. "I've added it to the mix."

Her mother smiles. "Thank you."

Sam brings the cup to her mother's lips, noticing how hard it seems for her mom to lift her head up. She takes a sip and falls back onto the pillow.

"A bit more?" Sam coaxes.

But her mother shakes her head, looking exhausted. "Maybe in a bit."

Sam hovers. Her mother's always so good with encouraging patients. They would've taken the second and third sip before they realized what had happened.

"You should have some more. Reishi mushrooms have been found to have a positive effect on white blood cells," Sam explains. "They alter inflammation pathways and increase lymphocyte levels."

Her mother grimaces. "They taste like it, too."

Sam sighs as she sits back down. Her father will do a better job of getting her mother to drink the tea. "How are your symptoms?"

"Still the same. Tight chest. Headaches. And sensitivity to light." Her gaze sharpens. "How is everyone else?"

Every day, a few more are reporting the same symptoms as Sam's mother.

The same symptoms as Seb.

Sam makes a fuss of ensuring the covers are smooth and tucked. "Everyone is being well cared for."

Which is the only truth she can muster right now. The infirmary is full while people are in the forest picking whatever herbs or plants or straw Sam has clutched at.

Her mother's frail hand clasps Sam's wrist. "How many? Who?"

Mostly the elderly and frail. Which makes even less sense why Sam's mother, the strongest woman she knows, has succumbed to this illness.

Sam is fast running out of hypotheses.

She smiles at her mother. "Aarov's still there. He's quite the grouch when he's sick." Her mother opens her mouth to speak, but Sam continues, having finally found a use for her ability to talk. "Charity has been a wonderful help. She's there as we speak, making sure everyone is keeping their fluids up. Speaking of fluids"—Sam grabs the cup of tea again—"maybe a little bit more?"

Her mother closes her eyes as her head sinks back down. "It's worse than I'd thought. They'll have a meeting of the leaders, soon."

This afternoon, in fact.

Sam will be there. Her mother won't.

Pushing the cup forward, Sam allows a hint of her desperation to creep into her voice. "Please, Mom?"

Her mother hesitates, then takes the cup with an unexpected show of strength. Sam watches as her mother takes two big gulps before handing it back.

"Thank you," Sam says quietly.

Please, let the reishi mushrooms be the missing ingredient.

Please let Sam save her mother.

Unlike Seb.

Her mother's eyes find Sam's. "I need a...favor."

"Anything."

"Go and check up on your grandmother. I need to know she's okay."

"Thea's doing fine, Mom. She was here earlier, remember?"

Sam frowns, worried that her mother's memory is fading as fast as her body.

But her mother waves a hand at her. "No, not my mother. Your father's."

Oh. Amity.

Despite being her fraternal grandmother, Sam hasn't seen much of Amity over her lifetime. When the old cruise ship, the Oasis, burned to the ground, taking her beloved Magnus with it, Amity withdrew from the world. Remaining in her hut on top of the hill, she seems more content to watch Askala than take part.

"I'm not sure I'm the best person to do that..." Sam says, wishing this is the one thing her mother didn't need her to do.

"Why not?"

It's well known Amity withdrew because she wants solitude. Peace. It's taken her a lifetime to try to heal from her loss. The last thing she needs is someone like chatterbox-Sam not knowing when to be quiet.

Sam shrugs. "She probably doesn't want to hear about the immune boosting effects of *Ganoderma lucidum*. Reishi mushrooms aren't exactly common, you know."

Her mother smiles, understanding blooming across her pale face. "I think you may have more in common than you realize." She squeezes Sam's hand. "And your father is busy enough as it is."

And worried enough. And if he discovers his mother is sick, it'll only add to his burden.

Sam nods, pulling up a smile. "Maybe you're right—we share genetic material, after all. I'll head there right now."

Her mother relaxes as her eyes flutter closed. "Have I ever told you how proud I am of you?"

Sam's glad her mother can't see her wince. She's done little more than fail her family. And Askala.

Seeing that her mother's already asleep, Sam tiptoes from the room. She has enough time to visit Amity before the meeting of the leaders.

Sam's chest aches as she makes her way past the kitchens and up a small hill. Everything is...quieter. More subdued. There are fewer people, and those who are making their way around seem to have less energy, less to smile about. People are getting worried.

Amity lives in a small hut at the edge of their gated community, closer to the fence that keeps them safe from hungry polar grizzlies than to the rest of Askala. Sam's parents are one of the few people who really see her, seeing as they're the ones who bring Amity food and necessities.

Sam finds her grandmother sitting outside, curled up in a chair in the midst of a small vegetable garden. The dark hair her father inherited has faded to gray, her skin has sagged with age, but she's still beautiful. She watches Sam approach, not getting up from her chair.

"Sam," she says as if she's testing the name. "Daughter of Kian." Her face twists. "Granddaughter of Magnus."

"And your granddaughter," Sam offers with a smile. "And daughter of Nova."

Amity's brows twitch up and Sam wonders if she's already managed to get her off side.

"I was sent to make sure you're okay. Is there anything you need?"

Suddenly, Amity sits up straighter. "Is my son okay? Is Nova?"

Sam's hands twist together in a knot. "Dad's fine. Mom's... not well."

Amity frowns. "The numbers are growing rapidly."

And yet Amity looks healthy, possibly because she's remained separate so she hasn't been exposed to whatever illness is spreading through Askala. Is that what they need to do? Isolate everyone who's sick? Including Sam's mother?

Sam sags, another looming failure weighing down on her. "Yes, they are."

"And what are you doing about it?"

Sam startles, her gaze flying to Amity's. "Me? I'm doing everything I can!"

She's spent hours in the forest, seeing if she might stumble across a new species. Late nights in the infirmary, creating tinctures and powders and oils. Too much time pacing their small hut, wracking her brain for whatever it is she's missing.

Amity glances behind Sam. "Without Hawk?"

Sam goes stock still, turning into the ice she's never seen. "I beg your pardon?"

"I've spent your life watching you grow up, granddaughter. I recognized the bond that you two have. I grew up with my one true love, too."

Sam tries to swallow, but her throat isn't working. "Hawk's a Seeker," she chokes out. "He's in the Newlands."

Amity nods, although her gaze has trapped Sam. She looks like she's waiting for more.

But for once, Sam doesn't have more words. What can she tell her grandmother? That Hawk is most certainly the one and only guy she'll ever love? And that he's doing what he was destined to do?

That it was Sam who didn't have what it takes?

"I…" she starts, only to fail.

Amity settles into her seat again, staring out over the community of Askala below them. "Do you know why I stay up here, Sam?"

"Grief?"

Sam's only tasted what losing Hawk feels like, and he's still alive. A part of her wants to disappear from the world, too.

"Yes, but only in part. Magnus was my world. My heart. I wholly believed he was my future." She sighs. "Did you know he lost hope? That he believed humanity couldn't overcome its selfishness?"

"No, I didn't." Although that sounds awful, for a fleeting moment, she wonders if Magnus met someone like Corbin or Raiden.

"He was so wrong. And do you know how I know that?"

Sam shakes her head.

"Because we had Kian."

Sam's father. One of the ones who fought for the Askala they have now.

Amity nods as she sees understanding dawn on Sam's face. "Kian knew our humanity is our strength, it's our ability to love. To connect. To come together. And he knew this because he fell in love with Nova."

Sam's knees feel weak. Amity can't be suggesting what Sam thinks she is...

"And you're their legacy, Sam. Just like Hawk is. And Mercy, and Luca. Each one of you are our future."

Sam's about to shake her head, but she stops herself. The other three are. There's a reason they're still in the Newlands. Instead, she looks away. "They really are. They'll find a way, you'll see."

Amity leans forward, her eyes narrowing. "Do you know that Kian went after Nova when she left for the Outlands?"

"I do." The story of her parents had always been a beautiful one, but Sam hadn't considered it relevant to what's going on now.

Amity nods. "He knew. He knew he couldn't do this without Nova. That a society that embodies love needs to be founded on...love."

Sam's heart thumps out one word. Hawk.

She takes a stumbling step back. She can't return to the Newlands. It's not safe for anyone if she does that.

She shakes her head. "And that's exactly what they did. Along with Dex and Wren and all the others."

"And when Askala came under threat again, what did they do?"

Another step and Sam's back on the path. Amity seems perfectly healthy, and she didn't take Sam up on the offer of needing anything.

And she has a leaders' meeting to get to.

Her grandmother's face softens as she watches Sam retreat. "They realized the answers were never here. They were with the people we haven't reached."

Sam turns too fast and she tumbles over her own foot, but she quickly rights herself. Trying not to look like she's running, she hurries back down the hill. Everything Amity just said seemed to speak straight to Sam's heart.

But what she's suggesting…Sam can't leave Askala, no matter how much her soul cries to be with Hawk. Especially not now.

Hurrying to the meeting of the leaders, Sam pushes the thoughts out of her mind. Of course she can't go back to the Newlands. Her inability to row that far shows she was never meant to be a Seeker.

And Hawk was.

A quick glance at the sun and Sam knows she's probably late. She doesn't like to be running behind for anything, but arriving late to the leaders' meeting means she won't be able to sit next to her father. Everyone would've taken a seat, and close to the older leaders is always most people's preference.

Sam pauses as she reaches the clearing beneath the trees, wondering if she got the time wrong. There are little more than a handful of people around the circular table.

Sam slides onto a stool beside her father. "Why are so many people late?" she asks him quietly.

Her father's face is lined with tension. "This is everyone."

Sam clamps her mouth shut, wishing she hadn't asked. People are sick. Dying. Or caring for the sick and dying. That's why there are so few here.

Her father stands. "This will be a short meeting. There are others we need to care for right now."

Sam's hands grip each other beneath the table. It must be so difficult for her father to be away from her mother, his beloved Nova, right now.

"I just wanted to see if anyone has any ideas or suggestions. Of anything else we could try."

Sam looks up to find several eyes on her. Dex. Wren. Jagger. Diesel. Zali.

"I'm starting to think it could be viral," she says quietly, knowing how lame that sounds. "Isolating those who are infected may be a good start."

Her father's jaw works. That means staying away from Sam's mother for the good of his people. Amity just told her how far he went to stay together.

Again, Sam's thoughts turn to Hawk. Was her one error dividing them?

"Unless it's not a disease," says another voice, quietly but fiercely.

Sam looks at Zali in surprise. "What else could it be?"

Zali's looking frail, like so many of the older people of Askala are, but she pushes to her feet. She lifts a trembling hand and points it at Jagger. "He's poisoning us!"

Sam gasps as several others do. Jagger's features twist into a ferocious frown. "I would never do that."

Sam's father reaches out a placating hand to Zali. "This isn't the time to be making false accusations. We need to think about this—"

"I have been thinking about it!" Zali almost screeches. "The Remnants have always wanted what we have. And they sent Jagger to infiltrate us. That's what stage one was. That raven they sent was meant for him!"

Wren shoves to her feet, but Zali takes a step away from her, looking like she expects Wren to pounce on her. "Don't you see? All he has to do is put something in our water, and we get sick and die, one by one. There will be no battle for Askala. There will be no one left to fight."

Dex stands too, slipping an arm around Wren's shoulder. "You have no proof. Jagger has done nothing but help Askala."

"Tell that to the dead," Zali spits.

Sam's gut clenches as she thinks of Seb. She looks to Jagger, registering how pale he is. Surely, he wouldn't...

Jagger leans forward, his hands pressing onto the table as he pins Zali with a glare. "You are worse than a Remnant. At least in the Outlands I knew not to trust those around me."

Zali's mouth works but no words come out. With a furious huff, she spins on her heel and strides away.

Sam's father sinks to his chair. "Jagger, I'm so sorry. I don't know how she reached such a conclusion."

Jagger's hands clamp into fists as he watches Zali leave. He looks angry. He looks betrayed. With a sharp nod, he turns and walks stiffly in the opposite direction.

Wren sighs. "I'll give him time to cool off and then I'll go talk to him. This illness is messing with people's heads."

"I'll come with you," Dex offers.

Sam's father nods. His eyes lift and stare straight ahead, glazed with pain. "As we continue to search for a cure, I suggest if anyone develops symptoms, they head straight for the infirmary."

One by one, everyone rises and leaves silently, their brows creased. Sam suspects that was the first meeting of the leaders where so little was decided. Where no one knows what to do next.

Where accusations as desperate as the ones Zali voiced were thrown across the table.

Sam's father sighs as he stands, looking like he just aged a millennium. "I'm going to take your mother to the infirmary."

He's gone before Sam can respond. She stands and starts to walk, but then hesitates. Her parents need time alone. Sam hovers, as uncertain as everything else around her.

Askala needs her. Her parents need her. And yet, the encyclopedia of knowledge in her head has led to nowhere but dead ends.

Does that mean leaving Askala and following her heart, just like her father did?

Sam looks up, realizing she's made her way to the beach. To the place that's just a few yards closer to Hawk.

Suddenly, she stops, her hand flying to her mouth.

Zali is lying in the sand, the waves lapping at her feet. But Sam knows she can't feel the acidic water corroding her skin. Blood pools around her, the garish cuts at her wrists unmistakable. Her eyes are open, but unseeing.

Sam's knees buckle, her mind stuttering as it tries to process what she's seeing.

Zali's dead.

MERCY

*M*ercy holds down Fleur's trigger, heart hammering as she watches a rod pull back to open some kind of valve.

She squeals as a burst of flame shoots from the end of the weapon, and lets her finger slide off the trigger, extinguishing the fire.

"Why did you scream?" asks Tarquin, forever curious.

"It gave me a fright." Mercy laughs. "Let's try it again, shall we?"

Tarquin nods enthusiastically. "Do it."

"Ready, Fleur?" Mercy asks, nodding at the weapon as she makes sure it's pointed in a safe direction. With nothing but rubble for miles ahead, she's unlikely to kill anything more than a few dozen mosquitos.

She pulls at the trigger again, holding her nerve this time, watching as the flame turns from red to orange then a pale yellow. The entire weapon burns in her hands as she becomes hypnotized by the sheer range of this thing. She could do some serious damage with it. Which means she should save the fuel for when she needs it.

"That's so cool." Tarquin's jaw has fallen as she stares at Mercy in awe. "Can I have a turn?"

"Definitely not." Mercy holds the flamethrower out of reach. "Fleur is dangerous."

"Why do you call it Fleur?" asks Tarquin. "It sounds a bit girly for a weapon like that."

Mercy lowers the weapon and bends down to eye level with Tarquin. "I'm going to tell you something really important, so I want you to listen hard, okay?"

Tarquin chews on her lip, listening intently.

"Being a girl doesn't mean you can't be fierce." Mercy narrows her eyes. "Men may have bigger muscles than us, but that doesn't mean they're more powerful. We can be just as strong. Just as brave. Just as intimidating."

Tarquin nods, her eyes lighting with excitement. "What does inminidating mean?"

"It means scary." Mercy glares at Tarquin, trying to demonstrate her point. "Can you show me your teeth?"

Tarquin gives Mercy a wide smile.

"No!" Mercy shouts, enjoying this far too much. "Not like that. Be fierce."

Shuffling her feet, Tarquin doesn't seem to know what she means, so Mercy makes a low growling noise, pulling back her lips to bare her teeth.

"Oh." Tarquin straightens her back and copies, having trouble holding her lips in place because she's laughing too much.

"Women are fierce." Mercy growls again. "I'm a fierce woman."

Tarquin pulls herself together and manages to get out a growl, her teeth flashing from her dirt-stained face.

"That's it!" says Mercy, smiling then remembering herself and fashioning her expression into a frown. "Do it again."

Tarquin growls and Mercy returns the sound, this time louder while she screws up her nose and narrows her eyes.

Luca chooses that moment to appear from the rubble. Thankfully, in the opposite direction to where Mercy had been pointing the flame only moments before.

Rather than ask why they're growling, he joins in, raising his hands with fingers bent like claws and making a low guttural sound.

It's actually kinda sexy.

Mercy shakes that distraction from her head as she focuses back on what they're doing here.

"We're fierce women!" snarls Tarquin. "Strong and inminidating!"

Luca drops his bear claws and holds up his palms. "Well, I'm certainly scared!"

"Good!" Tarquin lets her scowl slip as she fights a smile, winning the battle and snarling once more.

"What have you been teaching her?" Luca asks Mercy, shaking his head.

Mercy laughs. "Just a few important life lessons."

"Well, maybe it's time I taught you how to use that flamethrower you've been carrying around?" Luca suggests.

"Two things!" Tarquin steps in front of Luca and holds up a hand. "One. Her name is Fleur. Two. Mercy totally already knows completely how to use her."

Mercy giggles as Tarquin rolls her eyes dramatically.

"You used it without me?" Luca seems genuinely shocked. "You could have hurt yourself!"

"I'm an inminidating woman," says Mercy, using Tarquin's version of the word. "In case you hadn't noticed, I can do a lot of things around here without a man to help me."

Luca lets out a breath. "I feel like I've walked in on a women's rights meeting."

"You kinda did." Mercy puts a hand on his arm as she feels

the tiniest bit sorry for him. But as much as she wants Luca to feel strong and knowledgeable, she's not going to do that at her own expense.

"Are you going to train us now?" Tarquin asks, hopping from foot to foot.

"You sure you need a man to train you?" Luca frowns, although he's clearly not upset.

Tarquin throws her arms around Luca's waist. "We need you for lots of things."

Luca ruffles the small girl's hair. "Glad to hear I'm still useful."

"You're better than useful," Tarquin whispers in a revered tone. "You're the Falcon."

Mercy's heart lurches at these words. The admiration Tarquin has for Luca is off the charts. It almost rivals Mercy's own feelings for him.

"Then let's start with some basic self-defense techniques." Luca pries Tarquin off him and wipes his palms on his trousers.

"We don't want to defend." Tarquin crosses her arms. "We want to attack!"

Mercy sets Fleur down on a large rock beside her. "We won't be attacking anyone if our arms are pinned behind our backs."

Memories of her attack on the beach in the Newlands flood back. Being pinned down by that revolting excuse for a human as he tried to tear off her clothes. Luca's right. Defense is exactly what they need to know.

"Let me demonstrate," says Luca, coming up behind Mercy and gripping her around the waist.

This sends a whole range of feelings racing through Mercy's body and not one of them is screaming the word defense! The last thing she wants to do right now is break any contact between them. The firmness of his chest is pressed right up against her back and if Tarquin weren't standing right there, she'd find a way to spin around and kiss him until his lips go numb.

"What are you going to do?" he asks.

She gives her bottom the tiniest of wiggles and feels a shot of warm breath in her ear as Luca exhales.

"Behave," he whispers.

"Kick him in the nuts!" Tarquin cries out.

"That's a bit hard when I'm behind her," Luca points out. "Come on, Mercy. What are you going to do?"

Mercy tries to turn around but Luca's grip is too tight and he lifts her feet from the ground.

"Bend over," he tells her. "Shifting your weight forward makes you harder to carry."

She does as she's told, feeling like this really isn't anything a child should be witnessing. But Tarquin is squealing in excitement, unaware of the white-hot chemistry fizzing before her.

Now that she's created some space between their torsos, Mercy's elbows are free. Swinging one up, she connects with Luca's cheek.

"Ouch!" he complains but quickly recovers. "That was good, Mercy! See if you can do it again. Keep going until you're free."

"But I'll hurt you." She pulls her elbow back, not wanting to damage that face of his.

"Don't worry about me," he shouts, gripping her so tightly that now she's the one starting to hurt.

"Get him, Mercy!" Tarquin shouts, defecting from Team Falcon straight back to Team Woman. "Get him! Be fierce."

Mercy knows what she has to do. Tarquin's spent her life with her sister as her role model. A sister who let men walk all over her to get what they wanted. It's time this girl was not just told that women are capable and worthy of so much more. It's time she witnessed it with her own eyes.

Mercy lets her elbows fly, pummeling Luca's chest, his neck, his perfect face. Luca's groans tell her when she's hit her mark. But still, she's unable to break his grasp.

"Focus on one elbow and try to turn around," he says, breathing heavily.

Deciding that her right elbow is the one doing the most damage, Mercy drives it into Luca's chin. Over and over she lets her fury fly as she turns herself around.

Luca's hands break their grip from around her waist when she slams a final elbow into his throat.

She did it!

But her celebration is short, as now he grabs her again, this time pinning her arms to her sides, leaving her unable to attack.

"I give up!" she shouts, struggling to catch her breath. The feeling of being trapped is too much, making her memories of the Newlands all too real. "Let me go!"

Luca instantly releases her, his hands flying to her face as he gently trails his fingers down her cheeks, checking she's okay, even though his own face is the one showing signs of bruising.

"I couldn't do it," says Mercy, disappointment the new vice that's holding her tight. She hadn't shown Tarquin how strong women are. All she'd done was show her that they have no hope.

"You actually *did* do it," says Luca. "You just forgot the final move."

Mercy blinks at him as she waits for him to elaborate.

"Tarquin was right," he says, winking at the small girl whose face lights up immediately. "You should have kicked me in the nuts."

Mercy's not entirely sure that's an area she wishes to do too much damage to, but she nods her head in agreement. It's such a simple thing. If she'd managed to raise her knee when she had the chance, he'd never have been able to grab her again. She'd have had time to run. Her mom had taught her that since she was a tiny girl. She just needed to put it all together with what Luca just taught her.

"My turn!" shouts Tarquin. "My turn! Let me have a go!"

"Careful," warns Mercy. "Her elbows are pointier than mine."

Luca smiles as he obediently goes behind Tarquin and bends over to grab her around the waist.

Tarquin doesn't waste a moment. She thrashes out with one elbow, not tall enough to land any on Luca's face, instead pummeling his chest.

Mercy sees Luca loosen his grip, knowing he could hold on far longer if he needed to. It's quite sweet to see him let Tarquin get the better of him. Not that this little pocket rocket needs any more confidence.

Tarquin seizes the opportunity and spins around, slamming her foot directly into Luca's groin.

Hard.

He doubles over, this time without any need to fake, and howls in pain.

"I got you!" Tarquin raises her arms above her head and does a little jig as she dances away from Luca and goes to Mercy.

Mercy gives her a double high five as she tries not to laugh too hard. Luca really should've seen that coming.

"Again!" squeals Tarquin when Luca manages to stand up straight. "I want another turn!"

"I think that's enough training for one day," says Mercy. "We need to let the Falcon rest."

"She's right," groans Luca. "You got me good."

"Then I'm going to show Relic what I learned." Tarquin skips away toward her favorite way of entering Fairbanks—the slide.

"Don't kick him in the nuts!" Luca calls after her.

"Poor Relic." Mercy shakes her head, smiling.

"You mean, *poor Luca!*" He closes the gap between them and slides his arms around her waist, his touch a whole lot different to the one he'd used before.

"Poor Luca." Mercy steps up on her toes and trails gentle kisses across his face. "Poor baby."

Luca closes his eyes, feeding off her touch. Then, bringing his lips to her own, he kisses her in a way that's anything but gentle. It's a kiss fueled by passion and pent up frustration. A kiss that feels like their souls are trying to climb into each other's bodies.

"We really need to find Tarquin somewhere else to sleep at night," he groans against her lips.

Mercy giggles. Romance is hard to come by when you live a life without privacy.

But she's fine with kisses for now, realizing she may have pushed him too fast in the Newlands. Which only resulted in pushing him away. Sometimes it pays to keep a man wanting.

"Come here," she murmurs, deepening the kiss so that words are no longer possible.

She has her Falcon. The guy she's loved her entire life. She has Luca.

And there's no denying that he also has her heart.

"And by the way, that's gross!" shouts Tarquin from the entrance to the slide.

Mercy and Luca pull away from each other, laughing.

"We thought you left already," calls Luca.

Tarquin jams her hands on her hips. "Don't worry. I'm leaving now!"

She disappears into the tunnel and Mercy turns back to Luca.

"Thanks for the lesson," she says. "It was actually really helpful."

"I have a few other things in mind that I could teach you," he says, raising a brow.

She swats at his chest. "As a wise man once said…behave!"

"I don't know how." He bends to kiss her again and as she wraps her hands around his neck she has to admit she's glad.

Behaving really isn't any fun.

LUCA

*L*uca lifts his head with a groan. Mercy with a flamethrower is one of the most terrifying things he's seen.

And one of the sexiest.

He doesn't know whether he wants to wrap her up and hide her from a future where she'll have to use it, or kiss her until she realizes how hot she looks.

Unfortunately, he can't do either. Dropping his forehead so it rests on Mercy's, he sighs. "The memorial is happening soon."

"Oh, yes," Mercy says, now just as subdued as he is. "Good thing you came when you did."

"If I'd known this is what you were doing when you said you were going for a walk with Tarquin before training, I would've joined you earlier."

Mercy crinkles her nose. "That's exactly why I forgot to mention Fleur was coming, too."

Stepping away and gripping her hand, Luca shakes his head with a chuckle. "The white hot kiss right after you told me should've been a red flag."

Mercy skips a little, her beautiful face lighting up. "It was white hot?"

The sweet note of happiness has Luca stepping in front of her as he takes both her hands. "Every kiss burns me to my very soul, Mercy."

"Me, too," she breathes, her eyes shining like a galaxy was just born in them. She presses closer. "And curls my toes."

Stepping away before their chemistry ignites past the point of no return, Luca starts walking, Mercy's hand firmly clasped in his. "I don't think my toes have uncurled since our first kiss."

Mercy giggles, but the sight of the metal doors to the underground parking lot has the sound fading away. Dharma and Finn wanted a memorial for Aspen as an official goodbye. As painful as it was to deliver the news, Luca's glad they'll have some closure now.

He opens the door, locking it securely behind them. Gunnar and Vitron aren't due for three more weeks, which gives them time to prepare. Time to train Mercy and come up with a plan.

Inside, the parking lot is empty, but Luca was expecting that. Mercy glances around. "They're by the tree, aren't they?"

"Yeah. When someone dies here in Fairbanks their body is buried under rubble out in the ruins. There's a ritual to say goodbye." Luca's face twists. "Seeing as there's no body to bury with Aspen..."

"Then they're just having the ritual." Mercy's hand tightens around his. "But they get to say goodbye. That counts."

Luca nods, noticing how in tune their thinking is and surprised by how quickly it's happened. They're far more connected than he could've imagined. Tugging her in close, they make their way through the parking lot and up to the massive mangrove pine that's punched its way through the building above.

Dharma turns around as she hears them arrive and gasps

when she sees Luca's face. "What happened? Were you attacked?"

Luca smiles a little as he shakes his head. "I sure was. By two inminimating women."

"We were training," Mercy adds, flushing a delicate shade of pink.

Tarquin appears beside her, nodding furiously. "And we won."

Dharma relaxes. "Good. This world needs more people who are willing to do what it takes."

"Like Aspen," Luca says solemnly. "He was determined to keep the fight alive."

To keep the Falcon alive.

Dharma's eyes well up as she nods. She turns and heads back to Finn, who's waiting a little to the left. A beam of light spears through a hole in the fractured roof above them, embracing them as they embrace each other, Relic there with them. The other people of Fairbanks are spread around the area, faces drawn. Annabel is sobbing quietly as she clings to another woman.

Mercy tucks tight into Luca's side and he anchors her there. This is going to be painful to watch.

Finn picks up the scrap of material sitting on a rock beside them, his features drawn in lines of pain. Sitting in the center are the objects they're gifting their dead son. Luca's gut clenches when he sees the black feather sitting there, a tribute to what Aspen lost his life believing in.

Beside it are two cockroaches, and Luca nudges Mercy to see if she noticed. "They couldn't have done that without you," he whispers to her. Giving away two roaches is only made possible by the haul Mercy returned with. There's no way anyone could spare food without it.

Her shoulders pull back an inch as moisture pools in her

eyes. Luca presses a kiss to her temple, pride smoothing the edges of the sharp grief tangling in his chest.

Finn's just lifted the corners of the material as Dharma collects the string that will tie it all together when Annabel rushes forward.

"I want to add this, too," she sobs. She opens her hand to reveal a small carved object sitting in her palm.

Finn stills. "One of your treasures?"

She nods, her shoulders heaving with the tears she can't stop.

Dharma shakes her head. "You don't have to do that, Annabelle. These are precious to you."

Luca's never seen Annabel's treasures, although he's heard a lot about them. They sound as if they're little more than trinkets and scraps, but to her, they're her riches. In a world where people don't have much, Luca respects her ability to find beauty.

Annabel wipes her free arm across her nose. "I want to give one to Aspen. He was special, just like my treasures are."

Dharma's own tears spill over as her face crumples. "Thank you, Annabel."

Annabel reaches out and carefully adds her treasure to the feather and roaches. As she steps away Luca sees that it's a small, carved piece of wood. He squints. It looks like a...little boy?

"That is precious," Mercy whispers under her breath.

Finn ties up the small package, but even that brief glimpse was enough for Luca to see the detail in the small figurine. Whoever carved it was quite talented.

Dharma steps forward, the material balloon Luca was expecting in her hands. With Finn's help, they tie the pouch to the bottom, then light the small cup of mangrove pine oil just above it. They expand the balloon, capturing the tendrils of smoke as they curl up.

Silence descends as the balloon fills with hot air. The stained material expands, the glow of the flame flickering inside it.

Holding it on each side, Dharma and Finn lift it to the hole in the ceiling, bathing it in pale sunshine.

The lantern trembles then rises from their hands. It hovers in the air, the pouch a pendant beneath it.

"May your soul fly to a better place, Aspen," Finn and Dharma say in unison.

As if those were the words it was waiting for, the lantern lifts into the air. It glides upward and rises through the hole, free to float where Mother Nature wants to take it.

This time, it's Finn's sob that fractures the quiet. Dharma folds herself around him and they cling to each other. Relic buries himself between them and they hold him as tightly as they are each other.

Tarquin is clenching and unclenching her hands, probably unsure of what she should do. Luca doubts she's seen a memorial service. No one has the time to grieve in the Outlands. He places a hand on her shoulder and she tenses and relaxes all at once. Tarquin would struggle understanding support as much as she does grieving.

The anguish tangling Luca's insides is suddenly engulfed in white hot heat. Anger. Rage.

Fury at the senseless loss.

Gunnar and Vitron will pay for what they've taken from these people.

Mercy pushes up on her toes, her lips brushing his ear. "We're going to stop these bastards," she whispers fiercely.

Luca looks down, seeing the pain harden into determination in Mercy's eyes. The same need to make this right is burning within her.

And Luca knows he can't try to take that away from her. He blinks. Maybe they were destined to do this together all along.

He cups her face. "We will."

She nods once, short and sharp, sealing the promise.

Annabel's loud sobbing fills the air, and Luca and Mercy pull apart. "I'll go to her," Mercy says.

"Good idea," Luca agrees. Mercy's ability to say the right thing is probably just what Annabel needs right now.

Mercy takes Annabel into her arms. "You gave him one of your treasures," she murmurs. "That was very generous of you."

Annabel clings to Mercy. "I thought the little boy might keep him company. Look over him."

"I'm sure Aspen would love that."

Annabel tucks her face into Mercy's shoulder, her sobs starting to lose momentum.

Which means when another sound reaches them, it's undeniable. A sound that has everyone freezing.

A sound that has Luca's heart breaking into a gallop.

The loud banging on the metal door comes again, this time joined by a muffled shout.

Luca breaks into a run, wishing he didn't know that voice.

He finds Mercy right beside him. "They're not due back for another three weeks!" she mutters.

But it's Gunnar and Vitron's voices that are unmistakable as they demand the door be opened. Luca comes to a stop, seeing the other people of Fairbanks not far behind him. His muscles coil. "It seems they're not so good with counting time."

Another round of frustrated thumps boom through the door. "For every time I have to hit this door, I'm gonna kill one of you pathetic idiots and put you out of your misery!"

Luca glances at Mercy, conscious that they haven't had time to come up with a plan, let alone prepare her for this. They can't fight Gunnar and Vitron here in the parking lot. It's too dangerous for everyone else.

Mercy's face hardens. "They can take what little we have, but they won't get far."

Luca nods. "We'll follow them then finish this."

Knowing they're far from ready, he yanks open the door.

Vitron's fist falls to his side, having lost the chance to knock again. Luca steps back, hating that he has no choice but to allow them inside.

The two men strut through, lips curled as they scan the parking lot. The people of Fairbanks huddle not far away, even their chance to say goodbye to Aspen interrupted by these heartless men.

Luca stays by the door, hoping he can shut them out sooner rather than later. Mercy is tense and silent beside him.

Gunnar spins around, his gaze finding Luca. "I don't suppose you know anything about our missing bucket of food?"

Luca keeps his face impassive. "My bet is Vitron ate whatever was in there while you were asleep."

"Except someone took my flamethrower, too," Vitron snarls.

Luca waits for them to mention the feather Mercy dropped, but so far it seems they either didn't find it or don't have the brains to connect this back to his return to the Outlands.

Gunnar flexes his hands. "We've come so you can replace the food. We're hungry and no one wants that."

Tarquin shoves through the crowd, slipping out of reach of Finn. "If you lost your food, that's your problem."

Relic steps up beside her. "Yeah. Your problem."

Luca leaps forward, trying to break the deadly focus the two men just lasered on the children. "You're wasting your time. We have nothing."

Vitron spins to glare at him. "Liar! You're hiding food from us just like you're hiding my flamethrower!"

"We don't want any trouble." Luca waves an arm out wide. "Have a look around. Take what you want."

Like Mercy said. Even if they take what little food they have, Gunnar and Vitron won't get far. Luca's going to make sure of it.

And then the people of Fairbanks will be free of them.

Vitron's gaze skips around the parking lot, no doubt taking

in the rubble and decay and the wide, scared eyes watching him from gaunt faces. He glances over his shoulder to where Mercy is still standing by the door.

Something in the way Vitron pauses has Luca tensing. He has to resist sprinting back to her side.

When Vitron's gaze returns to Luca, a light has sparked in their dirty depths. "Whatever we want, you say…"

Gunnar sucks in a sharp breath as he realizes what Vitron is getting at.

Just like Luca does.

Vitron smiles, exposing his brown teeth. He lifts his arm and points behind him, toward Mercy, without breaking the victorious glare he's pinned Luca with.

"We'll take her."

HAWK

*H*awk wakes, unsure for a moment where he is. Then he feels the scorching heat, breathes in the cloying air and sees the flicker of dying flames before him.

He's in the Round House, having been dragged here from the beach by Raiden's men and knocked unconscious.

Gust is sitting beside him, true to his earlier statement that he's all Hawk has left.

"Thought you were never going to wake up," says Gust, his voice a little distorted due to a swollen lip. "Never wake up. Never."

Now that they've been caught in the act of trying to leave the Newlands, there's no more pretending they're trying to assimilate. They've graduated from being tolerated outsiders to prisoners. The only consolation is that Sam got away. And Mercy. It would be so much harder to see them locked up in here with him.

Hawk tries to sit up, but his sides are aching too much. Dammit! These ribs are taking forever to heal. Although, the rough treatment on the beach hadn't helped the process.

"We need to get out of here." Hawk puts his hands on his

bare chest and tries to feel if any further damage has been done. He really can't tell what the bruising is like underneath the tattoos he got courtesy of Corbin.

"There's no way out," says Gust, rocking back and forth. "No way. There's no way out. I checked. No way out."

"When's the last time you slept?" Hawk asks, wondering why Gust is behaving so strangely.

"I don't know." Gust shakes his head. "A few days ago. Yes, a few days. I slept a few days ago."

"A few days!" Hawk tries to sit up again, managing to prop himself on his elbows. Now that he thinks of it, he hasn't seen Gust sleep all week.

"No sleep." Gust's hands tremor as he talks, his eyes darting around. "They'll kill me if I sleep. I know it. Mustn't sleep. Sleep is a bad idea."

Hawk winces as he hauls himself into a seated position, concern for his friend his priority right now. "Gust, we need our strength if we're going to find a way off this island. You have to sleep."

Gust shakes his head, a crazed look on his face. "No way off. The boat wasn't real. There's no boat. They're going to kill us. No boat."

"We'll find another way," says Hawk. "We'll send that raven we spoke about."

"Raiden has the pendant." Gust's shaking intensifies as he launches to his feet and starts pacing. "He won't give it to us. No boat."

"A pendant's not the only shiny thing around here," says Hawk. "We'll find something else to attract a raven's attention."

"No pendant," says Gust. "Raiden has the pendant."

Hawk lets out a long sigh, regretting the action when it makes his sides ache further.

Knowing he's not going to get any sense out of Gust until he gets at least a few hours of sleep, Hawk pulls himself to his feet.

He looks at the fire wishing there was a way to put out the last of the flames. There are two piles of timber stacked up. One dry, which will only feed the flames further. And one damp, which will only fill the room with smoke.

Deciding he's going to have to put up with the heat, he heads to the door.

"Locked," calls Gust. "Door is locked. No way out. No way. Nothing at all."

Hawk tries the door anyway, not all that surprised to find Gust is right, but still unable to figure out why they're still alive. There's only one reason Corbin wouldn't have killed them already.

The Tournaments.

Corbin had said they were coming up and he was more than a little keen for Hawk to participate. In fact, he'd insisted on it. And Gust.

Hawk shudders as he remembers Corbin saying that an early kill will get the crowd excited. He can't let that happen to Gust. Especially not with the way he's behaving right now. He wouldn't stand a chance.

Trying the door again, Hawk is shocked when it pushes outward. It takes him a moment to figure out it's because someone has opened it from the other side.

"Alyx?" Of all the people, Hawk hadn't expected it to be her. Although she seems to have had some kind of history with Luca, Hawk hasn't had much to do with her at all.

She pushes past him and closes the door with a quick glance outside to see if anybody noticed her.

"Door is open," says Gust. "Get out. We have to get out."

But Alyx shakes her head. "The clearing is full of people. You'll be seen. Then you'll be killed. Stay here."

"Why are you here?" Hawk crosses his arms, wanting to get to the point.

"I brought you something." Alyx slides a bag from her

shoulder and passes Hawk a flask of water and Gust a small loaf of bread resting on a thick piece of bark. "You need to eat."

Gust immediately sets down the bark and tears off a chunk of bread. He shovels it in his mouth, but Hawk isn't so sure it's safe. Why would Alyx help them like this?

"Drink," says Alyx, pointing at the flask in his hands. "Before..."

Hawk's brows shoot up. "Before what?"

"The first Tournament is today." She sighs. "Corbin says you're fighting. You need some strength."

Unable to resist any longer, Hawk takes a sip of the water, knowing he can't survive much longer without it. He's no use to Sam if he's dead. What if Raiden were to find his way over to Askala and he wasn't there to protect her? He has no choice but to take the risk that Alyx wishes them no harm.

Stopping himself from drinking the entire flask, he passes it to Gust in exchange for the bread.

"Why are you doing this for us?" he asks Alyx, between mouthfuls.

She shrugs. "I'm not doing it for you. I'm doing it for someone else. Someone I wronged."

This doesn't make all that much sense to Hawk, but his stomach isn't complaining as he takes his first bite of bread.

"Luca's in Askala," says Gust, a droplet of water sliding down his chin. "Gone. Mercy, too. Both gone."

Alyx shakes her head. "Is that where you think he went?"

"Where else would he have gone?" asks Hawk, talking with his mouth full. "He wouldn't take Mercy to the Outlands."

"That's exactly where he went," says Alyx. "And he took my little sister, too. To punish me."

Hawk pauses his chewing, unable to imagine Luca doing anything as vindictive as kidnapping a child. "*That's* who you wronged? Luca? What in sweet Terra did you do to him?"

Alyx shrugs. "That's not important now. What's important is

that we go there to find him. I have plenty more food. Jewelry. Blankets. Whatever you want. But I can't get there alone. It wouldn't be safe. I need you to protect me."

Hawk laughs at this. "You actually think we're sitting in here when we have the means to get ourselves to the Outlands? Or anywhere for that matter? We're prisoners, in case you hadn't noticed."

"Prisoners," Gust repeats. "Prisoners."

"What's wrong with him?" Alyx asks with a frown.

"He hasn't slept in a week," says Hawk, surprised at how defensive he feels. "He's a bit confused, that's all. There's nothing wrong with him."

Alyx nods as she watches Gust pace in front of the statue of Ronan. "Well, I can't help him with that."

"We didn't ask you to," Hawk snaps, deciding Alyx is behaving even more strangely than Gust with these crazy ideas. "Thanks for the bread and water, but if that's all then it would be better if you just left us alone."

"I can get us a boat." Alyx grabs Hawk on the arm.

"Yeah, I hate to break it to you, but we've heard that one before." Hawk shakes himself free of her touch. "And it didn't go so well."

"You don't trust me?" Alyx shakes her head.

"I don't even know you," says Hawk. "You've walked in here telling us you wronged our friend and you think he's taken your sister and Mercy to the Outlands. And that we should jump on some mythical boat with you and chase after them. Face it, Alyx. Luca's back home in Askala. And if such a thing as a boat existed that's exactly where I'd be heading, too."

"There's so much you don't know." Alyx sits down and hangs her head in her hands.

"Let's hear it then." Hawk sighs. "I don't have much on my calendar today. Oh, apart from being murdered in a Tournament, of course."

Alyx looks up at him with tears in her eyes. "I sold Luca out. I told them he's the Falcon. I thought—"

"What the actual?" Hawk stands in front of Alyx, hands firmly planted on his hips. "Luca's the Falcon?"

"You mean, you didn't know?" Alyx turns an even paler shade than her already fair complexion. "I just assumed he'd have told you."

Hawk shakes his head as he tries to process this. "Why would he keep that from us? We've been trying to figure out who the Falcon is. Besides, we were told he's dead."

"Someone copied him," says Alyx. "They were killed in his place. The Outlanders didn't know the difference."

"And you told them that he's still alive?" Hawk's hands explode out. "They'll kill him for real now!"

"That's why he left," says Alyx, her tears running down her cheeks now. "He's gone to kill them first. I just don't know why he had to take Tarquin with him. I need to get over there, Hawk. I have to get my sister back. She's all I've got. Please, help me."

"Help!" Gust pauses his pacing. "Alyx needs help. We have to help Alyx."

"No, Gust." Hawk goes to his friend and places a steadying arm around him. "Alyx can use whatever it was she received in exchange for the information on Luca to get herself out. We're not getting involved in this."

"We need to send a raven to Askala," says Alyx, not giving up. "We'll ask them to send a boat to take us to the Outlands."

"They won't do that." Hawk finishes the last of the bread, wishing there was more.

"They will if they think Luca's life's in danger." Alyx stands, her face alight with determination. "His father is the leader. He'll want to save his son."

"Why does everyone think that?" Hawk asks. "Kian is one of the leaders. Not *the* leader. And he knows Luca can take care of himself."

"You'll see," says Alyx, heading for the door. "I have plenty of jewelry shiny enough to attract the attention of a raven. This will work. They'll send a boat and we'll go to the Outlands."

"Do whatever you like." Hawk presses at his temples. "But if I ever get myself on a boat again, I'm not going anywhere except home."

The thought of stepping off a boat onto home soil and seeing Sam's beautiful face pulls at him. He doesn't even care if it's just as friends. He misses her so much. If only he could be certain that might happen one day it would make it so much easier to live through this current nightmare.

"I need your protection," says Alyx, so sure that he'll do her bidding like all the other men around here. He's not being anyone's bodyguard, especially to someone who sold out a Seeker. "I'll pay you well."

Just as Alyx is about to put her hand on the door, it swings open.

Alyx dives to the side but isn't fast enough and Corbin's large hand seizes her by the back of her dress.

"What do we have here?" he sneers as he turns Alyx to face him. "A little bit of pre-tournament entertainment for our fighters?"

"Nothing wrong with that," says Alyx, her voice full of fear. "I took pity on them."

"Liar." Corbin spits directly in her face. "I see the water flask. You probably brought them food, too, didn't you? What a waste. It's like feeding a corpse."

Alyx wipes her face, remaining silent as she does her best to keep some dignity. Hawk feels a twinge of sympathy for her.

"Go to your hut and don't make any more trouble or I'll make sure every one of my men visits you after the Tournament. One. By. One."

He lets go of her, and Alyx scurries from the Round House while Corbin laughs.

The twinge of sympathy Hawk felt morphs into a surge. If he ever can get out of this place, he has to take Alyx with him. It's not right for anyone to be treated like that, no matter their past sins. Corbin has taken this way too far.

The sound of people gathered in the clearing filters through the open door.

"Are you ready?" Corbin asks. "The Tournament is about to begin."

"I told you last time. I'm not fighting." Hawk straightens his back and stares Corbin down.

"I wasn't actually talking to you." Corbin turns to Gust, who's stopped pacing and is staring at the open door. Maybe he should run. He might actually stand more chance of living.

"He's not fighting, either." Hawk steps in front of Gust. "Can't you see he's not well?"

"I never said it was going to be a fair fight." Corbin smiles, revealing a set of yellow teeth. "Best to put him out of his misery before he infects the whole island if he's not well."

"He's tired and starving," says Hawk. "Pretty sure your miserable island is already infected with that."

"I haven't got all day." Corbin tries to step around Hawk.

"Take me, instead," says Hawk, preventing him from passing. "Leave him alone."

Corbin jabs his index finger into Hawk's chest. "We have other plans for you, my friend. Today's not your day to die."

"What plans?" Hawk asks, hating that he's giving Corbin the power of knowing he has him curious.

"Raiden wants to finish you properly." Corbin smiles. "He just needs a little more healing time to even things out."

"You said these fights aren't supposed to be fair." Hawk glares at Corbin. "Or is it different when you're the one with the disadvantage?"

"Shut up, you Seeker scum." Corbin shoves Hawk out of the

way, sending pain radiating down his torso. "Get over here, Gust."

"No." Gust shakes his head as he backs away. "Not going over there. No."

Two of Corbin's men appear at the doorway and march over. Hawk stands in front of Gust once more, and the men make a grab for Hawk, pinning his arms painfully behind his back. Corbin takes hold of Gust and walks him over to the door. Gust drags his feet and fights back, but he's no match for Corbin, who's seeming to be exerting little more effort than if he were transporting a child.

"Gust!" Hawk is thrown to the ground and Corbin's men take off after their beloved Commander.

Scrambling to get to his feet, Hawk runs to the door just as it's slammed in his face and locked tight.

"Gust!" he shouts again as he bangs his forehead on the solid timber. "Gust!"

His friend is going to die, he knows it. And there's not a damn thing he can do about it!

Desperate to know what's going on outside, Hawk scans the Round House. There are no windows, but there are small gaps in the timber right near the top of the walls for ventilation. Not that there's much hope of getting fresh air in here with all the smoke that stifling fire puts out.

If Hawk can get up high enough, he might be able to see outside. Maybe he'll be able to shout out to Gust. Warn him or give him some advice. Something—anything!—that might be able to make the difference.

The only moveable object in this whole room is that blasted statue of Hawk's grandfather.

He goes to it, using all his weight behind it to try to push it.

It slides across the floor a few inches and he tries again, this time managing to move it a couple of feet.

With sweat beading on his forehead and his ribs crying out

in agony, he continues to move the statue until he has it pressed up against the wall.

Taking a moment to catch his breath, Hawk looks up at the giant silver effigy.

"Sorry, Gramps," he says, as he attempts to scale the statue.

But the surface is slippery and it takes him a few tries to figure out where to put his feet in order to get any kind of grip.

Slowly, he inches his way up, certain the great Ronan wouldn't be at all impressed with what he's doing. Aunt Wren would have a great laugh if only she could see, especially when he sticks a foot in the crook of Ronan's elbow and hauls himself up to sit on his grandfather's giant silver head.

He's almost at the perfect height. Pressing his face against the gap in the timber, he peers out at the clearing.

There's a ring of people, making the same large circle they did at the last Tournament. Gust is in the middle, turning around as he scans the faces, his tired, scrambled brain not able to make sense of what's happening. Hawk remembers feeling much the same when he was forced out there.

"You can do it, Gust!" Hawk shouts with no idea if his voice can travel the distance it needs. But Gust turns his face toward the Round House for just a moment, giving Hawk the hope that he can be heard. There are a few sniggers in the crowd, but Hawk isn't deterred. "You've got this, Gust!"

Raggid steps out into the clearing, greeted by cheers and whistles.

Hawk curses. Not Raggid! Corbin's right hand goon who can practically carry a whole tree under one arm. Anyone but that thug. Gust doesn't stand a chance! Perhaps he never did. And knowing Corbin, that's the whole idea of this evil farce.

Gust turns to see Raggid and it's like all his confusion instantly clears as a wave of pure terror washes over him. Hawk lets out a whimper as he sees a dark stain spread across the front of Gust's pants.

"You're a Seeker, Gust!" Hawk's throat sears at the volume he's using to project his voice. "The best of the best."

Gust turns to the Round House and suddenly doesn't look quite so afraid. He pulls back his shoulders and raises a fist.

"I'm a Seeker!" he shouts to Hawk. "The best of the—"

Gust's words are knocked from him as Raggid punches him square in the face.

"No!" Hawk cries as Gust slumps to the ground, unmoving.

"You fool!" Corbin scolds, running out into the clearing and glaring at Raggid. "That's not a show! You were supposed to give us a show! You've killed the guy with one punch!"

Hawk groans as he presses his face against the gap in the timber. Please let Corbin be mistaken. Gust can't be dead! Not like that.

Raggid says something Hawk can't hear, and Corbin marches back out to the crowd with his arms crossed.

Lifting Gust from the ground, Raggid hoists him until he's raised above his head. Hawk can't see any sign of life, but surely, Raggid wouldn't be doing this if Gust were already dead? Unless he's trying to give Corbin the show he'd requested.

The people cheer at the gruesome sight before them and Raggid does a victory lap, the shouts getting louder the longer he manages to hold Gust in the air.

Hawk considers climbing down from his vantage point. Whether or not Gust is still alive is of no consequence now. Either way the result will be the same. There's no hope. But it seems disrespectful somehow to give up on him now. There's nobody else out here on Gust's side. He's all alone on this island, except for Hawk.

"You're a Seeker, Gust!" Hawk shouts again, even though he doesn't believe Gust can hear him. The only consolation Hawk can take is that the last words Gust heard before he was knocked out were words of support.

Gust is a Seeker. The best of the best.

He may have used some questionable tactics to get here, but still, he proved he could do it. And that itself took courage and smarts. Hawk owes that guy his life. Which means he has to put the days he has left to good use. He has to get out of here. This whole disaster can't have been for nothing.

They may have lost the Newlands. And Gust. And Nikita. And Siena. But Hawk sure as hell isn't going to let them add him to that casualty list.

Raggid stands to one end of the circle and bends his knees, swinging Gust back slightly then launching forward, sending him flying through the air and landing heavily a few feet away. Still, he doesn't move.

The crowd goes crazy, whooping and cheering as Raggid goes to Gust and picks him up again, raising him in the air once more.

And Hawk knows he can't continue to watch. Gust is gone. Most likely dead with that first punch. If not, then in the series of hard impacts he's sure to face now as he's treated like a bully's plaything.

Climbing down from the statue, Hawk leans over and vomits up all the sustenance that his body had only just been so grateful to receive.

He looks up at his grandfather's silver face and shakes his head.

"This is all your fault," he chokes out. "You did this. Are you pleased with yourself?"

Ronan stares back at him.

"You're not my grandfather." Hawk kicks the statue, instantly regretting it when his toes hit the solid surface. "Your legacy may continue, but it doesn't live in my veins."

There's the sound of laughter and Hawk spins around to see Raiden leaning heavily on his cane by the door. He seems to be holding something behind his back.

"Nice speech, Hawk," Raiden says. "You should be proud to be the grandson of Cy."

"His name was Ronan." Hawk pulls back his shoulders. "The Mercy he claimed to love so much wanted nothing to do with him. He named himself after a delusion."

"What would you know?" scoffs Raiden.

Hawk rolls his eyes, about to protest that Ronan was his grandfather, but stops himself when he remembers that he just renounced him.

"Why are you here?" Hawk asks, having lost all patience. "Have you come to kill me?"

Raiden laughs at this as he pulls a sledgehammer from behind his back. "Not yet. I've just come to even the score a little before we fight."

SAM

Sam wonders whether she's worn a permanent groove in the path that takes her to the beach. Fifty-seven steps. That's how many it will take her to get to the start of the sand. Twenty more and she'll be standing at the edge of the waves on low tide.

Which will bring her to a total of seventy-seven steps closer to Hawk.

Her heart cries that it's not enough, that it wants to be whole again. It means her mind is experiencing something that Sam hasn't felt much in her life.

Indecision.

She smiles as she passes a woman, noticing the way she barely smiles back. In fact, the woman hardly glances at her. Sam drops her chin, maintaining her momentum to the beach. She just came from the infirmary, and although all the carers adhere to the strictest hygiene standards, the people of Askala are worried.

They're all wondering who will be next.

Especially after Zali's memorial this morning. It wasn't only her body that was weighed down and lowered into the ocean, but four others, too. Each one taken by the same symptoms that took Seb.

That has Sam's mother in bed, weaker and weaker every day.

As quiet sobs had crept over the sound of the waves, Sam wondered if people were more scared of the strange illness that seems to be spreading through Askala, or the undeniable truth that one of theirs had taken her life.

The sight of Zali's blood pooling around her has been branded in Sam's mind. Someone did that to her. Zali could no longer face a life in Askala.

As the people had walked back out of the sea, their difficult task complete, they'd moved in closer. Like the petals of a flower contracting around its central carpal, they'd comforted each other. Even Sam's father, without his beloved Nova, had people murmuring to him as they touched his arm.

As Sam stood there, alone, she realized she didn't have anyone to hold her. That there was no one she *wanted* to hold her. What's more, she felt...unneeded. As Sam had slowly retreated, she'd finally admitted it. She no longer fits in Askala. She never thought those words would gain substance, but they now run through her mind constantly.

The talk with Amity only made it louder. Sam's very own father left Askala to get her mother back because that was the best thing for their colony.

Sam's steps falter as she rounds a bend. Only fifteen more steps and she'll be at the beach. She can't leave Askala.

Can she?

The shouting reaches her at the same time as the sulfuric tang of the ocean. Sam hurries forward, frowning. Raised voices like that are uncommon in Askala.

Sam's toes touch the sand as she sees where the noise is coming from. Jagger is striding toward the partially-built boat, throwing his arms in the air.

"I told you that join isn't going to be waterproof, no matter how much sap we put on it!"

A man standing beside the steadily growing hull lowers his hammer and hunches his shoulders, turning away as if he didn't hear Jagger. Taking a step to the side, he starts banging again.

"Deniel, what are you doing? Didn't you hear me?"

Deniel spins around as Jagger approaches him. "How do we know you're not sabotaging the boat?"

Sam gasps. Deniel, Zali's son.

Jagger leans forward, standing over the slight man. "Because if I wanted to betray Askala, don't you think I would've done it by now?"

Deniel huffs and turns away, moving to the other side of the boat. Jagger's jaw is square and tight as he yanks his own hammer from his tool pouch and sets about fixing whatever error Deniel made.

Sam bites her lip. Askala is falling apart around her.

A mystery illness.

A suicide.

And now, suspicion.

"I thought I might find you here." An arm slips around Sam's shoulder and she instantly leans into her father's comfort.

"I'm just about to head back to the infirmary."

Her father's arm tightens, drawing her in close. "You don't have to work every hour of every day, you know."

Sam bites her lip. What else is she going to do with her time? Ruminate on the limbo she's living in? Not a Seeker, no matter how much her heart wants it. Which means no Hawk. And yet unable to find her place here in Askala. "I don't mind. I want to help."

"You always have," her father says softly. "And you are."

Sam shakes her head. Further down the beach, Wren is working with the strongest of Askala, teaching them how to use a slingshot. The weapons spin and fling over and over, rocks peppering the trees several yards away. Sam knew she wouldn't be of any use there, just like she wouldn't be of much help building the boat. She hoped she could find a cure, but she hasn't been able to do that, either...

"How are you, Sam?"

"I'm fine. No symptoms," she reports. "I'm going for a walk in the forest this afternoon, to see if I can find anything new."

"That's not what I meant," her father says on a sigh. "You're not eating much. I don't think you're sleeping a whole lot more. You can't be, you're either in the forest or in the infirmary from sunrise to late at night."

Sam looks up, finding her father's dark gaze on her. "You're worried about me."

Adding to her father's stress is the last thing she wanted to do.

He smiles gently. "You're my daughter, the worrying is inevitable." The smile fades as his brows wrinkle. "It's why I didn't want you going to the Newlands."

Sam turns to watch the boat building again, her jaw clenching. "You were right. I shouldn't have gone."

There's a pause and Sam hopes her father's going to let the topic go. She's about to step away, deciding she'll go back to the forest before heading to infirmary, when he speaks again.

"I'm not sure I was right."

Sam frowns. "No, you were, Dad. I wasn't very good at it." She only made things worse. "The others are doing a much better job."

"But, were you happy?"

She stills. "What?"

"Were you happy? Were you following your heart?"

Sam doesn't answer those questions. She's never felt more alive than when she was there. More infused with purpose. More...whole than when she was with Hawk.

But none of that matters. She only passed the second Proving because Kozue backed out.

Askala is about the greater good, and her being a Seeker isn't helping anyone.

Her father spins her to face him, clamping his hands on her shoulders. "Heart is the foundation of Askala, Sam."

She freezes. It's like her father knew exactly what she was thinking.

"That's what I learned when I went after your mother. I thought it was all about sacrifice, too. Except there is no Askala without heart."

"But..."

His hands tighten as his eyes blaze with intensity. "You saw what the Outlanders are capable of. What an invasion could mean for us, and everything we've built here."

Mother Nature wouldn't stand a chance. Neither would the people of Askala...

"You're saying I should go back?" Sam asks, confused.

Her father engulfs her in a hug, his strong body warm and soothing. "I'm telling you what I should've in the first place. Follow your heart, wherever that will take you."

Sam nods, her eyes stinging, knowing that's not easy. Her heart's torn. She desperately wants to do what's right. And she has no idea what that is.

Her father pulls back. "I'm going to check on Jagger and Wren, then go sit with your mother."

Sam steps away, nodding in thought. "I'm going to take a short walk in the forest."

Smiling, her dad's eyes soften. "Maybe just enjoy the forest for a moment? Try not to name everything you see?"

Her own lips twitching into a smile, Sam rolls her eyes. "I'll try."

"And don't fall over!" he says as he turns away.

Sam rolls her eyes, realizing that she hardly ever stumbles

anymore. She's not sure if it's because she's had to learn to cope without Hawk there to catch her or it's because becoming a Seeker gave her the confidence she needed. She's capable of so much more than she ever thought.

Her father heads down to the boat where Jagger is still hammering away. Her father would've noticed the way most of the workers are on the other side, meaning he's now trying to figure out what to do about it. It seems Zali's accusation has caught like a burr in some people's minds.

As Sam turns away, she still can't bring herself to believe Jagger would go to such lengths to destroy the people who took him in. Waiting almost twenty years to sabotage Askala and exact revenge? It doesn't make sense.

But then again, Sam assumed Corbin and Raiden had good in them, and look where that got her...

The cool shadows of the branches envelop Sam as she enters the forest, this time taking a sharp right and heading uphill as she leaves the path. Each time she goes into the forest she takes a different route to see if she can find any new plants. The answer has to be here among everything Mother Nature has to offer. It has to.

The land slopes even more uphill as Sam weaves her way between the broad trunks. *Pinus rhizophores* reaching up to the sky. *Bryophyta* moss clinging to the bark. *Neuroptera* with their large lace-like wings flitting above her in the foliage.

Realizing she's doing exactly what her father said she would, Sam stops and looks around. The forest is still and quiet, but she knows it's full of life. It's all light and shadows, simultaneously growing and gaining life as other parts die and decay. Pulling in a deep breath, Sam does a slow pirouette.

Such a beautiful, fragile balance. One she's a part of, mind, heart, and soul.

There's no Askala with no heart...

Sam freezes as she inhales sharply. Her father's right. There will be no Mother Nature without the heart to care for her. One can't exist without the other.

But there's no time to digest the realization because Sam's eyes narrow as she stops. There was a movement, a flash of material, to her left. Someone else is in the forest, too, despite the lack of path.

Cautiously, she moves toward them. As she creeps forward, Sam realizes how much her short time in the Newlands shaped her. She no longer trusts on face value. She no longer assumes.

Whoever it is, they seem unaware of Sam's presence as she slips behind a nearby tree. She lets out the breath she was holding when she sees who it is.

Charity's kneeling in the dry pine needles, picking something from a small bush. She holds her apron in front of her, dropping the small fruit into the pouch she's created.

Glad that someone else is working just as hard to find a cure, Sam steps around the trunk.

Her heart leaps as she registers what's happening. Charity's picking small, green, tomato-like berries. She's picking deadly nightshade.

Sam rushes toward her. "No!"

Charity leaps to her feet, her face stricken with fear. She stumbles backward a few steps, clutching her apron.

Sam stays back a short distance, surprised at the girl's terror. "Those berries. They're poisonous."

Charity looks down in surprise. "Surely, not?"

Sam watches her closely, not liking the suspicion prickling across her skin. "Yes, they're quite poisonous. Deadly, in fact."

And there's enough in Charity's apron to have it sagging with the weight.

Charity shakes her head. "I'm sure you're wrong. Why, they look just like little tomatoes." She picks one of the berries up and lifts it to her mouth.

"Charity!" Leaping forward, Sam knocks it out of her hand,

images of doing the same for Hawk flashing through her mind. "Even one deadly nightshade berry could kill you!"

Charity's eyes widen. "Deadly nightshade?" She drops her apron and the round berries tumble to the ground. "That sounds terrible!"

Sam's shoulders unwind. "Yes, *belladona* is called that for a reason."

"Thank goodness you came when you did, Sam." Charity's face crumples. "I was just trying to help. I thought maybe these were something we hadn't thought of." A fat tear trickles down Charity's cheek.

Sam blinks at the sudden change of emotion. "It's fine, you didn't know," she reassures. "Why don't you go back to the infirmary? I'm going to get rid of these so no one makes the same mistake."

Charity hesitates, her gaze flicking to the forest floor. "If you're sure..."

"I'm certain," Sam says firmly.

Charity takes a few steps away only to stop, her hands wringing her apron. "I really was trying to help."

"What else would you be trying to do?" Sam asks, making a show of being perplexed even as she wonders what she's doing. Charity almost ate a deadly nightshade berry. Of course she was only trying to help.

Charity smiles. "Exactly. That's what my mother sent me here to do, after all."

Turning away, Charity makes her way back to Askala. Sam watches her leave, conscious that her time in the Newlands definitely changed her. The Sam of before would've taken everything Charity said at face value. She never would've questioned the girl who's worked tirelessly in the infirmary and kitchens. And yet, Sam refuses to believe that Jagger would do what he's being accused of.

Sam sets about crushing each deadly nightshade berry

beneath her shoe, frowning at the destruction. Following her heart means following little more than instinct. It means ignoring her brain.

Glancing at where Charity disappeared through the trees, Sam bites her lip.

Askala is preparing for an attack. For a battle they hope never happens.

But what if the real threat lies within?

MERCY

ercy needs to make a choice. And she needs to make it now. A dozen thoughts race through her mind in far fewer seconds.

Vitron and Gunnar want to take her with them. And not for her sharp wit and kind heart. If she refuses, everyone here is in danger. They'll burn the place down with their flamethrower and take who knows how many of the women. But if she goes...she may never see Luca or Tarquin again. Actually, she may never see anyone again, given she'll most likely be dead. Because there's no way she's going to let them do what that creep tried to do to her in the Newlands. She'd rather go down fighting. Has Luca taught her enough in one short lesson?

Unlikely.

But her mom's been teaching her stuff her whole life. All she has to do is put it all together...

"I'll go," she says, locking her gaze on Vitron. "But you have to agree to leave these people alone. Not for another week. Or a month. *Forever.* Never come back here. Do you agree?"

"No, they don't," says Luca, stepping in front of her. "Firstly,

EXILE

because their word has no honor. Secondly, because that offer isn't on the table."

"Luca," Mercy hisses, trying to get back out in front of him. He has got to learn to have a bit of faith in her. He can't always swoop in like the Falcon and save her. She knows what she's doing. Or at least she thinks she does.

Luca's feet are planted firmly, and he uses his elbows to keep her back. Mercy's going to have to attack him first if she wants to get past.

Vitron lets out a low grunting noise and shoves the tip of his flamethrower directly at Luca. By the way he's pushed back, that thing has to be pressed right up against Luca's chest. After this morning's session with Fleur, Mercy knows just how much power those things pack. If Vitron pulls the trigger, there's zero chance of Luca surviving.

"Let's talk about this!" Mercy shouts.

Luca raises his arms above his head and Mercy is finally able to move forward to stand beside him.

Vitron is purple with rage. Not exactly the expression you want to see on someone's face when they have a deadly weapon pressed against the chest of the only man you've ever loved.

Gunnar is the one to turn to Mercy. He licks his lips as he sweeps his filthy gaze over her. "You heard what she said. She's coming with us."

"Get your eyes off her," snarls Luca.

"Be quiet," Mercy snaps at him. Luca's in enough danger already without angering Vitron further. One press of that trigger and it's all over.

"You can't take her!" Tarquin approaches, her fists held in front of her chest and growling in the same way Mercy had taught her earlier in the day. "We'll fight you!"

"Not now," Mercy hushes as she puts an arm around Tarquin, hating that this might be the last time she holds this precious girl.

"Let's go," says Vitron, not dropping his flamethrower from Luca's chest. "Gunnar, take our new friend out. I'll follow."

"Before we go…" Mercy lets go of Tarquin as she moves forward. "I have one condition."

Vitron rolls his eyes. "What?"

"Get that thing off Luca's chest so I can hug him goodbye." Mercy points at the flamethrower. "Please?"

"Aw, isn't that sweet," laughs Vitron. "She wants to give her boyfriend a hug goodbye."

"She'll be doing plenty of hugging later," says Gunnar, licking his lips. "May as well get some practice."

Vitron doesn't lower the weapon as Mercy had hoped. He keeps it pointed at Luca and takes two steps back to allow her some room. With the distance those flames can reach, she doesn't fool herself into thinking they're in any less danger.

Mercy slides her arms around Luca's neck and he pulls her to his chest.

"No, Mercy," he says. "This is a bad idea."

"Take care of Fleur." Mercy tries desperately to say what she needs to in a way only Luca will understand.

"Mercy?" Luca pulls back, his face full of confusion. And she knows she has to be clearer. Now's not the time to talk in code.

Standing on her toes, she presses her mouth against his ear.

"Follow me," she whispers, hoping it's loud enough for him to hear yet not anyone else.

"Enough!" Gunnar grabs Mercy around the waist and pulls her away while Vitron waves the flamethrower in Luca's face.

Mercy and Luca's eyes are locked on each other and it's only then she realizes that she didn't kiss him goodbye.

But it's not goodbye, she reminds herself. He's going to follow her. He'll bring Fleur. Together, they'll take these bastards down and Fairbanks will be free of the terror that's been brought upon their peaceful existence. They'll be able to eat the food they find for themselves and restore their health. Relic will have the chance to grow up into a strong man and then who knows what good he'll be able to do. Maybe Tarquin will stay on to live with them and she'll have the hope of a future as well.

It's these thoughts that keep Mercy's feet moving as she breaks Luca's gaze and allows Gunnar to lead her up the stairs.

"No, Mercy!" Tarquin calls up to her. "Don't go!"

Mercy tries to shake herself free of Gunnar's grasp. "Let go of me. I'm not going to run."

"If you run, we'll torch you," Vitron says and she feels the hard tip of the flamethrower pressing into her back. If only she had Fleur with her she'd spin around and turn his revolting beard to ash.

"I'm. Not. Going. To. Run." Mercy grits her teeth as she continues to climb the stairs. "Just get that thing off my back and let go of me."

"Ohh." Gunnar laughs as he lets go of her. "We've got ourselves a feisty one here!"

Mercy falls silent, deciding that it would be better if these oafs underestimate her. At least that way she'll have the element of surprise. But it might just be a little too late for that.

They step out into the bright sunshine and Mercy blinks as her eyes adjust. She wishes she had a long drink of water before they set out. The walk through the wastelands is going to be torture. Hopefully, she's not made to walk too far before the first stop. She's going to need all her strength for what she knows she has to do.

But instead of heading in the direction of the road the two men took the last time they left Fairbanks, they push Mercy the opposite way. Down the path through the rubble that will take them deeper into the ruins of the city that was once the thriving metropolis of Fairbanks.

Vitron pauses to unravel a long thin rope from around his waist. He ties the other end around Mercy's middle in a complicated knot that she knows she has no hope of unraveling.

"I already told you I'm not going to run," she says. "I'm well aware that if I do, you'll go back and hurt my friends."

"Hurt?" Gunnar laughs. "More like kill."

"Just making sure," says Vitron, testing the knot. "Not every day you get your hands on some sweetness like you've got going on there."

Mercy swallows, trying not to break eye contact but feeling ill at Vitron's sickening gaze.

He runs his tongue over his bottom lip. "The fact you're the Falcon's girl is going to make it all the more enjoyable."

"What did you say?" Mercy's jaw drops open at this revelation. If they knew Luca was the Falcon, why hadn't they killed him on the spot?

"You heard me." Vitron reaches into his pocket and holds up a single black feather. "Whoever took our flamethrower left this behind. Look familiar?"

Mercy doesn't say anything, which only seems to make Vitron angrier.

He glares at her. "Strange how the Falcon returned at the exact same time as your loverboy, isn't it?"

"Very strange," Gunnar adds with a sneer.

Mercy is flooded with dread and regret that she wasn't more careful with that blasted feather. The game is well and truly up. Now it's just the urgent matter of making sure the Falcon is the one who wins. And there's only one way to do that.

They have to do what they came here to do.

End it.

End *them*.

Eventually these men are going to have to stop somewhere and then she and Luca will roast them like the rats they are.

Vitron walks off, the rope pulling tight and tugging Mercy along behind him. She just wishes she could work out why they're going in the wrong direction. Is it to throw Luca off the scent? Perhaps these two are more frightened of the Falcon than they're prepared to let on?

"Why didn't you kill him?" Mercy calls out. "You had your chance back there."

This question seems to amuse Gunnar who trots off ahead to catch up to Vitron, leaving Mercy to trail behind them.

Stooping briefly, she picks up a small piece of crumbled red brick, dragging it across the surface of a concrete wall as she passes, pleased to see it leaves a mark. Quickly scribbling the letter M, Mercy hides the brick in the palm of her hand, looking for the next surface she can draw on. If Luca hasn't been able to keep up, then surely, he'll see her trail.

Then she reminds herself that Luca grew up with these ruins as his playground. She's certain he'll be close by. But she's not taking any chances. Her life, as well as all the lives in Fairbanks, depends on how this plays out.

Picking their way through the ruins, they make their way deeper into Fairbanks, Mercy leaving a mark whenever she gets the chance. She's never been this far into the crumbling city before and she notices the number of insects increase the further they walk. She's heard the story of how her grandmother, Avis, used to wear a skirt made from netting that she'd wrap around herself to protect from mosquito-borne disease.

Mercy swats away a bug that's just landed on her arm, wishing she had some of this netting now. It would certainly come in handy.

The insects are a large reason why the Outlanders choose not to live out here. That, and the danger of having a building fall on your head.

Daring to draw another letter M on a wall, Mercy stumbles forward, dropping her piece of brick as the rope gets pulled tight.

"Keep up, sweetheart," Vitron growls over his shoulder,

slowing his pace for a couple of steps. "You'll trip me up with your laziness."

Gunnar laughs like he does at all Vitron's jokes. But his glee is cut short as a steel beam falls across his path. It crashes to the ground, sending dust flying into the air and circling them like a cloud.

Mercy winces, wishing she hadn't paused to write on that last wall. If they'd been a couple of steps ahead, that beam would have silenced Gunnar forever and saved her a whole lot of trouble.

Gunnar curses and this time it's Vitron who laughs.

"Must've been your fat ass walking across that slab that set it off," he says, even though nobody in the Outlands has the luxury of being in possession of an ass that's anything close to being fat.

"Might as well stop here," says Gunnar swatting away a mosquito and ignoring his friend's remark. "This is far enough."

"You're planning to go back, aren't you?" Mercy glares at the two men. "That's why we're still in Fairbanks."

"Maybe we like it here." Vitron crosses his arms, blinking as a bug flies directly into his eye.

"If you think Luca's the Falcon, there's no way you're going to let him live," she says. "We had a deal that if I went with you, then you'd leave the people alone. And that includes Luca."

"As your boyfriend pointed out, our word has no honor." Vitron hoots laughing. "Seems like the Falcon got something right."

Gunnar sits down on a faded sign and Mercy strains her eyes to read it. Although there are no longer any buildings standing in their original form, there are remains of them all around. It's hard to imagine all these pieces put back together like some kind of jigsaw.

"What you staring at?" Gunnar asks her, sticking out his chest. "Do you like what you see?"

"Polaris," she says, pointing. "The sign you're sitting on. That building was once called Polaris."

"So?" He shrugs, looking at her like she's lost her mind.

"Polaris is the north star," she says, remembering the astronomy book Sam used to like quoting when they were children. "Wherever you are in the northern hemisphere, Polaris always points north. It's said that following it will lead you in a purposeful direction."

She can hear Sam's voice in her head as she speaks and it tugs on her heart, leaving a pain in her chest. She hopes her cousin is okay wherever she is right now.

Gunnar looks across at Vitron and they laugh yet again, seeming to find this piece of information hilarious. But Mercy doesn't. She sees Polaris as a completely fitting place for these scumbags to die. Maybe then they can all get on with the rest of their lives in peace.

Vitron pulls on the rope, dragging Mercy closer to him until she's pressed right up against his chest. "First, we're going to have ourselves a little rest. Then, you're going to show the both of us a purposeful direction, if you get my drift?"

Mercy blanches at the thought.

Vitron cups her face with his free hand. "Then, when all your little friends are asleep in their beds tonight, we're going to go back and show them how useless their precious Falcon is at protecting them. Got it?"

Mercy knows she should play nice. That she should go along with whatever they're saying while she waits for Luca. But how can she agree to any of that? The only reason they didn't kill Luca when they had the chance was because they wanted to make sure they took everyone else down with him.

"I asked you if your pretty little head understands what I just said?" Vitron squeezes her face harder, his filthy fingers in danger of snapping her jaw.

Mercy still doesn't answer, letting the fury in her eyes do the talking for her.

"You think a girl like you can tease a man and not get what's coming to her?" Vitron asks.

These words send a flare of anger straight to Mercy's gut. Those were the exact words Marr had used on the beach when he attacked her. And nobody is ever going to get away with saying those words to her ever again.

Her knee flies straight up and lands in Vitron's groin.

He howls, slipping his hands from her face to her hair and pulling so hard that a chunk comes out.

"Bitch!" he snarls, shoving her roughly to the ground and doubling over in pain.

Landing on a pile of bricks, she whimpers as the sharp edges cut through her clothes and tear at her skin. But it's still preferable to Vitron's lecherous touch.

Mercy bites down on her tongue to stop herself calling Luca's name. He's either watching from the shadows and biding his time for exactly the right moment, or he's still finding his way to her side. Either way, calling his name won't help.

Vitron hobbles over to sit beside Gunnar, still wincing in pain.

"Don't think we're sharing any of this with you," he says, taking a swig from Gunnar's flask and spitting some of the liquid out on the ground. "I'd rather give it to these blasted bugs than share a single drop with the likes of you."

"I'm not thirsty, thanks." Mercy gives him a defiant smile as she pulls herself into a seated position, keeping as far away from these two scumbags as the rope will allow.

Her throat burns at the idea of the water she craves, and she distracts herself by looking at the clouds, wishing the star of Polaris was shining at her now. She could sure use a purposeful direction to follow at the moment. Because it feels strangely like she's walking straight to her doom. Where in sweet Terra is Luca? Without him, she doesn't stand a chance.

Seeing the slightest movement from the corner of her eye, she shifts her gaze slowly, not wanting to alert her captors.

There's a flash of blond hair from the top of a nearby wall, and Mercy's heart rate picks up. That's not Luca. There's absolutely nothing blond about his hair. But whoever it is, she already likes them more than Gunnar and Vitron, which means she's not going to give them away. This could be just the distraction she needs.

She waits, trying not to make it too obvious that her attention has been distracted.

A shower of small rocks rains down on Gunnar and Vitron.

"What the hell?" shouts Vitron, jumping to his feet and looking up to find the source.

Mercy is just about to get up when something lands in her lap.

Looking down, her eyes widen as she sees it's a small knife, the handle intricately carved out of timber. She touches the tip and it immediately draws a pinprick of blood. This thing is sharp! Shoving it in her pocket, she rises to her feet.

Given that knives don't usually fall from the sky, it seems somebody has gifted this to her. Someone who threw a handful of small rocks at Gunnar and Vitron for nothing more than a distraction. But who? Relic has blond hair, but surely, it's not him? Where would he get a knife like that?

When Mercy's mom first arrived in Askala, she killed a leatherskin with a knife no bigger than this. And as menacing as her two captors are, they're far smaller than a shark. She'll be able to do some serious damage if she can manage to stick that thing in the right place.

Now she stands a chance.

"Stop being paranoid," says Gunnar, slapping Vitron on the

arm. "You know this place is falling down. It was just a few rocks."

"He followed us." Vitron pulls back his shoulders and twitches his nose. "I just know it. I can smell filthy Falcon blood."

Gunnar gets to his feet, scanning the ruins just in case Vitron turns out to be right.

"Get over here, girl." Vitron pulls on the rope and drags Mercy over to his side, while Gunnar takes the flamethrower and holds it out in front of them.

Mercy eyes the rope, knowing that she'll be able to slice through it when the time is right but having no idea when that will actually be. Being a Seeker has taught her many things, including the importance of picking your moment. Act too soon and she could wind up dead. Wait too long and she could also wind up dead. It has to be just right…

Then she sees what she's been watching for.

Not a flash of blond hair but this time a glimpse of movement behind a pillar. And she knows without a doubt from the shape of the shadow that it's Luca.

Her north star.

Her Polaris.

The guy she'd follow to the end of the Earth to be with. Which seems to be exactly what she did when she hid aboard his boat and wound up here. And even given the perilous position she finds herself in right now, she doesn't regret a thing.

With her heart thumping so hard it almost hurts, she checks to see if the two men holding her have noticed, relieved to find they're scanning the ruins in completely the wrong direction.

Mercy steadies her hand on her pocket, ready to pull out the knife.

Everything her mom taught her, everything Luca's ever showed her, all that she learned in the Newlands, it all comes down to this.

And she's never been more ready.

Luca runs from the shadows with Fleur held out in front of him.

Game. On.

LUCA

*L*uca's finger tightens on the trigger of the flamethrower as he flies over the rubble, one word propelling him.

Mercy.

He relishes the flash of satisfaction as Gunnar and Vitron spin around and see him coming at them like some avenging angel. Luca drops his head, his focus zeroed on them. Right now, he feels far more like a demon thirsting for a fight.

He leaps into the air, clearing a boulder of concrete, and as he lands, Luca sees the rope that ties Mercy to Vitron. Dammit. His finger slips off the trigger. He needs to get her away before he roasts these two bastards.

Vitron must realize the advantage that gives him, because he yanks on the cord. Mercy stumbles toward him, straightens, only to be roughly yanked again.

Adrenaline powers the fury through Luca's veins. He's determined that is one of the last things Vitron will ever do.

Gunnar looks from the fast-approaching Luca to his friend and back again, obviously calculating. Mentally, Luca dares Gunnar to come at him. To see if he can get to him in time. The butt of the flamethrower will be in his throat before he realizes what's happened.

But when Gunnar breaks into a run, it's not toward Luca. It's away.

He's fleeing.

"Coward!" shouts Luca.

Another tug from Vitron, and Mercy falls to her knees as she refuses to be dragged any closer. Vitron leaps toward her, knowing she's the only shield he needs.

Never pausing his sprint over the rubble, Luca tucks the flamethrower back over his shoulder. He can't use it, not with Mercy so close.

Vitron's lips are twisting in victory as he reaches a hand toward Mercy, only to draw back with a yelp. He clasps his hand to his chest. "Bitch!"

Mercy leaps backward, the rope trailing like an umbilical cord that's been cut. She streaks out to the side. "Now, Luca!"

Somehow, Mercy cut the rope. And Vitron's hand.

Leaving Luca with a clear line of sight.

There are only a few yards left, and Luca grips the flamethrower, pulling it back into position. Vitron's eyes widen as he realizes he just became prey.

In a flash of movement, he picks up a rock and hurls it. Luca ducks as it zings past his head. When he looks back up, Vitron is sprinting away. All it takes is several frantic steps and he disappears around a mountain of gravel, probably not far behind Gunnar.

Luca comes to a halt right where Vitron had been standing, breathing hard. He throws a disgusted glance at where he'd disappeared. Gutless prick.

But then, he's turning around, the men forgotten for now. His gaze searches the gray wasteland he's standing in, searching for her.

Finding her.

And striding toward her, the yards between them feeling like a mile.

Mercy must think so, too, because she breaks into a run and leaps. Luca catches her, welcoming the impact of her body against his. "Are you okay?"

Mercy burrows her head into his neck. "I am now."

"Did they..."

She shakes her head. "They're still alive, so obviously not."

Against the odds, Luca chuckles. He draws his arms tighter around her, wishing this is where he could keep her, always.

He pulls back, running his hands down her arms. "How did you..." Luca asks, noticing he's lost the ability to finish a sentence. The thought of losing Mercy short-circuited his brain. Finding the trail of clues she left him is the only thing that kept him sane.

Mercy holds up a small knife with a grin. "I found this."

Luca gapes, knowing there's no time to figure out how she could've been that lucky. He presses a fierce kiss to her lips. "Remind me to never underestimate you."

Stepping back, he takes her hand. "Now, we need to get back to Fairbanks." Where it's safe.

But Mercy doesn't move. "What about Gunnar and Vitron?"

"They can get lost in the ruins for all I care. If they make it back to their villages, I'll deal with them there."

Mercy shakes her head. "We can't let them get away."

There's an urgency in Mercy's tone that has Luca stilling. "Why?"

"The feather that I had, they found it. They know you're the Falcon, Luca."

Luca blinks, a small part of him hoping he heard that wrong. "They know?"

"They were planning on coming back tonight and killing you." Mercy bites her lip. "And everyone else in Fairbanks."

His jaw so tight it feels like his teeth are cracking, Luca

straightens. "Looks like they're dying sooner than I thought." He lifts the flamethrower strap off his shoulder and passes it to Mercy. "You'll need this."

She takes the weapon, hefting the weight like it's familiar. "Hello, Fleur. You and I have got a job to do, girl."

Simultaneously, they turn and head in the direction Gunnar and Vitron disappeared. Luca glances at Mercy. Giving her the weapon is a no-brainer. Without fighting skills, this is the best way she can protect herself. But being willing to use it might not be something Mercy is ready for. "Hopefully you won't have to use your new friend."

Mercy's hands tighten around her weapon. "When I pull this trigger, it will be for every girl who has been hurt by men like Gunnar and Vitron."

And Marr.

Luca nods, wishing there was time to tell her how proud he is of her. His beautiful, fierce warrior. He wonders if even Mercy realized she had this in her.

But they both stop as they see what's ahead. The path ahead splits into two, branching around a mountain of rubble that probably used to be a building. Luca glances down, but the gravel makes it impossible to track which way the men went. There are no footprints in the dust, no grass or vegetation to disturb.

Gunnar and Vitron could've gone either way.

The tracks look like they may converge on the other side, but there's no way to know for sure. Luca's about to suggest they try the right track first but Mercy speaks first.

"We need to split up."

"No." Luca doesn't know how he didn't shout the word. "Not happening."

"You know I'm right. We can't afford for them to get away, Luca. Fairbanks is in danger."

Because if Gunnar and Vitron don't attack themselves, then

all they have to do is tell someone Fairbanks has been the Falcon's base and his friends will never be safe.

Not until every one of them is dead.

Luca grips Mercy's shoulders, his heart screaming a denial as his mind knows she's right. "You call me the minute you think you might be in danger."

Mercy nods, her eyes determined even as she bites her lip.

"And you shoot first and ask questions later."

She nods again.

"And you remember that I refuse to consider a life without you in it."

Her face softens. "I'm not likely to forget that."

Pointing the flamethrower like a rifle, Mercy heads down the path. Luca watches her, resisting the overwhelming urge to follow. With a quick glance over her shoulder, she disappears around the pile of rubble.

Luca turns left, his hands clenching compulsively at his side. If either of those bastards hurt her…

Stalking like the predator he just became, Luca continues around the other side of the mountain of broken buildings. He scans ahead as much as he can, flicks his gaze over the ground for any sign that someone else has been here, listens beyond the sound of his own controlled breathing. He even scents the air, trying to detect dust or sweat or unwashed body.

The sooner he knows whether this is the way the bastards came, the better he'll feel.

At the first bend, Luca presses himself close to a slab of concrete, glancing around the corner. He jerks back when he realizes someone is there.

It's Gunnar. And he's lying in the middle of the path. Vitron is nowhere to be seen.

Hoping the crumbling city of Fairbanks has done his job for him, Luca steps out. Except Gunnar is already moving. He groans and lifts a hand to his head. A second later, he leaps to his feet, frantically looking around. Like the Outlander he is, he sees a length of metal nearby and scrabbles to pick it up, stumbling once.

Righting himself, Gunnar looks around, spotting Luca. He grips the pole with both hands, ready to defend himself, probably before he's even fully conscious. His fair hair blows in the wind that's picking up, making Luca wonder if a storm is coming.

Luca keeps his gaze on Gunnar as he takes in their surroundings. Rubble on the right, a massive beam on the left. There's nowhere for Gunnar to escape.

Neither can Luca, but that's fine. He doesn't want to.

Gunnar waves the steel pole like a bat. "Hello, Falcon."

Luca narrows his eyes, trying to understand why Gunnar is here, alone, with a bleeding wound to his head. He straightens as he realizes. "You didn't want to give up the flamethrower, did you?'

Gunnar doesn't answer, but the tightening of his jaw says it all.

Luca shakes his head. "So, Vitron tried to kill you instead."

"Shut up, bird boy." Gunnar flexes his shoulders. "That doesn't matter. This way, I'm going to be the one who takes down the Falcon."

Luca snorts. "If you're actually lucky enough to kill me, do you really think Vitron is going to tell everyone that's how it went down? He'll finish what he started before you squawk a word of this to anyone."

Gunnar's eyes blaze, the pain that must be permeating from his cracked skull being steadily pushed back by hatred and fury. He swings the metal again in a smooth arc, like he's warming up.

Luca takes the risk of breaking eye contact for the briefest of seconds. He can't run at Gunnar while he has the pole and hope to come out unscathed. Children in the Outlands are given weapons instead of toys. Gunnar was probably swinging metal lengths just like this one in games against his siblings. If anyone was hurt, they were rewarded.

But Gunnar was waiting for even the slightest of distractions. He runs at Luca, his dirty face twisted with the need to kill.

Luca thrills at the jolt of surprise across Gunnar's face as he breaks into a run, too. Straight for him.

Gunnar lifts the pole over his shoulder, winding up to strike. He's probably expecting Luca to try to duck. Maybe even jump over it. He'd be waiting to alter the trajectory of the deadly swipe in the blink of an eye.

But Gunnar doesn't know that Fairbanks was the playground of Luca's childhood. So was every tree, hill, or hut in Askala. Each time he challenged himself to climb higher, leap farther, run faster was preparation for moments like these.

Luca steaks toward Gunnar, who slips on a rock but maintains his momentum. His mouth twists in a snarl as the pole begins its savage swing.

It reinforces what Luca suspected. Despite the show of strength, Gunnar's still groggy enough that Luca could probably do what he expects—leap high or duck low.

But where's the fun in that?

With a roar, Gunnar swings, the metal pole ringing as it slices through the air.

Luca launches left, his feet and hands slamming into the smooth surface of the beam and gripping. He contracts in and pushes out again, twisting in the air as he does so. Gunnar disappears beneath him, the pole whistling uselessly across the path.

For long seconds, Luca's flying, arms extended, body arcing and spinning.

For breathless moments, he is the Falcon.

He lands behind Gunnar in a crouch, his body absorbing the impact.

Gunnar halts, confused as his muddled brain tries to process what happened. And that's all Luca needs.

He vaults forward, grabbing the man from behind. A short scrabble and Luca has a hold of the metal bar. He jerks it backward before Gunnar has time to react, slamming it across his throat.

Gunnar breaks into a frenzied struggle, his hands grasping at the pole, his body coiling and contorting as he tries to free himself.

But he's trapped. Luca holds the filthy man against his front, increasing the pressure on Gunnar's throat. A strangled gasp draws in.

And doesn't have the chance to exhale.

"Please," Gunnar wheezes.

But the begging falls on deaf ears. Just like the pleading of every one of Gunnar's victims would have.

His movements become smaller, weaker, as his body is starved of oxygen. Luca grits his teeth and hardens his heart. He wants this to be as quick as possible.

"Your mother," Gunnar chokes out. "I know who she is," he gasps, only to discover there's no air to find. "And your father…"

Luca's hands loosen but don't relieve the pressure.

Gunnar's probably lying.

But…what if he's not?

And how does he know about Luca's mother?

And his father…

Gunnar could have the answers Luca's been looking for all his life.

Except Gunnar planned on hurting Mercy. And if he manages to escape after he feeds Luca his lies, then everyone will be in danger again.

Luca leans down, whispering in Gunnar's ear. "My mother would never know someone like you."

It only takes a handful of seconds. Gunnar's words used up the last of his oxygen, probably speeding up his death. His body goes limp, the weight sagging down on the metal pole.

Luca waits for a few more, knowing Gunnar isn't beyond faking his death. But the man doesn't move, his body sagging as his weight multiplies.

Releasing him, Luca watches as he crumples into the dust. He should feel some remorse, but he doesn't. The world is a better place without Gunnar.

Breathing heavily, Luca spins around. He needs to find Mercy.

Before Vitron does.

Luca's just broken into a run when he hears it. A roaring. The crackling of flames.

Then silence.

A renewed burst of energy pumps through his veins, this time powered by icy cold fear.

Someone just deployed a flamethrower.

HAWK

*H*awk inwardly groans as he sees the sledgehammer Raiden is holding, having just told him he'd come to the Round House to even the score.

"Raiden, I'm not sure how many of my ribs you broke, but I can assure you that we're even." Hawk holds his ground, not wanting this rat to sense any kind of power over him.

Raiden uses his spear to hobble forward. "Has my father told you that we're going to fight in the next Tournament?"

Hawk sighs loudly. "Isn't life already hard enough out here? Why make it worse with these senseless fights?"

Images of Gust's body being flung around like a sack of wheat send a sick feeling to Hawk's gut.

"The Tournaments are about power," says Raiden. "I'll be the Commander one day. It's in my blood. I need to earn respect."

"Actually, it's in *my* blood." Hawk points at the giant statue he just climbed down from. "Maybe it's time I claimed my position."

"You wouldn't dare." Raiden's nostrils flare, betraying his fear at this thought.

Hawk stares him down, even though he has no intention of

trying to become the Commander. He'd rather die than align himself with these murdering bastards. But it doesn't hurt if Raiden believes that. Actually, maybe it does hurt given it's one more reason for Raiden to want him dead.

Changing tack, Hawk holds up his palms. "I don't want to be Commander. I just want to live in peace. I don't want to fight you."

Raiden smiles. "You're afraid of me."

"Should I be?" Hawk looks at the sledgehammer he's certain was brought here to break his ankle.

This makes Raiden laugh. "I'm going to give you a choice. You can sit like a good little boy and let me do this quickly…"

"Or?" Hawk asks, already deciding he'll take Option B.

"Or I'll get my men to hold you down and instead of just breaking your ankle, I'll crush the bone so you'll never walk again." Raiden taps his spear on the ground and Hawk has no doubt he intends to come good on that threat.

"Looks like you'd better get your men then." Hawk crosses his arms as his mind swirls, searching for a way out of this predicament. "Because I will never sit still for you."

"I thought you might say that." Raiden takes a few steps back and turns toward the door.

Hawk swoops down and picks up the piece of curved bark Alyx had used to carry the bread and shoves it into his shoe so it wraps around his ankle. Covering it with the leg of his pants, he quickly stands up.

"I changed my mind," Hawk calls out, not wanting more than one person to have to come up against. He's got more chance against this one spineless wimp. "I'll sit for you. Just do it fast."

Raiden turns back to Hawk, the smile on his face sending a shiver down Hawk's spine. He doesn't just want to break his ankle. He's going to *enjoy* doing it. This guy is even sicker than Hawk thought.

"I have a condition," says Hawk.

Raiden swings the sledgehammer as he approaches, still leaning heavily on his spear. If Hawk has any hope of getting off this island, he needs to make sure he keeps both his ankles intact. He's just not exactly sure how he's going to do that right now. The plan forming in his mind is flimsy at best.

"You're not the one who gets to make conditions around here," says Raiden.

"I'll let you have one swing at me, but after that you let me out of here," Hawk says. "It's not like I can run off anywhere—broken ankle or not."

"We burned your hut down." Raiden widens his grin. "You have no shelter."

"I don't care if I get wet," says Hawk, hoping Raiden will see this as a further opportunity to weaken him. "I want to see the stars again before I die."

"Fine," says Raiden. "My father was going to kick you out of here, anyway. It's far too nice a prison for scum like you."

"Fire's nearly out," says Hawk, nodding toward the dwindling flames.

"Then put some wood on it." Raiden rolls his eyes.

Hawk ignores the pile of dry wood, and goes to the collection of damp bark next to the fire. He picks up a few pieces.

"Not that wood," shouts Raiden. "It will make sm—"

Pretending not to hear, Hawk throws it on the fire and turns to Raiden, trying his best to look surprised as clouds of smoke spill into the room.

"You idiot Seeker!" screams Raiden. "It's going to give me great pleasure to rid the world of someone as stupid as you."

Hawk sits down and puts out his right leg, keeping the one with the bark around it tucked underneath himself as he banks on Raiden's mistrust.

He gives Raiden a nod and a smile, despite the terror that's coursing through his blood "I'm ready. This leg will do."

Raiden positions himself and swings the sledgehammer a few times as a warm-up.

Hawk nods encouragingly, praying his gamble pays off.

Raiden swings the sledgehammer again and Hawk's heart beats so hard he's worried it's going to break another rib.

Raiden's not taking the bait.

"Unless you want my other leg?" says Hawk, deciding someone as thick as Raiden needs subtlety a little more like the weapon he's brandishing. "Actually, no. Forget I said that. This leg is fine. Just do it fast."

Raiden stills his weapon and Hawk holds his nerve, waiting for Raiden to play right into his hand.

"What?" asks Hawk. "I said this leg is good. Let's just get it over with. Do it."

"Swap legs," barks Raiden. "I like the other one better."

"This one's fine," Hawk argues. "It's the same one as yours. We'll be like a mirror out there in the Tournament."

"I said I like the other one." Raiden grits his teeth, coughing as the smoke continues to drift over. His brain is working so hard right now Hawk can practically see it ticking over.

"No, Raiden," Hawk pleads. "Please not the other one. I'll do anything. Just let's stick to this leg. I'm begging you here."

Raiden laughs. "Save your begging for the Tournament. Now swap legs before I call in my men to swap them for you."

Hawk makes a show of not wanting to put out his other leg, buying time until there's enough smoke in the room that visibility is severely hampered, hoping like sweet Terra that Raiden won't see the bulge of the thick bark underneath the leg of his pants.

With no time to reposition it, Hawk holds his foot out in what he hopes is going to be the safest position given a sledgehammer is about to come down on him.

He winces as Raiden swings the weapon into the air, letting out a grunting sound as it arcs and comes down hard.

There's a loud crunch and a crack as pain shoots through Hawk's ankle. But nowhere near enough pain for that sound to have been bone rather than bark.

Hawk howls as he pulls back his ankle, clutching it as he continues moaning.

Raiden stands over him, a look of sick satisfaction on his face. "Now you know what it feels like."

Hawk can only pray that Raiden doesn't decide to take another swing at him, so he curls himself over his ankle and nurses it, sobbing as loudly as he dares.

"You're free to leave." Raiden steps back and sweeps out his hand.

"I can't walk," Hawk yelps. "I think you crushed the whole bone!"

Actually, his ankle does feel a little sore and he's certain to get a nasty bruise, but that bark had taken almost the full impact. He just needs Raiden to look away for a moment so he can slip the broken pieces out from underneath his clothes.

"Well, you're not having my lucky spear to lean on," says Raiden. "Nikita sharpened it just for me."

"You killed her, didn't you?" Hawk asks, shaking his head as he pretends to wipe away tears.

"She asked for it," Raiden sneers. "Classic case of a pauper who thinks she's a princess. I need myself a real queen."

Hawk swallows, realizing just how deranged this guy is, having just promoted himself from future Commander to King.

"After I kill you in the Tournament, I'm going to go and get that bitch Sam back," says Raiden. "She owes me. I'm thinking five sons at least."

Hawk blanches at the thought. Not Sam. Not *his* Sam. The only girl he's ever loved. The only girl he's ever going to love! The thought of getting back to her to protect her from scum like Raiden is the only reason he's still choosing to breathe right now. And maybe the thought of holding her in his arms once more. Even if it is just as a friend…

And this is why Hawk has to get out of the Newlands. He can't stay here. He has to get to find a way out and it seems he only has one hope left.

Alyx.

The woman who proved she can't be trusted by selling Luca out is now his Plan A, B and C. There's literally nothing and no-one else left.

Doing his best to act distracted, Hawk turns sharply to look at the door and raises his eyebrows.

Raiden looks to see what has his attention and Hawk slips the broken pieces of bark out of his clothing and kicks them aside. It feels almost cruel to fool this imbecile with what must be one of the oldest tricks in the book.

"Thought I heard someone," Hawk says.

"Get out of here." Raiden pokes Hawk with the sharp tip of his spear. "Before I decide to break your other ankle."

Hawk pulls himself to a stand, wincing dramatically and being careful not to put any weight on his supposedly broken ankle. He hops to the door while Raiden hoots with laughter. Hawk's not feeling so gleeful given the real pain that radiates through his joints with each jolted movement.

"I've never seen a one-legged hawk before," Raiden jeers.

Hawk gets himself out of the door and drags in some clean air, grateful to be out of that Round House of Hell. He hops toward the charred remains of his old hut, not wanting Raiden to receive any reports of him having walked on two legs.

The clearing is full of people and Hawk avoids looking toward their focus. He knows what they're looking at and he can't bear to see it. Or rather, him. Or whatever is left of poor Gust.

Waiting by the only remaining post of the Seekers' hut, Hawk looks around to see if anyone is watching him. Raiden leaves the Round House and limps to the home he shares with his parents, no doubt to brag about what he just did to Hawk.

Hawk is going to need to move fast before Corbin decides that letting him go wasn't such a good idea. He looks at Alyx's hut, which is positioned behind the other dwellings, marking her as a woman of disgrace. She really does have to get out of here. She should never have come in the first place. Grace has some protection being the wife of the Commander but Alyx is just too vulnerable out here on her own.

He gets himself to her hut and leans heavily on the doorjamb.

"Alyx!" he calls through the flap of thick leather acting as a door. "It's Hawk."

Nobody answers so he steps inside, sighing with relief as he sets both feet on the ground, and looks around.

Alyx's hut is far nicer than any of the others he's seen around here. It looks almost cozy. He'd love to lie down on the pile of blankets in the corner and just close his eyes for a few hours. Or maybe days. He's beyond exhausted.

But that's not going to happen. He has to find Alyx. They have to send a raven and get themselves out of here.

There's a small table in the corner of the room with a scrap of paper and a piece of charcoal.

Dammit! Alyx must have already written her note for the raven, begging Kian to come and rescue Luca from the Outlands. That's never going to work! Kian knows Luca can take care of himself. He's not going to abandon his people to chase after him. Alyx has no idea how things work in Askala.

But he does.

Picking up the charcoal, he scribbles his own note on the remaining scrap of paper.

Send help! Only one Seeker left. No boat. Life in danger. Hurry.

He debates putting his name on it but decides against it in case the note is intercepted. Besides, maybe it's better if the leaders in Askala aren't sure which Seeker survived. It means more leaders will vote in favor of the recovery mission if they think it might be their child's life hanging in the balance.

Shoving the paper in his pocket, his eyes turn to a mug of water on the table. He downs it quickly before he can consider whether it's stealing and limps out of the hut, heading toward the tree line. Once he's in the safety of the canopy of the forest, he runs, certain that Alyx will be on the beach.

With most of the population of the Newlands in the clearing, he doesn't see another soul out here. He crashes through the trees, knowing this is his one chance at escape.

His feet hit the sand and he scans the beach from left to right, looking for Alyx. There's a figure standing on some large rocks out in the water down the other end of the beach and he stumbles forward, hoping it's her.

As he gets closer, his heart pounding with both exertion and desperation, he sees a mane of blonde hair and knows it's Alyx. She's holding something shiny above her head and it's catching the sunlight and sending it out in sharp rays.

"Alyx!" he shouts between breaths. But she can't hear him over the crashing of the waves, so he presses forward.

There's a bird circling high up in the sky and he can only hope if it's the raven she's seeking that it takes its time to land.

"Alyx!" he calls again as he gets himself to the wet sand where he can move faster without his feet sinking with each step. He kicks off his shoes and runs to her, waving his hands. He can't let her send whatever note she's written. They might only have one chance at this. His note is the one that will get acted on, not a request to rescue Luca from a land he's already proven he can survive in.

The bird swoops down and lands in front of Alyx just as Hawk steps onto the rocks at the shoreline. They're sharp and he instantly regrets leaving his shoes behind. But at least he doesn't have a broken ankle.

Hobbling over the rocks he calls Alyx again, but his words get swept away by the wind as she squats down and encourages the bird to approach her.

"Alyx!" he cries as she ties her note to the raven's leg.

This time she turns to see him.

"Don't!" he shouts, slowing his speed so he doesn't scare the bird away. "Wait!"

Alyx considers him for a moment, then turns back to the bird. Just when he thinks she's about to shoo it back into the sky, she grabs hold of the raven and tucks it firmly under her arm.

Hawk closes the gap until he's standing before her.

"We need to send this note," he pants, waving his scrap of paper at her. "Trust me. They'll come for us if we send this note. I know what to say."

"How did you get out?" she asks, staring at him like he's a ghost.

"Long story," he says. "Raiden let me go."

"Talk about cutting it fine." She smiles. "One second more and you'd have been too late."

"I know," he says, trying to get his breathing under control.

Alyx is wearing a necklace with a large blue gemstone dangling from it, no doubt part of her payment for her betrayal of Luca. It must have been worth a fortune in ancient times when things like money still existed. But it's worth even more now as it's possibly just saved their lives.

"Help me untie the note," she says, holding the unimpressed bird out to him.

He quickly does as he's told and replaces the slip of paper with his own.

Without hesitation, Alyx throws the raven into the air. It squawks as its wings stretch out, propelling it into the sky until it's a mere shadow amongst the clouds.

"How do we know it's going to Askala?" Hawk asks, as they stand, watching the magnificent bird.

Alyx shrugs. "We don't. It could go anywhere."

Hawk groans to hear this.

"I'd say we have a fifty-fifty chance," says Alyx. "Not bad odds."

Normally Hawk would agree, but those aren't just the odds of which direction the bird will fly. They're the odds for what chance he has to live. Because if that bird flies anywhere except Askala, he's as good as dead. Which means he'll never see Sam again.

"Why didn't you ask to read my note first?" Hawk asks as they begin picking their way back across the rocks, surprised that she'd trusted him like that when they barely know each other.

Alyx gives him a strange smile. "Look at my note that you took off the bird."

Hawk unfolds the piece of paper he has crunched in his hand and pauses his steps. There's no writing on it at all. Just a crude drawing of a boat with a stick figure of a person beside it.

"I don't understand," says Hawk, taking a few steps to catch up to Alyx. "This is what you were going to send?"

She lets out a long sigh. "Hawk, I didn't read your note because I don't know how to. I can't read. I can't write either. Nobody ever taught me how."

Hawk shakes his head as he processes this. Of course, she never learned to read. Literacy is just another privilege he'd taken for granted growing up in Askala. He can't imagine Tarquin learned to read either. There are so many more important things to think about in the Outlands than learning your ABCs.

Like surviving.

"You thought a drawing of a boat would be enough for them to send help?" he asks.

"I hoped it would be enough." Alyx avoids his eye. "I didn't exactly have a lot of choice."

"You don't need to be embarrassed," says Hawk, putting a hand on her shoulder. "It's not your fault."

She nods. "I know."

"I'll teach you to read," he says. "When we get to Askala."

She gives him a sad smile. "But I need to go to the Outlands and find my sister."

"Luca will bring her to Askala eventually," he says, still not understanding why Luca took Tarquin in the first place. "He always returns there."

"What's it like?" Alyx asks, as their feet touch soft sand once more.

"You'll see for yourself," Hawk says. "It's beautiful."

"Did Raiden really let you go?" she asks.

"Sort of," he says. "But he thinks I have a broken ankle. I can't go back or he'll break it for real. I need to hide while we wait for a boat."

"Then we hide together," says Alyx, nodding. "I'm not going back either. Not after what Corbin threatened me with in the Round House."

"But where?" Hawk doesn't like their chances of hiding in the forest. And it's far too open on the beach.

"Follow me." Alyx smiles widely. "We'll hide in the Falcon's nest."

SAM

*T*he people of Askala are dying.

There are no more herbs to be found.

And the building of the boat has slowed as fewer and fewer people trust Jagger.

As Sam walks down the path, she notices that smiles are becoming harder to find. That somehow, Askala feels quieter. More...fragile.

But Sam has a hypothesis.

She hesitates outside of Dex and Wren's hut. A hypothesis that involves snooping. She glances through the front door, not surprised to find the hut empty. Wren would be training the able bodied people they have left, Dex would be helping her, proving that a missing hand isn't enough to stop anyone from fighting for what's right.

It was this assumption that has Sam standing here, knowing she'd have the place to herself. She spent all day considering her options. Deciding how she could gain evidence for her hypothesis.

Searching Charity's room had been the only logical conclusion. Askala doesn't need any more accusations founded on little more than suspicion thrown around. The foundations of Sam's beloved colony are already eroded enough.

But she's never done anything so...underhanded. Sam always thought honesty was best, as was a far more direct approach.

Except Sam's learned she doesn't live in a world of black or white. Good or bad. Right or wrong. Mother Nature created as many shades of gray as she did shades of green. If Sam can appreciate the fragile shades of an aphid through to the deepest emeralds of *Didymodon* moss, then she needs to embrace the shades of ash and shadow that make up this world, too.

Straightening her shoulders, Sam steps through the doorway. She needs to put the itchy suspicion that keeps pricking under her skin to rest.

Charity's room is Mercy's old room, and Sam finds that it's still mostly the same. A bed by the window, shelves on the wall for the few belongings that each person in Askala owns. Sam's shelves are stacked with books. Mercy's were littered with trinkets she liked to put in her hair, small stones or pretty flowers she was planning on giving someone, her mother's slingshot even though she had no idea how to use it.

With a pang, Sam wonders how her cousin is faring in the Newlands. Did she and Luca sort out their differences?

Now, though, the shelves are bare. Sam slides a hand over each surface, just to make sure, but there's nothing. It seems Charity hasn't accumulated anything she wants to keep in the time she's been in Askala.

A quick glance around shows the room is clear, the floor as bare as the shelves. Mercy used to have the few clothes she had strewn everywhere. Sam would've preferred that. Right now, she's running out of hiding places to search.

Not that she knows what she's looking for.

A part of her is hoping she won't find anything. Just because Charity came from the Outlands, just because she's Corbin's daughter, shouldn't make her a cause for suspicion. And Sam didn't have any misgivings, until she found Charity in the forest with an apron full of deadly nightshade...

Turning to the bed, Sam pulls back the blanket. She lifts the sheet and shakes it out. She squashes and compresses the pillow, trying to see if there's anything hidden inside it.

Except she doesn't find a thing.

In fact, the place barely looks inhabited. Charity is obviously used to living simply. Or she's never considered this place home.

Sam shakes her head, trying to push away the unkind thought. She may have discovered that humans can carry deeply rooted hatred, but she's not going to jump to the conclusion that Charity is one of those.

Not sure how relieved she's feeling, Sam starts to remake the bed. It looks like Charity was innocently picking those berries, which is why she almost put one in her mouth. But finding nothing also means Sam's just run out of hypotheses.

She's got nothing.

Sam's just tucked in the blanket when she hears the sound of footsteps approaching the hut. She straightens in a hurry, spinning around as she tries to figure out whether she needs to hide or come up with an explanation. Her knee crashes into the side of the bed and Sam bites down on the yelp that shoots up her throat. But it's too late.

The bed bangs softly into the wall on the other side.

"Who's there?"

Wren's voice has taken on the edge Sam's only heard a few times in her life. A hard, cold edge.

An edge that makes Sam think of Outlanders.

Her hand fluttering to her throat, she swallows. "Ah, it's just me, Wren."

There are striding footsteps and the small woman appears in the doorway of Charity's bedroom, the ferocious look on her face slowly fading. "Sam? What are you doing here?"

Sam hesitates, swallowing again. She needs to think up a lie, and fast. What's more, she needs to make it believable. "I, ah, was looking for Mercy's slingshot. The one that used to be yours. I thought I might use it to practice."

Wren arches a dark brow and Sam can't help but flush. Even she knows lies need to be plausible to be believable. And Wren would be well aware that the world is a safer place if Sam doesn't have a slingshot in her hand.

Wren glances around the room as she hikes her hands on her hips. "You're suspicious of Charity, too, aren't you?"

Sam stills in surprise. Wren doesn't trust Charity, either? She frowns. "What have you noticed?"

Wren shrugs. "Very little. It's more of a gut thing. I've learned to never ignore it, no matter how improbable things seem. It saved me many times in the Outlands."

Sam's starting to understand that. She nods as she looks around, realizing she's not willing to voice any theories without some evidence. "Well, I didn't find anything, so—"

She stops when she sees that the bed has moved after her knee knocked it. It's only shifted a couple of inches, but it's exposed a small corner of white. A slip of paper.

Wren must see it, too, because she strides over, frowning. Her heart thudding, Sam squats down and holds the protruding corner. "Can you lift the bed?"

Wren's already done it before Sam finishes the sentence, and Sam pulls it out. Little more than a folded square, she pauses before she opens it. "Maybe one leg was shorter than the others?"

"No way, Phee built that bed," Wren scoffs.

And Wren's twin is a master craftsman. It's where Luca learned everything he knows about building anything he puts his mind to. Then why was Charity hiding a small slip of paper under it?

Wren moves around so she's standing beside Sam. "It looks just like…" Her eyes widen. "Like the notes that we used to send with ravens."

Does that mean Charity's been in communication with the Newlands? She certainly hasn't mentioned it.

Realizing she's potentially holding a piece of evidence, Sam unfolds the note slowly.

Wren gasps at the same time that every molecule of air leaves Sam's body. She reads the words again. And again.

But they don't change. Neither does their gut-wrenching impact.

Send help! Only one Seeker left. No boat. Life in danger. Hurry.

"Mercy," moans Wren.

Hawk! Sam's heart cries. *Sweet Terra. Luca! Even Gust!*

Sam's hand trembles. "We don't know who the note is referring to."

Just that there's only one Seeker left in the Newlands. Sam's knees go weak. What's happened to the others? And who remains?

The one who has her heart? Her best-friend? Or her brother? Or is it Gust who has managed to stay alive…?

Sam shakes her head. The others aren't dead. They can't be.

Wren seems to have turned into a piece of cold, hard steel. "We need to find out," she bites through clenched teeth.

Sam grips the note in her palm. "We need to tell the others."

They need to find a way to help the Seeker who sent this note.

Wren nods. "Let's find your father."

She strides out the door, Sam close behind. At least her family's hut isn't far away. The sense of urgency in the note was undeniable.

Life in danger.

Hurry.

For some reason, the words feel like they're just for Sam. Like Hawk is calling for her. But she knows that any of the Seekers could've written it. And that if it was Hawk, then the others could be dead...

Bile burns up Sam's throat. She left so no one would be in danger. She was so sure they'd be safer without her.

As they reach the hut, Wren slows so Sam can go in first. Two steps in and Sam stops.

Her father is at the table, his head in his hands. She doesn't think she's ever seen his shoulders so low.

He looks up as he hears them enter, quickly smoothing away the haggard lines on his face. "Hey, Sam." His brows hike up. "Hi, Wren."

Sam glances at the doorway to their bedroom, even though her mother's now in the infirmary. "How's Mom?"

Impossibly, her father's shoulders drop another inch. "She's still refusing to eat."

Sam's chest constricts. "Not even the tea I made her?"

"She had a mouthful or two. But she says she can't stomach the broth from the kitchens."

Sam takes the seat beside him. "That's something. We just need to keep trying."

Her father nods, his eyes a strange mix of helplessness and determination. He watches as Wren takes a seat at the table, too. "What's up?"

There's a guardedness to her father's words that has Sam wishing she could bring good news for a change. Instead, she passes him the note. "We found this in—"

"It's a note. From the Seekers."

Sam glances at Wren, conscious she cut her off before she mentioned Charity's name. Wren shakes her head imperceptibly.

Her father's hands tighten around the note. "Who sent this?"

Wren leans forward. "We don't know. But we do know we need to help them."

The intensity in Wren's gaze is powered by her love for her daughter. By her fear that it was Mercy who sent it.

By her panic that it wasn't...

Sam's father nods thoughtfully. "Of course we do. We were the ones who sent the Seekers in the first place."

Sam's muscles unwind a little. The Seekers are going to be okay.

Wren clamps her hands together on the table. "I'd like to go tonight—"

"No," her father scowls. "The Newlands are even more dangerous than we could've imagined. We need to send a rescue party." He glances out the window at the sinking sun. "Tomorrow, at first light."

The tension is back, contracting through Sam. "But they said hurry. We don't know how long ago this was sent."

Her father turns his tortured eyes to her. "It's going to be dangerous to return. We can't lose even more people trying to get this Seeker back."

Wren's quiet voice climbs between them. "If too many arrive, it will be seen as an act of war." She clenches her jaw. "Is Askala ready for that?"

Sam's father doesn't respond, although the answer hangs undeniably in the air.

Askala isn't ready. Not even close. Their people have to get well. The boat has to be complete. They have to be able to defend themselves.

For some reason, Sam senses that her father wants to sink his head in his hands again. Instead, he stands up. "We'll convene a meeting of the leaders. Tonight."

Wren pushes to her feet, too. "And if they vote that we remain here, Kian?"

Sam's father can't hold her gaze. "Then we must respect that." He strides to the door, his spine as straight as a spear.

Sam almost reaches out to him as he passes her. Even though he's making this a democratic choice, she can see he's shouldering the outcome of this choice himself.

"Says the guy whose daughter is here, safe and sound," mutters Wren as he passes her.

Sam's father's shoulders tense like each word was an arrow jabbing into his back, but he continues to walk out the door. "I'll tell the others."

A moment later, Wren spins on her heel and strides out, her body vibrating with anger. Sam collapses back into the chair, suddenly understanding why her father was nursing his head.

So many decisions.

So many lives.

No way to know which is the right choice.

Glancing out the door, Sam sees that dusk is spreading its peace through the colony. A vote at the leaders' meeting is the democratic thing to do. The decision will be accepted as the best thing for Askala.

She takes a step toward the door. Except Hawk could've written that note. Or Luca. Or Mercy.

Her heart knows without a doubt that they need her.

And Askala was built on heart.

Her decision made, Sam hurries out of the hut and down the path. She doesn't go inland, to the table where the leaders will be starting to congregate.

She goes to the place her soul has been drawn to since she returned to Askala.

The beach.

As she expected, it's empty. People are either attending the leaders' meeting or heading to the kitchens for their evening meal. Or they're in the infirmary.

Sam walks further down the sand to the place where the

partially built bridge juts out over the water. It feels like a lifetime ago that she sat here with Hawk, wondering if they've passed their Proving.

She thought she knew so much, and yet she knew so little. She had no clue that she'd find so much...more in the Newlands. More love. More hate. More purpose.

Hurrying down the bridge, Sam falters when she looks ahead and discovers she's not alone. She frowns in frustration until she realizes who it is.

Wren is squatting down, unwinding a rope from the railing of the bridge.

She looks up and she sees Sam. She frowns, resuming her task. "I'm not waiting for some vote that I'm probably going to defy anyway."

Relief has Sam smiling. "Thank Terra. I can row as well as I can shoot a slingshot."

Wren's eyes widen in surprise. "You're coming?"

Sam shrugs. "My heart is in the Newlands," she says simply, recognizing the words for what they are.

The truth.

Wren grins. "Can you navigate?"

Sam glances at the indigo sky, noting which stars are already visible. "If I can't find ursa major then I'll use Cassiopeia to find the north star. Then we just need to stay due east."

Wren's grin grows. "I'll row, you get us there."

Squatting down, Sam helps Wren unloop the rope, a potent mix of excitement and apprehension tangling in her gut. The boat waits below in the water, two oars resting within. She's going back to the Newlands.

Please, don't let her be too late.

Sam and Wren still as a sound reaches them. Footsteps on the bridge, rattling the timber as someone approaches.

Sam straightens, her stomach sinking at the thought her

father is here. Will he try to talk her out of this? When all she's doing is following her heart?

But it's not her father who's coming toward them. It's Dex.

He takes in the boat bobbing on the dark water, the rope in Wren's hand. "I just spoke to Kian. I came here as quickly as I could."

Wren's lips curl up, her small smile sad yet full of love. "You know me too well."

"I want to come."

"You know someone needs to stay here," Wren says quietly. "Just in case Mercy is already on her way back. And to let Kian know where we've gone."

And keep her father busy while his daughter is gone. Again.

Dex sighs. "I can't change your mind, can I?"

"Have you ever been able to?"

Dex's eyes close on another sigh. As he opens them, he engulfs Wren in a hug. "Stay safe," he whispers. "Bring our daughter back."

Wren clings to him for long seconds. She pulls back, pressing her lips to his. "Don't let Charity out of your sight until we get back."

Dex nods even as it's obvious he has more questions.

With a flash of movement, Wren climbs down into the boat. Sam clambers after her, her stomach noticing the moment her feet leave solid ground. Settling herself in the center of the boat, she keeps her gaze on the horizon. She should've packed some ginger.

Wren grabs the oars, only to pause as if she just thought of something. "What will happen if you go back, Sam?"

Raiden will demand they marry. He'll threaten the Seekers. He'll try to hurt them.

But it seems the Newlanders already have.

Sam's hands clench around the boat as she glances over her shoulder. Dex is standing up on the bridge, little more than a shadow in the dark. Behind him, the scattered lights of Askala are starting to come to life.

But beyond that, there's another light. Up on a hill. And another lone body.

Amity raises her hand, waving once. Somehow, it feels like all the blessing Sam needs.

She turns back to Wren and passes her an oar. "I'll be fighting for what's right."

MERCY

*M*ercy ducks just in time, sending the flames stretching their hungry fingers above her head and scalding her skin.

The bastard! Vitron fired directly at her. Not that she should be surprised. He'd planned to do far worse earlier.

Holding Fleur firmly in front, Mercy takes aim. There's no time for hesitation.

It's kill or be killed.

She pulls the trigger and Fleur fires, her flames meeting Vitron's in the middle of where they stand amongst the rubble of Fairbanks. But instead of swelling into a ball of fire like she'd expected, the flames are dragged down to the ground as their streams of fuel join and fall.

Tilting Fleur upward, Mercy tries to send the flames shooting higher but Vitron does the same, nullifying the effect. She has to get this right! Thoughts of Avis rush to Mercy, the scarring covering one side of her grandmother's body evidence of the damage a flamethrower can do. And Avis was one of the lucky ones…

Vitron lowers his weapon and Mercy mimics him, knowing

it's her only way of keeping the flames from reaching her. Then disaster strikes.

Mercy's flame begins to die out as Fleur runs low on fuel.

Letting go of the trigger, she tries again. But no fire appears.

Fear pools in Mercy's gut as she drops Fleur, turns, and runs.

The small knife she was mysteriously gifted is no match for a flamethrower. Her only chance of surviving this situation is to get away and come back for Vitron later. Or hope that Luca can get to him first. But who knows what he's facing right now. Or where Gunnar is. Maybe splitting up wasn't such a great idea.

Darting across the rubble, Mercy jumps off the edge of a large slab of concrete and pushes forward, wincing as her shin scrapes against a metal pole.

She can hear Vitron grunting behind her, but the sound of the hungry flames has vanished. He clearly had to choose between firing his weapon or keeping up with her. And she's not sure which option is worse.

One thing she's certain of, though, is that she needs to keep running. It's the only chance she has right now.

Scaling a pile of crumbling bricks, she drops to the other side and takes a sharp left that opens out to a section of what must once have been a road. Being out in the open is risky but there's less chance of hitting a dead end.

Pounding the ground, she increases her pace, ignoring the wind that's been increasing in strength since this chase started. It whips at her hair, sending it flying into her eyes. She's younger than Vitron, and less weighed down without her weapon. But she's also dehydrated, not having had the same replenishment he did when they'd stopped to rest. Maybe if this storm that's brewing takes hold it will give her an advantage. At the very least, she might be able to catch some raindrops on her tongue. And maybe it will be enough to put out Vitron's flame.

She can hear him cursing behind her as they run on. Frightened he's gaining on her, she turns to the right, slipping between two slabs of concrete that are leaning on each other. Surely, Vitron will be too large to follow?

The rough surface drags on her arms as she darts through, but she has no time to care. She bursts out on the other side and takes a narrow path ahead, hoping the maze of rubble is enough for her to lose her pursuer.

There's a crash behind her as a concrete slab falls and the grunting sound of Vitron once more.

Dammit! Those slabs must have been more precariously positioned than she'd counted on.

Scrabbling her way across the uneven terrain with her heart thumping wildly, she sees a wall ahead. This time it's a vertical one. If she can manage to scale it, there's a chance Vitron won't be able to follow. Not with a heavy weapon strapped to his back.

But will she be able to do it? She doesn't even know what's on the other side. And then there's her fear of heights...

She runs forward, still not certain if she should veer left or attempt the climb.

Slamming into the wall, Mercy jams her toes into a foothold, realizing there's one thing that frightens her far more than heights.

Death.

This is her best chance and she has to take it.

Reaching up, she finds a piece of brick that's jutting out and she hauls herself up the wall. Over and over she looks for places for her feet and hands, getting herself higher off the ground. She only has maybe a minute at best to get enough distance to avoid the worst of Vitron's flames if he decides to shoot his weapon instead of climbing after her. Her father's warned her many times how flammable their hemp clothing from Askala is.

"No risk, no reward," she mutters, certain that if she'd kept running through the rubble, Vitron would have closed the gap and she'd already be dead by now.

And where in sweet Terra is Luca?

The wind picks up force, threatening to blow Mercy right off the wall as the first raindrops fall. It seems that Fairbanks is no more immune to Mother Nature's sudden bursts of fury than Askala is. This storm is going to be a big one. But will it be her friend or foe?

Glancing down, she sees Vitron at the base of the wall. His flames could still reach her from this distance. He swings his weapon to his front and plants his feet just as the rain increases in intensity. It comes down hard, obscuring Mercy's vision.

Rivulets of water are running down the wall now and Mercy presses her lips against the bricks and takes in a mouthful of sweet liquid, not caring what the acid content might be. It soothes her dry throat and she focuses back on her task, hoping that the rain will also protect her from Vitron's flames.

Near the top of the wall, she spots a metal bar sticking out. She grabs hold of it, using it to swing herself up until she's straddling the wall.

Panting for air and enjoying the feeling of the warm rain soaking her depleted body, she dares to look down. Even with that mouthful of water, she can't run much further. Please, let this chase be over soon.

On one side of the wall, she can see Vitron climbing up after her. And on the other is a drop so much further down than she expected. But the thought of Vitron getting hold of her is far more terrifying, so she squeezes her eyes closed, ignores the way her body is shaking and lets herself fall.

She lands on a steep slope of concrete that's so worn by time it almost seems polished. The rain makes it slippery and she half scrambles, half slides her way down, aware that Vitron is heavier than her and will likely move at a greater speed when he gets to this point.

Looking back, she sees Vitron scale the top of the wall in what feels like impossible time.

"Get back here, you bitch!" he shouts, his words muffled by the wind and pelting rain, but his intent is clear. This guy is not giving up.

Mercy scrabbles down the rest of the slope, rights herself and runs toward a gaping black hole in the rubble, once again debating her options. She's exhausted now, almost at the point where she can't continue on, no matter how frightened she is. Her body is at its limit.

This mysterious black hole is her last chance. It will decide her fate.

Mercy launches herself forward, pulling up her legs as she disappears through the abyss and prepares to take the fall.

She lands on a hard surface below, pain jarring through her feet and radiating up her body as it absorbs the impact.

It's pitch dark and she stumbles forward, certain that Vitron will follow her. She crawls until she makes contact with some kind of steel wall and crumbles into a heap, knowing she can't possibly go on.

This is where it ends.

Drawing in deep breaths, she tries to steady the gasping noises climbing up her throat as she takes her small knife from her pocket and holds it in front of her. Maybe she'll be able to injure Vitron as a farewell gift before she leaves this world. Everything is aching, her muscles trembling and sweat pushing precious moisture from her body as it mingles with the acid rain coating her skin.

At least she knows she did her best. She conquered her fear of heights. She fired her weapon with the intent to kill. She ran when she had to run. And now, she's letting go when she has no other choice.

And she did it all alone. She proved that women can be just as capable as men. If only Tarquin were here to see it. Although, she wouldn't want her to see what she's certain is about to come next.

"Luca," Mercy whispers in the dark, wanting to keep the memory of him close. It's quiet in here, the howling of the storm insulated by the thick concrete walls.

Then comes a loud crash and the sound of Vitron grunting.

He's here.

Which means soon she won't be.

Stilling her breathing, she waits.

"I know you're in here," Vitron says, his voice full of menace. "I can smell you."

Mercy pulls herself into a ball, biting down on her lip to stop herself from making any sound.

"Wait until the others hear that I killed the Falcon's girl," he says. "That will give them a real boost to their plans."

Cringing, Mercy wonders what plans he's talking about. They'd thought if they got Vitron and Gunnar out of the way that they'd be safe.

"We're going to take Askala," he growls. "And kill every last member of your precious colony. Selfish pricks."

She hears him spit on the ground as if the mere mention of Askala is enough to make him ill. Mercy swallows down her anger at hearing her people being called selfish. She never even knew the meaning of the word before she arrived in the Newlands. He couldn't be more wrong.

The sound of a flamethrower echoes off the walls and a sharp burst of fire ignites a few yards away. It lights up the cavernous space and Mercy sees they're in some kind of ancient parking lot. Like Fairbanks, yet completely empty with no sign of any tree winding its way through the structure.

She also sees Vitron, his face as furious as the flames that light the room.

"Aha!" he calls, moving toward her. "I see you."

She squeezes her eyes closed as she clutches her knife, thinking of Siena and the way she was charred to death on the beach. Then she thinks of Avis, her brave grandmother who experienced the same torture, yet somehow lived.

Vitron moves closer and the heat of the flames sting Mercy's face.

This is it. It's really it. She's actually going to die.

The steel wall Mercy's leaning against falls away as it swings open and she realizes it was a large door. A gust of wind sweeps in as if it's being sucked into the room, and Mercy gasps in surprise.

Strong hands grab her and pull her through the door just as the wind picks up even more force. It blows at Vitron, collecting his flame and pushing it back toward him.

Vitron is fast enough to let go of his trigger but nothing can stop the flame that engulfs him. He screams as it lights up the matted dreadlocks of his beard. The fire catches on his clothing, refusing to let go and soon Vitron is the ball of flame. Finding its way into his weapon, the fire explodes his fuel tank, making a thunderous boom as the sound echoes through the parking lot.

There's no chance in Terra Vitron could survive that.

"Mercy!" cries Luca, scooping her up into his arms and carrying her up a flight of stairs.

She buries her face in his chest and allows herself to be rescued, not caring in the slightest what that might mean for the girl power she'd just been celebrating. Luca might have helped get her out of this mess, but she'd never have been alive for him to rescue if she hadn't done everything else first.

They make a great team.

"Where's Gunnar?" she asks as they burst out into the storm.

Luca blinks away the raindrops running down his face.

"Heading to the same place as Vitron," he says. "It's what they both deserve."

Mercy lifts her eyes to the angry gray clouds above, grateful for the storm that saved her life. Well, after Luca opened the door that is.

"It's over now," says Luca with a sad smile. "It's over.'

She knows she should tell him what Vitron said. That this is so much bigger than just Gunnar and Vitron. That it's anything but over.

But she can't.

She just wants him to have a few moments of peace. Some happiness to feed his soul and prepare him for the battle she knows lies ahead.

"Are you going to put me down," she asks.

He smiles at her in the exact way he always does just before he's about to kiss her.

"Not on your life."

LUCA

*P*ressing his lips to Mercy's mouth is all Luca wants to do right now. Needs to do.

He doesn't think his heart has thudded out a beat from the second he heard the flamethrower deployed.

Even as he'd run faster than he ever has in his life.

Even as he'd caught a glimpse of Mercy, climbing the wall in the rain, then leaping into a gaping black hole.

Even through every never-ending second as he'd circled the pile of rubble, looking for another way in.

His heart had held still, holding itself in suspended animation, waiting to see if it's worth beating again.

It had finally shuddered out a thud when he'd opened the door and found her.

Now, his heart is hammering at him to hurry up. To touch Mercy. To feel her breath. To draw her in.

She sighs as their lips touch, sweet air brushing his mouth. Rain slicks over their faces as he tastes her, savors her. Reminds himself Mercy is okay.

Luca pulls back, pressing his forehead against hers as they

both breathe heavily. The desperate run, the fight to live, have both taken their toll. "Let's get back."

Mercy nods, unwinding her arms from around his shoulders. "Yes, the others will be worried."

She looks up, waiting to be put down, lashes dark with moisture. But Luca winks at her as he starts to walk. "I kinda like doing it this way."

Mercy doesn't even bother to object. With a little hiccup, she tucks herself against his chest, her face nestling in the crook of his neck. "Me, too."

Luca presses a kiss to her forehead, feeling her unwind even further. His warrior woman is physically and emotionally exhausted. "You did good."

Mercy's hand flutters to his cheek. "We make a good team," she murmurs.

Trudging over the muddy path, Luca walks as quickly as he can. Although Gunnar and Vitron are dead, being out in the open feels unsafe. Every pile of rubble feels like a threatening gray hulk. Blinking through the water streaming down his face, Luca determinedly makes his way back to the parking lot. Mercy's been through enough for today.

He almost trips when Mercy's tongue flicks against his throat, making his pulse skyrocket. "Stop it," he growls.

"What?" Mercy asks innocently. "I'm thirsty."

"I'll trip because my toes are all curled up."

She giggles, a sound that dances down Luca's spine, only for her smile to slip away as she leans back. "I have to tell you something before we get back."

Luca slows. "It can't wait until we're with the others?"

Mercy shakes her head. "Vitron said something before he…"

"Was stopped from hurting anyone ever again," Luca says flatly.

Mercy blinks. "Yes." She pauses and Luca knows something significant is waiting to be told. "Vitron said they had plans to take Askala." Her eyes pool with dread. "That they're planning to kill every last member of our colony."

Luca's gut contracts like he was just punched. He catches his breath before it whooshes out, not wanting to overreact. "He said that?"

"Yes. He called us selfish."

Luca clenches his jaw. He's heard the Outlanders talk about the people of Askala like that before. They believe Askala is keeping its wealth to itself. At first he used to defend the society he grew up in. Any Outlander was welcome to join Askala. But he was faced with too much disbelief. Too much hatred.

When Luca doesn't say anything, Mercy narrows her gaze on him. "My mom was right. They're planning a war, Luca."

Kian. Nova. Seb. Every gentle soul who's trying to heal the wounds humanity inflicted.

They're all in danger.

The outline of the parking lot, the massive mangrove pine spearing through its center, appears ahead through the curtain of rain.

Luca comes to a stop and lowers Mercy to the ground. "How tired are you?"

Her eyes are grave as she regards him, water streaming down her face. "It's amazing how rejuvenating being carried by the man you love is."

A blossom of warmth spreads through Luca's chest at Mercy's words. He grips her hands in his. "We have to go back."

She nods. "We need to warn them."

"And we need to protect them."

Mercy's beautiful face turns fierce. "Damn straight, we do."

A quick kiss blessed by the rain, and holding hands, they walk to the large doors. Luca hopes Mercy is feeling as refreshed as she says she is. He wishes it were otherwise, but they have a long trek ahead of them. They can't afford to wait.

Shoving open the door, Luca ushers her in. Instantly, the

deluge of rain is cut off, becoming little more than a low hum as he shuts the door. Water sluices down their bodies, puddling at their feet. Luca frowns. Mercy's not only drenched, she's also pale.

Is leaving Fairbanks so soon asking too much of her?

"They're back!" Annabel rushes at them, engulfing Mercy in a hug. "We were so worried!"

Mercy's face relaxes into a smile as she hugs Annabel back. "I'm fine."

"Actually, she kicked butt," says Luca.

"That's because she's the Peregrine!" shouts Tarquin, slamming herself into Mercy's side like a child-missile.

"The who?" Luca narrows his eyes at Mercy. "Peregrine?"

Mercy waves a hand dismissively before wrapping her arm around Tarquin. "Just a little name I gave myself."

Luca's not too sure how he feels about this.

"I bet you were an inminimating Peregrine," says Tarquin.

Before Mercy can answer, Tarquin launches herself at Luca, drawing an "oomph" out of him. Her arms become a vice around his waist. "Because the Falcon and the Peregrine will always win, right?"

His heart constricts as if Tarquin's arms have squeezed that, too. The addition of the final word turned the statement into a question.

The little girl they've grown to love was worried about them.

Luca hugs her back, finding Mercy enfolding them both. "They'll always fight for what's right," she murmurs.

Tarquin grins up at them. "Damn straight."

Mercy giggles and Luca has to suppress a smile. He shakes his head but there's the sound of someone clearing their throat before he can decide whether this is the moment to correct Tarquin's cursing. They look up to find several people surrounding them, Finn and Dharma smiling at the front.

"It's good to see you back," says Finn warmly.

Dharma looks at them anxiously. "The men?"

"Vitron and Gunnar are dead," Luca assures them. "They won't bother Fairbanks again."

There's a collective sigh of relief from the people around them. Annabel claps her hands in delight. "We get to keep our food?"

Mercy nods as she smiles. "The way it should be."

But Finn is watching Luca closely. "There's something else."

Luca nods, realizing the tension must be apparent on his face. "We learned the Outlanders are planning an attack on Askala."

Dharma's hand flies to her throat. "No."

Finn nods solemnly. "You need to go back."

Tarquin had just moved away a few inches, but she quickly presses herself between Luca and Mercy. "I'm coming, too."

Luca kneels down beside her. "It's safer to stay here, Tarquin. There could be a lot of fighting in Askala."

A battle.

A war for resources.

Tarquin frowns fiercely at him. "What they're doing is wrong." Somehow, her brows sink even lower over her determined eyes. "I'm coming with you."

Luca glances up at Mercy, whose gaze is a mix of tenderness and worry. Tarquin really would be safer here in Fairbanks.

Tarquin crosses her arms. "I'll just follow if you leave without me."

"You would, wouldn't you?" Luca asks with resignation.

"Dam—"

Luca shoots his hand up to stop her. "Okay! You can come."

Tarquin's body unwinds and she puts an arm around his shoulder. "Of course, I was coming."

"We need to go now," he warns.

Tarquin nods so vigorously her wild hair flops over her eyes.

"But..." Luca stands up to find Annabel wringing her hands

as her lip trembles. "You can't go, yet. I didn't get to show you my treasures."

Luca and Mercy glance at each other. Time is the one thing they don't have much of at the moment, but upsetting Annabel isn't something either of them want to do.

"You do that," Finn offers. "And we'll get you some supplies together for the trip."

"Thank you," Luca says quietly, feeling a little humbled by the support he's being shown. The people of Fairbanks have so little, but they're still willing to share it.

Annabel's face lights up. "Wonderful!" She spins around, her skirt twirling out wide. "This way!"

She skips away, leaving Luca and Mercy little choice but to follow.

Tarquin grins. "I want to punch Relic one more time before I go." Before anyone can answer, she's once again a blur of movement.

Annabel leads them down the ramp to the sleeping quarters, grabbing a candle made of mangrove pine sap along the way. Mercy slips her hand into Luca's as they make their way through the maze of roots that mold the beds of the people of Fairbanks. They pass their own little nook, the place where Luca got to hold Mercy for entire nights, Tarquin tucked between them. It was a sweet slice of paradise while it lasted.

Mercy squeezes his hand, probably thinking the same thing.

Luca stifles a sigh. How long before they can have that again? How long until they can have even more?

Annabel stops beside her own sleeping quarters and kneels down. She pushes the blanket aside with her free hand and reaches into what must be a little crevice, then pulls something out.

Her eyes aglow, she sits and crosses her legs. In her lap she holds a dented tin box. "My treasures," she whispers reverently.

Mercy tugs Luca's arm and they sit down beside Annabel in

the cramped little space, the glow of the candle like a halo around them.

One by one, Annabel lifts out her most precious belongings. Mercy makes all the right noises at each one, passing them to Luca once she's admired them. A rock in the shape of a heart. A strip of ribbon so faded it's hard to tell what color it used to be. A shiny piece of metal that Luca isn't sure what it's supposed to resemble.

Impatience is just starting to tug at his muscles when Annabel looks up. "And then there's these."

She opens her palm, and Luca squints, surprised at what he's seeing. A small carved animal—an elephant—sits cradled in Annabel's hand.

Mercy lifts it carefully. "It's beautiful," she whispers in awe.

She passes it to Luca, who silently agrees. The detail in the small figurine is impressive. Next, Annabel passes them a monkey. Then a flower. Each one just as exquisite as the last. He realizes that the figurine of the boy that Annabel sent at Aspen's memorial was probably carved by the same hand.

Luca holds the fragile bloom up so he can see it better. "Who made these, Annabel?"

Annabel's eyes shine. "The Ghost of Fairbanks."

Luca blinks. "Fairbanks has a ghost?"

"No one's seen him but me," Annabel says proudly. "Everyone thinks I made him up."

Luca smiles fondly. He's not surprised that Annabel has an imaginary friend. But the smile quickly fades. It still doesn't answer who made these finely crafted figurines. Is someone at Fairbanks playing a prank on Annabel?

"I believe you," Mercy says quietly.

Luca glances at her in the half-light, wondering at the catch in her voice. But Mercy shakes her head imperceptibly. It seems it's not something she wants to discuss in front of Annabel.

"There's one more," Annabel says. Her lashes flutter and

Luca thinks he sees her cheeks flush in the gloom. She reaches in and grabs something. "This one is yours, Luca."

"Mine?"

Annabel doesn't answer, simply passing him the object. It lands in his palm, and Luca looks down, realizing it's a...shell.

Well, he assumes it's a shell, just like he assumed the others were an elephant and a monkey. He's never seen any of those because they're all extinct. But he's seen photos in Sam's books.

"I can't take this, Annabel."

Annabel's face crumples. "You have to."

"Why?" Mercy asks her, her concern and confusion evident.

Annabel's gaze slides away, the flush returning. "Because I took it from you on the day you arrived."

Luca's stunned into silence. Into stillness. "The day I arrived?" he chokes out. "When I came back from Askala?"

Annabel shakes her head. "The day you came here as a baby." She glances down at the shell. "You were crying. A lot. Avis picked you up from where you'd been tucked into a little hidey hole. The shell fell out so I picked it up."

Mercy's hand falls on Annabel's arm. "And it's so pretty."

"Yes!" Annabel straightens, glad that someone understands. "And Avis was busy trying to make Luca stop crying. No one saw the pretty little shell but me." She straightens. "But I was wrong to take it. That's why I'm giving it back before you go."

"Thank you, Annabel," Luca says quietly, not sure what to think of it all. The shell in his hand was a gift.

A gift from his mother.

And Gunnar mentioned he knew who she was before he died.

Luca frowns. He'd decided that his search for her was futile. That she was probably dead. That there were more important things to focus on.

Annabel shoots to her feet, quickly tucking her tin box back in its crevice. "Well, you'd better get going." Picking up the candle, she steps away, looking over her shoulder expectantly with a smile. It seems Annabel's done what she needed to do.

Luca follows Annabel and Mercy, still trying to process the small wooden carving burning a hole in his palm.

They've just reached the next level when Mercy presses a hand to his forearm. "Luca."

He turns around, registering the somber expression on her face. He steps closer. "Is everything okay?"

Reaching down, Mercy draws something out of her pocket. A knife. A small knife with a wooden handle. The one that she used to cut the rope tying her to Vitron.

And the patterns etched in the handle are very similar to the shell.

Glancing over his shoulder, Luca sees that Annabel has skipped away, whatever guilt she was carrying now lifted.

"There wasn't time to tell you," Mercy says. "But this practically fell in my lap when Gunnar and Vitron weren't looking. I caught a glimpse of a man before he disappeared." She swallows. "A man with blond hair."

Luca's lost the ability to breathe. The same man who carved the knife that helped save Mercy's life also carved the shell that was left with Luca when he was abandoned as a baby.

He swallows, the world around him contracting.

Mercy's eyes fill with the knowledge that he can't bring himself to admit. "Luca, The Ghost of Fairbanks is connected to your mother."

HAWK

The Falcon's nest is a little bit like paradise right now. Hawk hasn't felt this safe since he arrived in the Newlands. And that's saying something, given how much actual danger he's in right now.

Alyx is taking a turn of acting as lookout in the desperate hope they'll see a boat on the horizon in the moonlight while Hawk rests. They've been here two days and he's starting to feel a bit better now that he's stopped moving about so much.

He hopes Alyx is being careful to keep herself hidden. They know there have been men out searching for them. It's just fortunate that with thanks to Tarquin, they have possibly the best hiding spot on this whole island. The Falcon's nest is so well hidden that even the Falcon himself doesn't know about it.

This small cave sitting amongst the rocks was where Tarquin used to come when she was playing at being the Falcon. Alyx said she'd sit in here for hours, pretending to be on a stake-out. The only reason Alyx had found the cave at all was because Tarquin had jumped out once when Alyx had been looking for her, tackling her to the ground wearing her mask made from leaves.

Hawk shakes his head, still trying to come to terms with the fact that Luca is the Falcon. He can guess why he kept it secret, though. Not just to protect himself, but to protect the rest of the Seekers. The way he treated Mercy is starting to make some kind of sense now. And the reason behind why he had to flee.

He's even gladder now that Sam got away when she did. She'll be far safer back in Askala than here now that Alyx sold Luca out.

Hawk's heart hurts at the thought of Sam. This is the longest they've ever been separated by far and it's even more difficult than he imagined. He'd give anything to look into those soulful eyes of hers right now. Or have her tell him one of her many amazing facts. Maybe he could even dare to hope she changes her mind and lets him kiss her again one day. Or is she better off if he walks away from her?

No.

Hawk isn't the Falcon. The best way he can keep Sam safe is to be right by her side no matter what kind of relationship they have. Which means when he finds her again, he's going to make sure they're never separated.

Hawk gets to his feet and stretches, being careful not to hit his head on the low roof of the cave. It's been raining all night. Before sunset, he could see a storm in the distance over the Outlands, but it never seemed to make its way here. Which is just as well. If the ocean levels were to swell, this cave would be washed out, including all the supplies Tarquin had so carefully hidden amongst the rocks. There are jars of fresh water, some blankets and even a bag of almonds. If Hawk ever sees Tarquin again, he owes her big time.

Stepping out of the cave into the moonlight, he glances around cautiously.

"I'm here," Alyx whispers and he sees her crouched just to his right.

He rubs at his eyes. The rain has stopped, the clouds clearing to allow the light of the stars to filter down.

"You look like a red-headed polar grizzly emerging from his den," Alyx laughs.

"I feel like one, too." He runs a hand through his hair. "Except there aren't too many deer out here for me to eat."

"What's a deer?" Alyx asks.

"A large animal." Hawk swallows as he realizes just how privileged he was to grow up with such beautiful creatures in his life. There was a time when they'd thought the deer population had become extinct in Askala, but over the past couple of decades, they've been increasing in numbers as the people have given them space to thrive.

"We need to send another note in the morning." Alyx sits on the rock beside him and pulls her knees up to her chest. "That first one must have gone missing."

"We don't have any paper," he reminds her, being careful to keep his voice down. "The only thing we have is that note you tried to send first."

"Then maybe we send that." She tugs at the blue gemstone around her neck, her hands trembling as it glints in the moonlight. "Otherwise, I think we wait for a boat from the Outlands and hide on board. Might be hard to hide a polar grizzly, though…"

He huffs as he sits beside her. "I'm not half as threatening as a polar grizzly."

"Hawk, I'm scared," she says, her face reshaping into a serious expression. "What if nobody comes? What do we do then?"

Hating to see her so upset, he wraps an arm around her shoulders in the same way he used to do to Sam or Mercy.

Alyx freezes, then seeing the innocent offer of comfort behind his gesture, she relaxes into him.

"Sorry," she says. "It's just that men always want something from me. I'm not used to...this."

"Not all men are like that," he says. "We're not all bad."

She rests her head on his chest. "Luca was the first decent guy I ever met. I liked him the moment I first saw him."

Hawk smiles. "I found him a bit of an acquired taste. But you're right. He's a decent guy."

"I thought I was in love with him," she says, her revelation making Hawk a little uncomfortable. "I thought what we had was special. But it wasn't. He loves Mercy, not me. And to be honest, I'm not sure I'm capable of loving anyone like that. Not after what I've lived through."

Hawk rubs her arm, trying to think of something he can say in reply. Being a Seeker has taught him that sometimes words are necessary, even when he doesn't feel like parting with any.

"Sam told me she doesn't love me," he says, trying his best to open up. "Which means I'm not capable of loving anyone like that either. I can't. Not if it's not Sam. It's always been only her."

"She's a lucky girl." Alyx sighs. "And a crazy one if she doesn't love you back."

He smiles, hoping that Gust was right when he said he didn't believe what Sam told him. That maybe she was lying to protect him. That maybe there's still hope. But the reality is that he's not going to find the answer to that question until he sees her again. If he ever sees her again.

"You'll find love one day," he says. "There are plenty of guys with kind hearts in Askala."

"There are things I need to tell you, Hawk." She turns to him underneath the blanket of stars. "Things about the Outlands. Things about the Commander...I want to be honest. I've never been part of a team before. It's always just been me. And Tarquin."

"You can tell me all of this in Askala," he says, as if speaking these words out loud will make them happen. "We have plenty of time."

"I need to tell you now," she says, her voice breaking in pain. "Because I'm not going with you."

Hawk's arm falls from her shoulders as he pulls back. "What do you mean you're not going with me? You have to! They'll kill you out here. You said so yourself."

"I have to find Tarquin," she says. "I can't go to Askala without her. She might not find me there, and I can't bear the thought of never seeing her again. She's the only other person in the world I care about. Surely, after what you just told me about Sam you can understand that?"

Hawk hangs his head. Sam might be the only girl he's in love with, but she's far from being the only person he cares about. He loves his parents and his sisters. And Mercy. He doesn't want to tell Alyx that, though. She's feeling alone enough already.

"I can't let you stay here," he says.

"I'm not staying here." Now she's the one to reach for him in comfort. "I'm going to hide on a boat to the Outlands, just like I told you. I'm going to find my sister."

He shakes his head. "Why did you send the raven if you weren't planning to go with me?"

"Maybe I'm hoping you'll feel guilty and convince them to head to the Outlands," she says. "Or maybe that's where they'll insist on going anyway when they hear that's where Luca is."

"They've never chased after him before," says Hawk. "I'd say it's more than a little unlikely they'll start now."

"Then I'll set myself up here." She smiles. "I'll go back to my hut when everyone's asleep and get what I need. A boat will come eventually. I know it will. Or maybe Tarquin will find her way back. She'll know to look for me here."

"I'll help you get your things," he says, accepting she's firm in her decision. "It's quiet here tonight with all the rain."

At least if he can carry what she needs, she'll only need to risk returning once. And he'll be there to protect her if she gets caught.

"No." Alyx clutches his arm and shakes her head.

Hawk's genuinely confused by this reaction. "You don't want my help?"

She shakes her head again, seeming adamant. Then she points out to the ocean with a shaking hand. "There's a boat."

Hawk's heart leaps at these words. He's not sure if he dares to believe it.

Alyx gets to her feet, no longer caring about staying hidden and walks to the shoreline. Hawk follows. If there are any of Corbin's men out here looking for him, they'll see the boat anyway. He can only hope the rain has kept them hiding in their huts.

Squinting at the horizon, he sees it. The unmistakable shape of a boat. And it's coming from the direction of Askala.

"They got the raven," Alyx breathes. "It actually worked."

"You mean, you've never sent one before?" he asks, surprised. He'd thought she'd known what she was doing.

"Never." She grins at him. "But maybe I'll try again now that I know it works."

Hawk reaches into his pocket, pulls out her crumpled drawing of the boat, and gives it to her. "If you're in trouble, you send me this, okay? I'll come back for you."

She looks at him strangely before screwing the note into a ball and tossing it into the ocean.

"What did you do that for!" Hawk stretches out his hands.

"Never come back here," she says, her eyes glued to the boat. "Be with Sam. Be happy. There's no happiness in a place like this."

"Please, come with me," he says.

"I can't." Her voice breaks. "Tarquin needs me."

He nods, trying his best to understand, even though he doesn't. If Tarquin really is with Luca, then she's safe. Alyx needs to get herself to safety, too. But having grown up in a house made up mostly of females, he knows a losing battle when he sees one.

"Will it be Luca's dad rowing?" Alyx asks. "Or one of his men?"

"I have no idea." Hawk shrugs as he squints at the boat drawing closer with each moment that passes. Then he breaks into a smile as he realizes he knows exactly who will be rowing that boat.

Wren.

The same person he discovered the Newlands with all those years ago will be the one to take him home. There's not a chance she'd let anyone else head out here if she thought her daughter was in trouble.

And when Wren gets here, she'll take him home to Sam.

Everything's going to be alright.

Hawk's body trembles as the emotion of the moment washes over him. He's been through so much out here and only a couple of days ago he'd been certain he was going to die. And now... now there's a boat coming. Which means he gets a second chance to set all of this right.

Alyx holds her gemstone in front of her, catching the moonbeams.

"What are you doing?" he asks.

"Trying to direct them." She concentrates on her task. "So they know where to find us."

Hawk waits in silence as they watch the small boat crest the waves as it draws closer. It's very possible that tomorrow he'll be able to hold Sam in his arms. And even if she only hugs him back as a friend, that's enough. Because it's a whole lot more than he'd thought he was going to have.

"There's two people," says Alyx, her eyesight seeming far sharper than Hawk's.

He fights the urge to wade out into the water, needing to see what Alyx can.

Half of him hopes it's not Sam in that boat. It's not safe for her out here. But the more selfish half of him can't help but soar with the thought it might be her. He misses her with every cell in his body, his stomach contracting at the thought of pressing her to his chest and resting his face on her head.

The boat surges forward on a wave just as a moonbeam hits it, illuminating a girl with golden flecks in her hair.

"Sam!" he gasps, not feeling the sting of the water as he steps into the ocean. Let the ocean eat at his skin. He really doesn't care. All he wants is to reach that boat. To reach the girl in the boat. To be reunited with Sam once more.

Wren is seated beside Sam as they haul on the oars.

The boat is pushed forward again, and Hawk launches himself, grabbing the gunwale and pulling it to shore until it's beached.

Sam flies out of the boat and straight into his arms. He hugs her back with one arm and uses the other to scoop her up so her sensitive feet don't touch the water.

Sam. His Sam. She's back with him at last.

"I missed you so much," he says into her ear.

"I knew it was you who sent the note," she says, tightening her grip around his neck like she never plans to let go. "I knew it."

Hawk looks over to the boat and locks eyes on his aunt. She's not smiling at the sight of him. The usual proud look on her face when she sees him is absent. Instead, her face has fractured into pieces as her palms remain pressed to her cheeks. She's devastated.

He wades over to the boat, still holding onto Sam.

"What happened to her?" Wren asks, blinking back tears. "What happened to my girl?"

"She's okay," Hawk rushes to tell her, guilt washing over him as he realizes it was his note that frightened her like this. "Mercy's okay. She's with Luca. She's alive."

Wren tips back her head and looks at the stars. "Oh, thank Terra! I thought when I saw you that... I thought..."

"She's okay," he says again, realizing that Alyx must have been right in her guess that Luca and Mercy went to the Outlands. "You raised a strong woman."

"What about Gust?" Sam asks.

Hawk shakes his head, letting the sadness in his eyes tell the story.

"We could go to the Outlands to find Mercy," says Alyx. Hawk spins around to see she's come up beside him. "We could find her and bring her back."

"Who's this?" Wren asks, directing her question at Hawk and Sam, as mistrusting of someone new as always.

"This is Alyx," says Hawk. "She helped me send the note. She's been hiding me."

"Alyx helped you?" Sam lifts her head from Hawk's shoulder and stares.

Is she jealous? Sweet Terra, he hopes so.

"We can't go to the Outlands," says Wren, biting out her words. "As much as we might want to. Askala needs us. Luca will look after Mercy."

"Mercy can look after herself," says Hawk. "You'd be proud of her, Wren. She's grown so much out here. We all have."

"Yeah, so Sam keeps telling me." Wren frowns. "I'd like to see for myself, though."

"Then let's go," says Alyx, not giving up. "We can find her."

"We don't have time to stop and discuss this." Hawk sets Sam back down in the boat. "Corbin's men could find us any moment and kill us all. We have to get going."

"I'll go to the Outlands if that's what you want, Wren," says Sam. "We can find Mercy and bring her home."

Wren shakes her head, resolutely. "When I was Mercy's age, I left the Outlands to come to Askala. Nothing and nobody could have changed my mind. Mercy's more like me than people realize. I have to let her do whatever it is she thinks she has to do. We're returning to Askala. Mercy will find us there when she's ready."

With Sam and Wren already in the boat, and the acid water starting to prick at Hawk's shins, he shoves the boat off the sand.

"Come with us." He turns to Alyx, pleading with his eyes for her to follow.

But she shakes her head. "If you see Tarquin before I do, make sure you tell her that I love her."

Hawk pushes down his anguish at her decision, certain it's the wrong one. "Please, be careful. And get out of this water before it eats you alive."

She smiles and holds up her hand to wave as she steps backward toward the shoreline.

"And... thank you," he calls. "You saved my life. Despite what you did to Luca, you're my hero."

Then, without waiting for her reply, he shoves the boat further out and leaps inside, picking up an oar. Wren is used to exerting herself, but Sam must be exhausted by now.

"What did she do to Luca?" Sam asks, as Hawk sits beside Wren and hauls them out to sea.

"Oh, Sam." He shakes his head. "I've got so much to tell you."

"Me, too," she replies with a shy smile.

As he focuses on the task ahead, he feels the warmth of those two words inside his chest, hoping they mean what he wants them to. It's only then that he realizes Alyx never got to tell him the secrets she claimed she had. About the Newlands. And more specifically, about the Commander. And now who knows if she'll ever get the chance.

"Come on," says Wren, nudging him. "Let's go home."

SAM

*S*am knows she should be looking at the sky so they can navigate their way back to Askala, but she can't tear her eyes away from Hawk.

He's thinner than when she last saw him. Yet somehow stronger looking.

And so beautiful it makes Sam's entire thoracic cavity ache.

Hawk's gaze seems just as trapped as hers. Even in the dark, Sam knows his eyes are full of questions.

She wants to reach out to him, but she stops herself. How does Hawk feel about her after what she said to him? Will a lifetime of apologies ever be enough for the hurt she's caused him?

"Sam, where are we heading?" Wren asks sharply.

Snapped out of her reverie, Sam looks skyward only for a fat droplet to splat in her eye. In the short time they arrived and left, a storm has crept in. She frowns as the pinpoints of light that guided them here wink and flicker. Only about half the stars are visible as they're progressively obscured by clouds as black as the night.

Focusing, Sam does some mental calculations. She finds ursa major, then ursa minor. As the boat jostles with the growing waves, she follows the pointer stars, Merak and Dubhe. The boat dips into a trough and she loses sight for a precious moment. Maintaining her focus, Sam stares hard at the sky. She finds the constellation of Cassiopeia and realizes she's gone too far. But before her eyes can dart back, desperately seeking the north star, the tiny guiding lights disappear.

Plunged into darkness, rain peppers Sam's head and shoulders. She just has to hope the brief glimpse was enough to point them in the right direction.

"Sam?"

It's Hawk's voice, laced with worry. Is he concerned about her, or about getting home?

"I saw a glimpse of ursa minor." Sam points in what she hopes is due west. "We need to head that way."

"I can't see you well enough. You'll have to move closer."

Despite the growing gusts of wind, Sam hears the note of vulnerability in Hawk's voice. It pulls at her soul, and she's shuffling to where he's sitting without a conscious decision to move. She sits across from him. "Is this better?"

"If it gets any darker, I won't be able to see you pointing at all."

Sam's heart soars. Hawk wants her to move closer!

Drawing in a breath for courage and as she hopes she hasn't read this wrong, she scoots forward and tucks herself between his legs. "This way you'll be able to feel me point."

Hawk doesn't say anything for a moment and Sam stills. She moved too fast. She's hurt him too much. He probably meant for her to sit next to him.

"I can feel you," he says huskily.

And Sam can feel him. Her shoulders press against his thighs, his warmth wrapping around her. The sounds of the storm mushrooming around them fades away.

Sam's home.

"And it feels good," Sam replies quietly.

A crack of lightning splits the sky, an echo of thunder rumbling shortly afterward. Sam flinches and Hawk wraps around her. "Hold on."

He starts to row, his upper body leaning forward then backward in rhythmic movements. Sam tucks herself as small as she can, not wanting to obstruct him.

Wren moves to the bow, balancing their weight. "Let me know when you get tired, Hawk. We need to get back fast."

Hawk doesn't say anything, but he doesn't need to. They all know the less time they spend out in this storm, the better.

Sam keeps her gaze on the rumbling clouds above her, waiting for any gap where she'll be able to catch a glimpse of the stars. She's not strong enough to row in this sort of weather, but she could be of some use if she can navigate.

Except the obsidian mass above them is only multiplying, feeling closer and closer by the minute. It's like staring into the mouth of a black hole. A gust of wind buffets the boat just as Hawk digs the oars into the water and the boat surges forward. Further out to sea.

With no way of telling if they're still going in the right direction. Whether they're heading to Askala.

The rain increases, becoming a deluge that plasters Sam's hair and clothes to her body. The boat rises a little bit higher with each wave, and her stomach bottoms out each time it plunges down again. At the head of the boat, Wren's gripping the sides as she scans the darkness around them.

Behind Sam, Hawk starts to grunt with each pull of the oars. The legs braced on either side of her feel like warm steel. Strong. Stable. Steadfast.

Another bolt of lightning has Sam instinctively ducking. She turns to blink up at Hawk through the rain. "I can't see the stars to navigate. What else can I do to help?"

Water is running in rivers down Hawk's face, his features tight in the dark as he continues to pull them over the agitated ocean. "Just stay where you are, Sam. Having you here makes me strong."

Sam's breath catches in her throat as Hawk's words sing through her veins. She wishes she could kiss him. Hold him. Explain.

"Well, I'm not going anywhere, so you're about to be the strongest man on Earth." Before Hawk can answer, Sam tucks herself in, her heart hammering.

They're in danger. A lot of danger.

But she's with Hawk.

Which means they'll get through this. They have to.

As Hawk rows steadily, fighting the waves, ignoring the rain, and Wren keeps a lookout at the bow, Sam makes a note of what they're up against.

They're in the middle of the ocean, somewhere between the Newlands and Askala…she hopes. There's no way to tell considering she can't see the stars to navigate. Which is just as dangerous as the storm itself. Hawk's powerful strokes could be taking them away from home for all they know.

And right now, Askala needs them as much as they need its safe shores.

Sam frowns, focusing. The wind is gusting hard, consistently in an easterly direction, the waves tossing them up and down. The storm isn't going away, but it isn't getting any worse. Realization spears down her spine. Mother Nature is helping them!

"Hawk!" she calls out over the wind. "As long as we keep the wind at our back, we should be heading in the right direction!"

Hawk's teeth glint in the dark as he flashes a smile. "That's the clever Sam I know."

More warmth cascades through Sam at those words, but it's quickly doused. That's assuming Sam's right.

And assuming the wind doesn't change direction.

Hawk spears the right oar deeper into the water, angling the boat slightly to the left. The wind slams into his back, propelling the boat into an oncoming wave. Water explodes over the sides, saturating them both.

"Stay where you are, Sam," calls Wren. "I'm going to bail some of this water. I can't see anything, anyway."

Sam's about to get up when Hawk's legs tighten. "There's probably only one bucket."

Another bolt of lightning illuminates the scene and Sam's pulse leaps. The waves are so high. The clouds are so low. They're surrounded by the unforgiving, punishing might of Mother Nature.

Sam's hands clench as she focuses on the feel of the wind so they can maintain their course. They have to get back to Askala. They absolutely, categorically, unequivocally have to. She can't have Hawk back only for them to…

She shakes her head. Refusing to let that thought finish.

Tense minutes pass. Hawk rowing. Wren bailing. Sam pushing a little on Hawk's right or left leg as she keeps them heading west. The wind and rain are a relentless force throughout.

It means none of them are ready when something slams into the side of the boat. Hawk instantly contracts around Sam. Wren cries out in alarm only for the sound to be abruptly cut off.

It's followed by wind-whipped, rain-drenched silence. Fear tsunamis through Sam. Would they even hear a splash in this weather?

"Wren!" Hawk calls out. "Wren!"

"I'm still here." Her reply sounds like its ground through clenched teeth. "What the hell was that?"

Hawk's stopped rowing as he glances frantically about. Sam crawls out from her safe haven, doing the same. She sees they're in a trough, the space between waves. And apart from ink-colored water on all sides, she can't see a thing.

Wren scrambles back to the head of the boat. "Keep rowing, Hawk!"

There's a desperation in her tone. The pitch heightened with fear.

Lightning strikes again, illuminating the world for a second.

It's then that Sam sees it. A fin riding the wave, as dark as the water it's carving.

"Leatherskin," Sam moans.

Hawk must hear her, because he goes still. Sam lifts an arm and points, although there's no way to see anything as they're plunged into darkness again. "North east!" She raises her voice so Wren can hear, too. "Leatherskin!"

The next collision is like a battering ram, but they're ready for it. Sam grips Hawk as he hunkers down around her. The boat rocks wildly, water splashing over the side and soaking Sam's feet.

She's about to straighten when a second blow hits the boat from the other side, somewhere near the stern. This time, the boat not only rocks, it's thrown into a turbulent twist.

"There's more than one!" shouts Wren.

Sweet Terra. How many?

The boat settles just as a wave lifts them. Sam peers out from the Hawk-armor around her, but all she sees is night.

"Can you hold on?" Hawk asks hoarsely.

"What are you going to do?"

"See if we can scare these sharks away. You said their eyes are their sensitive spot, remember?"

Of course, Hawk is the one person who seems to remember everything Sam says. Fighting the leatherskins is going to mean standing in the boat that feels like a rollercoaster Sam once saw in a book. It would be dangerous. Far too risky.

And right now, their only hope.

Sam nods and she's about to say something, to tell him she loves him, but Hawk's already moved away. Tucking one oar into the boat, he braces himself on his knees. "Let me know if you see one!"

Sam and Wren move to opposite sides of the vessel, scanning the angry waters. Sam squints, resisting the urge to lean out. The surface of the ocean is a moving monster, pockmarked by the stabbing rain. There's no way to see into its depths.

"There!" Wren screams just as the boat is slammed again.

It tips wildly, and Sam's stomach bottoms out as she finds her side of the boat plunging down. Closer to the water.

It means she sees the jagged flash of teeth just below the surface. Watches with terrified eyes as a head materializes, a pointed nose coming at her like the tip of an arrow.

Another leatherskin is right here, propelling itself toward her.

Sam rears back as it breaks the surface and launches into the air.

"Hawk!" she screams so loud it burns her throat.

But he's going to be too late. The leatherskin's mouth opens, exposing rows of pale, dagger-like teeth. Beyond it, Sam stares into the abyss of its throat.

The passage that will be her tomb.

She scrambles backward, fighting the inevitability as she futilely holds her hands up as if she can stop the hundreds of pounds coming at her.

"No!"

Hawk's roar is louder than the storm. An oar slices through the air, slamming into the leatherskin's mouth.

The predator's jaws clamp shut as if the movement was instinctive. The oar splinters, the paddle lodged in its mouth. But it's enough for the leatherskin to lose momentum. With a furious flick of its head, it drops back into the black waters.

Breathing as if she's just run the circumference of the ocean, Sam looks up at Hawk. He's panting just as hard, the oar in his hand now nothing but a handle.

And then he's holding her, stroking the wet hair back from her face. "Sam…"

Curling up as if she wants to crawl into him, Sam's lips find his jaw. His cheek.

His lips. "Thank you," she murmurs against them.

Hawk's breath puffs against her face. "I thought—"

But whatever he was going to say is cut off by another shark colliding with the boat. The impact is hard enough to have it rocking wildly again. For the sound of splintering wood to seep through the drumming of the rain.

Before the boat can right itself, there's another blow. And another.

There are more than two leatherskins. Possibly an entire school of them. They only have one oar to fight off any more that try to take one of them.

Another collision and the boat tips far more than it has before. Water sloshes over the side, flooding around Sam.

"Wren!" Hawk calls, probably making sure she hasn't tumbled out.

"Just hold on!" she shouts back.

Except the boat is tilting, leaning. Reaching the point of no return.

In a few seconds, they'll be holding onto a capsized vessel.

And they'll be in the same waters as the leatherskins.

Sam moans. They can't save themselves, let alone Askala. She and Wren are the only two people who really know Charity is up to something. Sam's mother will die without a cure.

This can't be happening.

The arms around her tighten as the boat slams back down, still upright. But before any sense of relief has a chance to flicker, there's another blow. Just below Sam. Just off center.

With the precision of a torpedo.

It launches the boat up out of the water, where there's no water to suck them down, to stop their momentum.

The boat tips and twists. Sam holds tight onto Hawk as they tumble out. For breathless seconds, they're held by air. No longer in the boat. Not yet in the ocean.

Sam wishes she could cry out, but she knows she needs to keep her mouth shut as gravity does the inevitable. As the water closes around them, she feels her heart splinter long before her body is about to be shredded.

She just found Hawk again.

And she hasn't told him she loves him.

MERCY

"*L*uca, I'm trying to talk to you." Mercy puts a hand on Luca's shoulder as they walk, but he ignores it, deep in thought.

"Yeah, Luca," says Tarquin, her short legs moving fast to keep up with them. "She's trying to talk to you."

Luca huffs. "Is there an echo out here?"

"We're ganging up on you," says Tarquin proudly.

"I can see that." Luca gives her a weak smile.

"We really do need to talk." Mercy tries touching Luca again, pleased when he reaches for her hand and holds it.

He slows his steps. "We can walk and talk."

Mercy looks at Tarquin and rolls her eyes. Tarquin returns the gesture somewhat dramatically and Mercy tries not to smirk. The whole point of Mercy wanting to talk is that she's not sure walking anywhere is such a good idea.

"We should stay in Fairbanks and look for the Ghost," she says. Luca hadn't listened to her the last six times she'd suggested this. But you never know. This might be a case of lucky seven.

"Thanks," he says, keeping his eyes ahead. "I do appreciate

your persistence with this suggestion, but we need to get back to Askala."

So, he had heard her the other times.

"But this is the closest you've ever come to finding your mom," says Mercy.

"Everyone we know and love is in danger right now." He shifts his dark eyes and locks them on her, squeezing her hand gently. "I can't keep chasing after a ghost for the rest of my life."

"But it's not *a* ghost anymore," says Mercy. "It's *the* Ghost. We know he's out there. I've seen him."

"I've never seen a ghost." Tarquin pouts.

"He's not really a ghost," Mercy points out. "That's just what Annabel called him. He's a real man."

"My mom's a ghost." Tarquin's mood picks up as she skips along beside them. "Well, she's dead so that kinda makes her a ghost, doesn't it?"

Mercy's not sure how to answer this. Nobody had given her a handbook on how to be a quasi-mother to this complicated girl. She asks questions that Mercy's never even considered before. Where's Sam when she needs her? She'd know how to answer this one.

"If my mom was out there, I'd go and look for her," says Tarquin, not seeming to have needed an answer to her question. "I'd never stop until I found her."

"Why did you leave Alyx then?" Luca asks, clearly trying to keep the conversation away from himself.

Tarquin's eyes fly open. "She's not my mom! Besides, I didn't leave her. We'll go back to the Newlands, won't we?"

"Maybe one day." Mercy lets go of Luca's hand to ruffle Tarquin's hair, not wanting to tell her the truth. They can never go back there. Not now that they know Luca's the Falcon. It would be far too dangerous.

Luca looks at Mercy, his eyes warning her not to give

Tarquin false hope. But Mercy's not too sure. Sometimes false hope is better than no hope at all.

"You two aren't going to let up, are you?" Luca throws out his hands as he shakes his head. "Let me try to explain."

Mercy holds her tongue. She's learned with Luca that when he's ready to talk, she's best to listen.

"I know I'm closer than ever to finding my mom. I get that." Luca stops walking for a moment to look at them. "But I also get that Askala is in danger and I have a responsibility to protect the only mother I've ever known."

"Nova," breathes Mercy.

"That's right," he says. "And Avis. Without either of those women, I wouldn't be standing here talking to you. That means more to me than blood."

Mercy nods, even though she isn't quite sure she believes him. Luca's spent years looking for his mother. She might not mean as much to him as Nova, but she's still important.

"Will it matter if we take an extra day or two to return to Askala?" she asks, wincing as she anticipates his passionate reply.

He starts walking again and she follows, glad she'd had something to eat and drink in Fairbanks to restore her energy before they'd set out.

"It was just a suggestion," Mercy protests.

"A day or two could be all the difference," he says. "You know that."

Mercy lets him walk off ahead as she waits for Tarquin to catch up.

"Maybe he doesn't want to find his mother," Tarquin says. "Maybe he just likes the idea of it more than actually the doing part."

Mercy's eyebrows shoot up as she considers this.

Tarquin lowers her voice so only Mercy can hear. "Maybe his mom's like my dad."

"What do you mean?" Mercy adjusts the bag of supplies on her shoulder then puts a hand on Tarquin's arm.

"Maybe Luca's scared his mom isn't very nice," she says, blinking up at Mercy. "She left him when he was a baby. If she didn't want him then, maybe she doesn't want him now."

Mercy looks at Luca's back as he walks. She doesn't think he can hear from this distance, although with nothing but dirt surrounding them it's possible Tarquin's words have carried in the breeze. Tarquin might just be right. Mercy's only ever known two parents who love her. She'd never stopped to think what it might feel like to have a parent leave you for dead in a pile of rubble. Not knowing who his mother is would be difficult for Luca. But perhaps knowing might turn out to be even worse.

A hammering sound in the distance has Luca holding up his hand to silence them.

"What is that?" Tarquin asks as they draw to a stop.

"Shh." Mercy tilts her head and listens. Is somebody building something?

"It's over those hills," says Luca. "We should check it out."

Tarquin jams her hands on her hips. "But that's the exact opposite direction to the water."

"It's not, actually," says Luca. "It's just a bit further down the coast from where we arrived."

"Like a lot further down." Tarquin's hands slide to cross over her chest as she taps a foot on the ground.

"You could have stayed in Fairbanks," Mercy reminds her. "We can still take you back if you like?"

"I'm fine." Tarquin remembers herself and replaces her frown with a smile.

"We'll check out what the noise is," says Luca. "Then we can follow the coast down to where we hid the boat."

"What do you think it is?" asks Mercy. "Are they building huts?"

"It sounds like it." Luca scratches at his chin. "They must be using timber sent over from the Newlands."

Mercy shakes her head. Those beautiful trees need to stay in the ground, not be harvested like that! After all the suffering the Outlanders have experienced out here, have they really not learned to have a bit more foresight? Sam would have conniptions if she were here.

They veer off the path they'd been on and walk toward some hills in the distance, the hammering sound getting louder with each step they take. Whatever is being built, it must be huge.

By the time the ground begins to slope upward, Mercy's exhausted, clearly not having had enough rest before they'd set out again. She hadn't counted on this detour on the way to the water, thinking she'd have a chance to rest in the boat. Warning the people of Askala had seemed so much more important at the time. But there's no choice now. They have to push on.

Luca reaches for her bag of supplies and adds it to the heavier bag he's already carrying. She lets him take it, shaking her head at how he'd noticed the way she was tiring without her even needing to say anything. Since arriving in Fairbanks they've become so attuned to each other. She understands now how Hawk was able to reach out his arm to stop Sam from falling before she'd even begun to trip. When someone is your whole world, the tiny details get magnified.

Following Luca up the hills, she finds she's able to keep up now the weight of the bag has been lifted from her shoulders. If only he'd decided to kiss her as he'd taken the bag, she's certain she might even be able to run from the energy she gets from his touch.

"Do you think they're building the bridge?" Luca asks.

"Oh." Mercy runs a hand through her dark hair. "Maybe?"

A bridge was started back when Mercy was only a baby to connect Askala to the Outlands. It was supposed to replace a bridge from decades ago that Sam's grandfather burned down.

But the Outlanders pilfered so much of the timber on their side that the construction never got very far.

They walk up to the top of the steep slope, falling into silence so they can approach unnoticed. Mercy tries not to pant too hard from the exertion.

Luca motions to a cluster of rocks on top of the summit and Mercy nods. It will be a good spot to observe what's going on without being seen.

Stooping to a crouch, the three of them squat behind the rocks.

Luca holds a finger to his lips, his gaze on Tarquin. She nods, her eyes wide and her mouth firmly closed. She knows how serious this is.

They jostle into positions where they can lean out to peer down the other side of the hill to the coast, and Mercy has to stifle a gasp when she sees exactly what the Outlanders are building.

It's most definitely, one hundred percent, absolutely not a bridge.

"Sweet Terra," Luca says under his breath. Frankly, Mercy is surprised he hadn't used stronger words, which would be more than warranted in this situation.

On the sand at the bottom of the hill is a beach.

And on that beach are dozens of men.

And the men are building a fleet of boats.

"Holy crap," says Tarquin, using the words Luca should have.

If Mercy weren't so concerned by this discovery, she'd talk to Tarquin about her language. But right now, she isn't sure what to say. Or what to think. A fleet of boats could mean a lot of things but there's only one likely conclusion.

The invasion of Askala is real. And it's going to happen soon.

She watches as the men hammer boards into place, framing the skeleton of some boats, while filling in the hulls of others.

There must be more than twenty vessels in various stages of construction.

Mercy tears her gaze away to look at Luca, only to find him already staring at her, his soulful eyes full of worry.

"It's real," says Mercy, keeping her voice down. "The invasion is happening."

Luca nods slowly, his mind sure to be whirling.

"How long do you think we have?" Mercy asks.

"Hard to say." Luca looks back at the boats. "Weeks maybe? Sooner if they're organized."

Mercy sits down with her back against the rock and reaches for the supply bag that holds their water. She passes a flask to Tarquin.

"Drink," she says.

Tarquin gulps down the water and Mercy watches her, wondering how she can keep this small girl safe. Nobody deserves to be caught up in an invasion, especially a child.

"That's enough water for now," says Luca. "We need to save some for later."

Tarquin nods obediently and hands the flask to Mercy for her turn.

Luca then takes a few sips and puts it back in the bag. But as he does, his carved shell falls out.

"What's that?" Tarquin's eyes fly wide. "That looks like one of Annabel's treasures!"

"It is." Luca passes it to Tarquin to look at. "She gave it to me."

Tarquin studies it carefully and Mercy takes a deep sigh, avoiding the conversation they need to have. How can they possibly save Askala from what's being planned here?

"Is this the thing you were left with when you were a baby?" Tarquin asks. Clearly, she's been piecing together fragments of their conversation on the way here.

Luca nods.

"What's it supposed to be?" Tarquin turns it over, frowning. "It's too pretty to be a rock."

"It's a shell," says Mercy. "People used to find them on the beach."

"Before the acid ate them all up?" she asks.

"That's right." Mercy smiles. "When we get to Askala, Sam can show you a photo of a shell in one of her books."

"Books are for burning, not reading," says Tarquin, as if by rote.

"You'll change your mind once you look at a book properly." Luca gets to his feet, making sure to stay low. "Come on, we need to get moving. Now more than ever."

"So, we stick to our plan of returning to Askala?" Mercy asks.

Luca nods. "We need to warn everyone. At least now we know what to expect."

"Can I carry your precious shell?" Tarquin stoops as she stands, even though she's small enough not to be seen at full height.

Luca nods and Mercy knows what a big deal that is for him. That shell is the only clue he has that has any hope of leading him to his mother one day.

"And Tarquin, you were right," he says, crouching down in front of her. "I am scared that maybe my mom might not want me."

Mercy's hand flies to her lips as she realizes he'd overheard their conversation.

Tarquin leans forward and kisses Luca's cheek. "Mercy wants you. And so do I. If your mom doesn't want you, then she's a holy crap."

"Tarquin!" Luca forgets to keep his voice down for a moment. "We really need to talk about your newly acquired vocabulary."

"Was that a rude word?" she asks, innocently. "Relic taught it to me."

Mercy stands and winces as her feet protest at being made to walk again.

They begin the walk down the slope of the hill with Tarquin skipping ahead.

"I'm scared Luca," Mercy says when Tarquin's out of earshot. "There were a lot of boats."

"We'll think of something." He wraps an arm around her shoulder and she wonders if he's as confident as he sounds.

Mercy fights back a flood of tears, wanting to be stronger than this. Askala is a peaceful society. They can't fight back against that many boats holding that many men. Their people and the land will be decimated just like the Newlands.

Tarquin lets out a little scream as something flies out of her hands.

"The shell," says Mercy, watching as the small object rolls down the hill.

Tarquin chases after it, slipping and stumbling as she tries to go faster than the slope will allow.

"Don't run!" Luca slips the supply bags from his shoulders and chases after her. "We'll get it at the bottom."

But Tarquin either hasn't heard him or isn't prepared to risk the shell falling into a hole or getting damaged as it bounces off the stones.

The shell gathers momentum and Mercy watches its shadow tumbling down. Picking up the bags, she follows slowly, hoping Tarquin doesn't fall and scrape the skin from her knees.

Just before Luca reaches Tarquin, she makes a dive for the shell, flying through the air and landing on it, causing Luca to trip and go crashing to the ground beside her.

Mercy quickens her pace to get to them, hoping there are no injuries. When she reaches them, she thinks the worst.

Tarquin has crawled onto Luca's lap and has buried her face in his chest and is sobbing loudly. He looks equally as solemn.

"Tarquin!" Mercy cries. "Where does it hurt? What happened?"

"She's okay," says Luca. "She's not hurt."

"Then what?" Mercy crouches down next to them and sees that Tarquin has something clutched in her hand. "What do you have?"

Tarquin's hand falls open as her face remains glued to Luca's chest and Mercy sees the crushed remains of the shell. It's been smashed right open and lies in several pieces in the palm of Tarquin's hand.

Mercy takes it from her and studies the pieces, her heart breaking then leaping when she notices something more than a little unusual.

"Look, Luca," she says holding out her hand.

"I know," he says, not seeming to want to. "It's broken. It's okay. It was just a shell."

"No, Luca," says Mercy practically waving her hand in front of his face. "Look closer. There was a note hidden inside. It must be for you."

LUCA

A note?

Luca stares at the crumpled slip of paper sitting in Mercy's palm. There was a note inside the shell that his mother left with him as a baby...

Tarquin's sobs come to an abrupt halt as she realizes the significance of what they've discovered. It could be a message from his mother. A clue to her identity.

With trembling fingers, Luca picks up the scrunched piece of paper, seeing that it's been folded tightly multiple times. There's no way to tell if there's anything written on it.

"Open it, Luca!" Tarquin demands impatiently as Mercy hushes her.

That's exactly what he needs to do. Open it. He's been waiting for something like this all his life.

And yet, he's hesitating. Just like Tarquin's perceptive little mind guessed, a part of him is scared at what he's going to find. In the Outlands, happy endings are only found in dreams. Reality is just too harsh for anything good to survive.

"You need to know," Mercy says quietly. "You need answers."

Luca looks up at her, finding her warm gaze on him. He

realizes despite the violence and desperation, the Newlands and Outlands only made him and Mercy stronger. This was where their love was born. Maybe there's still hope...

With a quick nod, Luca carefully unfolds the note once, twice. His heart drums against his ribs as he sees faint black lines. Letters.

A message.

But suddenly the breeze is no longer silent.

"Over there! That's where the noise came from!"

The distant voice has them all stilling. The Outlanders must've heard Tarquin cry out as she'd fallen down the hill.

Clenching his hand around the slip of paper, Luca does a slow spin. The ashen plains stretch out as far as the eye can see to his right, any place they could hide destroyed long ago. The encampment building a fleet to destroy Askala is ahead. Outlanders are on their tail.

Which means stop and fight. Or find somewhere to hide.

His first instinct is to fight. If there are only two or three Outlanders, Luca can probably deal with them. Except he's not alone. Mercy's exhausted. Tarquin's a child with more courage than sense.

And if those men don't return, the others will know something is up.

Which leaves hide.

Luca jams the note in his pocket. "We need to run." Grabbing the supply bags, he breaks into a jog in the direction they just came—back up the hill. "This way."

Mercy and Tarquin leap into action. Luca takes them in a diagonal line across the hill—making their way up, but also away from the Outlanders looking for them. They flee over rocky soil, Luca keeping one eye on their destination at the top of the hill, one eye on the two people he'll do anything to keep safe.

Tarquin stumbles and Luca quickly catches her before she

falls again. He swings her up and she clambers onto his shoulders. Barely breaking stride, Luca powers forward up the hill, Mercy by his side.

When they reach the rocks they left not long ago, Luca comes to a halt, breathing hard. Mercy stops beside him, resting a hand on his shoulder as she works to catch her breath. "What…now?" she pants.

He jostles Tarquin as she perches on his shoulders. "Hopefully they'll continue around the base of the hill."

Luca eyes the stand of rocks. Jagged and harsh like everything else in the Outlands, there's not enough of them to hide three people, even if one is a child. On the other side is a steep drop, carved out by the ocean winds. The other side is also where the other Outlanders are.

But as long as the Outlanders following them remain below, this is as good a place as they can hope for as they wait them out.

He hears the sounds before Mercy or Tarquin do. Footsteps crunching over gravel—two men, one breathing heavily.

"Going to the lookout was a great idea, Dunn."

The panting becomes louder. "Well, I ain't walking the whole way around the stupid hill."

Mercy and Tarquin freeze.

"They're coming," Mercy mouths.

And they're not far behind. Luca slips Tarquin to the ground and runs over the rocks, clambering as he desperately searches for somewhere to hide them.

But there's nothing. Not even a crevice large enough to tuck Tarquin in.

"Dammit," Luca breathes. Fighting is fast becoming his only option, and that runs the risk of being found. Any advantage they had discovering the boats will be lost.

Or someone could get hurt, or worse…

Tarquin comes to stand next to him, looking south instead

of at the boulders or the men about to stumble across them. She points to her feet. "We need to go down."

Down? But that's the side that faces the beach. Luca glances over his shoulder, seeing Mercy running her hands over the boulders as if she'll miraculously find a door to get them the hell out of here.

Luca turns to Tarquin. She's right. They need to go down. There's no other choice.

A few steps forward and Luca discovers it's not a very palatable option. The hill has practically been shorn away by the ocean winds. The small droplets of the acidic water whipped against the hill have gouged away little more than a cliff face.

"There'd better be someone here," pants one of the men. "Or I'll be pissed I did all this walking for nothin.'" There's a hacking cough. "And they'd better have food on 'em."

Their supplies!

Luca drops to his stomach as he crawls to look over the edge. His eyes light up when he sees what he's looking for. A ledge! A little further down than he'd hoped, but a ledge, nonetheless.

He indicates for Mercy and Tarquin to join him, swinging his feet around.

"Luca," Mercy hisses, but he ignores her. There's no time for her to point out how dangerous this is, and for him to retort that he did foolhardy things like this as a kid all the time.

He lowers himself, his fingers clamped tightly onto the edge of rock he's about to dangle off. His feet swing down and he stretches, trying to find anything but air. His breath catches when his toe scrapes over solid ground, only to slip back out into nothingness. Dammit. The ledge is not only further down than he'd hoped, it's tucked into the cliff face, making it harder to reach.

Luca presses his fingers into the rock as if he can grow roots and anchor himself there. "Climb down," he mutters through gritted teeth.

He doesn't have to ask Tarquin twice. She clambers down him like the human ladder he is, and Luca pulls his legs forward as she passes his waist. He hears her drop onto the ledge.

"Mercy, your turn."

"But..."

"Now."

The sounds of the men's footfalls are a countdown to the moment they're discovered. Mercy curses, the surprise making Luca blink. A second later, she's shimmying down his back, holding onto him for dear life.

The strain on Luca's fingertips multiplies, and he can feel the tendons on his neck standing out as he strains to keep them from slipping. Mercy slides down quickly, and Luca curves his body so she can step onto the ledge safely. She lands, sending small pebbles skittering over the edge.

"What was that?" one of the men demands.

Luca stops breathing. He can't let go. Not only would it be hard to land on the ledge, but he can't do it silently.

Which leaves his fingers visible.

Heavy footsteps rush over, and Luca guesses they must be standing by the boulders. "I wouldn't go too close to the edge," one of them mutters. "These cliffs crumble all the time." The man coughs then spits. "Which is probably what you heard, fool."

Luca still hasn't taken a breath. All the men have to do is look down.

"I saw someone! I know I did!" the second man half-growls, half-whines.

Gravel crunches as they move but Luca can't tell if they're coming closer or moving away. "Or you're seeing things again cause you're so bloody hungry."

The increasing voices tell Luca they're moving in his direc-

241

tion. He keeps his gaze up, waiting to see a dirty face peering over the edge at him.

"Come on, we need to get back."

"What the hell for? We can't finish it until—" The man's words are cut off as he breaks into hacking coughs.

"Point that mouth of yours the other way! I don't wanna catch nothin'. Not when we're so close to seeing more food than we can ever eat."

The men's footsteps fade, but Luca holds on for several more minutes, the muscles in his arms screaming with the strain. When all he can hear is the wind whipping the cliff face, he pulls himself up, inch by painful inch.

The moment he has his torso over, he collapses onto the rock-strewn dirt. He pulls in lungfuls of air, wishing away the darts of pain shooting down to his fingers as blood flow is restored.

Four breaths are all he allows himself before he lowers himself again. "Climb up," he tells Mercy and Tarquin.

"Quick, Tarquin," Mercy says. "Luca won't be able to hold on much longer."

Tarquin scrambles up him like the nimble creature she is. Her weight is slight enough that Luca barely feels it. Mercy's climb is slower and heavier and the pain in his arms returns, shrieking up and down his muscles.

But she does it as quickly as possible, reaching for the ledge the moment she can and hauling herself up. Seconds later, two sets of hands clamp onto his forearms and help Luca back onto solid land.

He flops onto his back, breathing like he just ran to the beach and back. Two faces appear above him, Tarquin smiling, Mercy frowning.

"I'm totally going to be the Falcon when I grow up," Tarquin says with relish.

Mercy's hands flutter over his face. "Are you okay?" He nods, pressing a kiss to her fingertips. She relaxes only to tense again. "We need to get moving."

Because they may have been spotted out on the cliff face.

Luca rolls over and gets to his feet. His arms feel like the squishy bodies of pteropods, but his legs will work just fine.

Except...

Mercy takes Tarquin's hand. "The boat isn't far away." She walks a few steps only to realize Luca isn't beside her. She looks around in alarm. "They're coming back?"

Luca shakes his head. "No." He lets out a breath. "Did you hear what they said, though?"

Mercy frowns. "I only caught little bits down there."

"They said they're waiting for something before they can finish."

Mercy's free hand hikes up to her hip. "And?"

"I'm going to stay," Luca says quietly. "I have to find out what they were talking about. There might be a way to stop this." He strides forward, taking Mercy's hand. "You and Tarquin get the boat. I'll meet you on the beach where it's hidden at midnight."

Mercy chews her lip, not keen on the idea of being separated, but probably realizing the value in seeing whether they can learn anything else before they leave.

Tarquin shoves herself between them. "We can help. We're fierce women."

Luca raises his brows at Mercy. There's no way they can bring Tarquin closer to the Outlanders. It's just too dangerous.

Mercy's shoulders drop as she realizes he's right. A second later, she straightens again. "Tarquin, our job is to get the boat. That way we can meet Luca and get out of here."

Tarquin's brows scrunch down. "Are you sure?"

"I'm positive. In fact, I think this job is best done by fierce women. It's the only way we can show Luca we row as well as he does."

Tarquin straightens, growing an inch. "True." Her grip tightens around Mercy's hand. "We'd better get going."

Mercy's gaze returns to Luca's and his heart feels like it just tripped over itself. She looks determined but scared, and if that's not courage, he doesn't know what is. "Stay alert, I doubt you'll see anyone, but you never know."

She presses her lips to his briefly, but it's still enough to brand. "I'll see you at midnight."

"I'm already looking forward to it," Luca says with a grin.

Spinning on her heel as if she needs to get going before she changes her mind, Mercy makes her way back down the hill.

"You're going to love Askala," she murmurs to Tarquin, her voice fading away, taking Luca's heart with him.

How odd. He spent so long fighting what he felt for Mercy, then fighting to keep her tucked somewhere safe and away from danger. And now, as he watches her walk away, being apart feels so wrong. In fact, she's one person he'd have beside him in a battle.

Once they're out of sight, Luca returns to the boulders, watching the Outlanders down by the beach for long minutes. They move around, working on the boats, showing no indication that they saw three bodies clinging to the cliff not long ago. Letting out a sigh of relief, Luca sits and leans against the hard rock. He lets his head fall back, noting it's late afternoon.

A couple more hours and twilight will be here, giving him the cover he needs to get close to the encampment. Luca uses the time to rest in the same way everyone else does in the Outlands—with one eye open, always scanning. Always expecting an attack.

But one doesn't come as evening settles over the ash-colored wastelands. As Luca makes his way back down the hill, he hopes Mercy and Tarquin found the boat easily. As he'd sat there, he'd thought of all the ways this plan could go wrong. They came across some nomads. They arrived only to find the boat was stolen. Tarquin tripped and this time, seriously hurt herself.

Shoving away the uncomfortable thoughts, Luca makes his way to the camp. Night closes around him, the only thing that's hiding his presence right now. There are no trees, no rocks, no huts to dart between and hide behind. Creeping forward, he pauses regularly, ears straining. But all he can hear are the rhythmic breaking of the waves to his right and the odd sound of the men.

Ahead, a few fires dot the sand, the men lounging around them. Luca hunches down as he jogs toward the closest boat, then crouches low. This one isn't much more than a skeleton, though, affording little cover. Seeing a completed one not far away, he darts forward.

Ready to run at the first sign he's been sighted, Luca ducks behind it. He frowns as the tumble of the waves obscure any other sound.

But there's nothing. No shouts. No sudden movements. No one has seen him.

Allowing his breathing to slow, Luca waits. Several men look like they're asleep, the others are mostly quiet, probably too hungry to talk. Glancing above, Luca calculates the time using the Big Dipper and the North Star like Sam taught him to. He has a couple of hours before he needs to leave to meet Mercy and Tarquin. Hopefully, this little expedition hasn't been a waste.

Someone spits into the fire, sparking a handful of embers into the air, then nothing. Luca shifts his weight, leaning a little more against the boat as he tells himself to be patient. Surely he didn't send Mercy and Tarquin off alone in the Outlands for nothing...

"How much longer?" grumbles a man, looking like he's chewing on a twig.

"Gunnar and Vitron said the stuff would get here about the same time they got back with the food," snaps another.

Grim satisfaction settles in Luca's gut at the thought that Gunnar and Vitron will never return, quickly followed by disgust. This is what the people of Fairbanks were forced to support? Their food provided the sustenance to build these boats. The boats that will bring war to Askala.

"Shut up," rumbles someone else on the other side of the fire and Luca recognizes the voice of one of the men who was up on the hill. He coughs and spits again. "A man needs his sleep."

"You do if you've got one foot in the grave," mutters someone else.

Coughing is a common sound in the Outlands, despite the warm humid climate. The weak, malnourished bodies of the people here struggle to fight off even the most common illnesses.

The sick man rolls over, facing his back to the others. "I'll be holding on till the sap gets here, then when we get to Askala and I get better, me and me spear will show you who's the strong one around here."

Sap! That's what they're waiting for from the Newlands!

Luca rubs his hand over the side of the boat, feeling the roughness of the timber. These vessels can't go out on the water until they've been covered in mangrove pine sap, protecting them from the acidic ocean.

Which means they still have time to stop this!

He grips the wood, his heart hammering. He needs to tell Mercy. They don't need to go to Askala. They need to get to the Newlands. Tonight.

Exhilaration thrums through his veins as Luca prepares to push to his feet. If he leaves now, he'll get back early. He can't wait to see Mercy's face when he shares the news.

Except, as Luca releases his grip on the boat, something

clamps around his wrist. Another hand. With a punishing grip that refuses to let go.

"Oh, no you don't."

Instantly, Luca yanks his arm as hard as he can, but the human shackle doesn't release him. The man shouts, and in a blink, the Outlanders swarm toward him, a human wave of fury.

The fight is rough but short. Luca kicks and swings wildly, trying to keep the men at bay. But there are too many of them. A punch to his face has him reeling. A foot lashes out and slams in the back of his knee and he crumples. Dirty, smelly bodies land on him, hands taking hold of his limbs.

Another fist collides with his face, snapping Luca's head to the side. When he turns back and looks up, the sharp end of a spear is hovering between his eyes.

Luca knows he has to think fast. "You don't want to kill me. Not yet."

"Seems like a mighty fine idea to me," growls a voice above him.

"I suspect there are people out there who would pay handsomely for the Falcon."

"The Falcon?" The tip of the spear moves back a few inches.

"You heard me." Luca's voice turns hard as he realizes he has no other choice but to do this. "I am the Falcon."

"Prove it."

"The Falcon stole the girl Vitron was given in a trade. He rescued two women who were about to be stoned to death because they stole a slice of bread. He stole a hare when Gunnar's village refused to give any to three orphans and left it in their hut. Plus, who else would be stupid enough to claim being the Falcon? It's little more than a death wish."

There's silence as they all digest this. Enough of them would know those stories are all true.

"Gunnar and Vitron will be back soon," says someone in the group. "With food."

"And Vitron's desire to kill me is personal," points out Luca.

The spear draws up another few inches, and the man's eyes turn assessing as he chews on his lip.

"You'd be given extra rations for your forward thinking," Luca adds. "For giving Vitron a chance to kill me himself."

The next thing he knows, Luca's being hauled to his feet, his arms yanked painfully behind his back. Rough rope is tied around his wrists before he's shoved back down into the sand.

"If Gunnar and Vitron aren't back by morning, you're dead," says a threatening voice.

The intent to follow through with his promise is unmistakable.

One of the men crosses his arms and leans against a nearby boat. "I'll take the first shift."

The men move away, one loudly clearing his throat and spitting. Luca hears the glob of saliva land beside him.

As the gentle break of the waves becomes all that fills the air, Luca lets his chin drop to his chest. He needs to find a way to escape before morning. He works his hands in the rough rope, feeling how tight it's been knotted as it chafes his skin.

"Vitron's gonna be happy to see you, dead or alive, if you ask me," growls the man in the boat.

Gritting his teeth, Luca acknowledges the pickle he's in.

These men know he's the Falcon.

Gunnar and Vitron won't be returning seeing as they're already dead.

He won't be meeting Mercy and Tarquin as he'd promised.

Luca's jaw clenches. And the note is still in his pocket.

Unread.

HAWK

*H*awk holds Sam with all his strength as they're thrown from the boat.

Seconds seems to take hours, or is it the other way around? He loses sense of time and place. All he knows is that he has to keep Sam in his grasp. It feels like the most important thing he's ever had to do. If he lets go, he might never get the chance to hold her again.

They hit the water and Hawk squeezes his eyes closed in anticipation of the sharp sting of the acid.

But instead of being swallowed up by the waves, his rear end hits sand, sending a ricochet of pain through his still-healing ribs.

He spins around in the darkness, his heart beating fast as he tries to work out how he's sitting on sand in the middle of the ocean. This isn't possible! Although, he doesn't have time to figure this out right now. All that's important is that Sam is still in his arms.

Safe.

But for how long?

"It's a sandbank!" Wren shouts from somewhere near Hawk's left. "Get moving! Now!"

Hawk doesn't have time to question what in sweet Terra a sandbank is doing here. All he knows is that it just saved their lives.

A flash of lighting forks across the sky and Hawk sees a dark fin slice through the water. He pushes Sam back out of harm's way.

"We need the boat!" Wren calls over the noise of the storm, appearing beside him as they're plunged back into darkness.

"Take Sam!" Hawk thrusts Sam in Wren's direction and spears his body toward the upturned boat, just managing to grip it before the current drags it away. He hasn't come this far to perish on a sandbank, even if Sam is with him. That boat is their only chance.

His injuries scream at him and he knows he's going to pay for this in the days to come. If he's lucky enough to see those days...

There's another lightning flash and Hawk turns his head to see Sam dart forward, wrenching free of Wren's grasp to pluck their remaining oar out of the water. As much as he hates that she risked herself like that, he can't deny they're going to need that.

A huge wave surges toward them, picking up the boat and hurling it into the air. Hawk hangs on, almost relieved when both he and the boat are slammed onto an expanse of damp sand.

"Sam!" he cries. "Wren!"

But without another bolt of lightning, he has no hope of seeing either of them.

He squints into the darkness, hoping that wave hadn't dragged Sam and Wren under. He knew he should never have let go of Sam!

"Hawk!"

His eyes widen at the sound of his name just as more lightning splits open the sky. Wren and Sam are wading through the shallow water toward him.

There's enough light for Hawk to lock eyes with Sam for only a second, but it's enough for the story he needs to pass between them. He sees the worry on her face, and the relief when she sees him. Just before her image is plunged back into the darkness, he sees something else.

Love. Regret. Fear.

He closes the gap between them, putting his arms around the only girl he'll ever love, and pulls her to his chest. If they don't get hit by lightning, they'll survive this storm to see the sun rise again. The leatherskins can't get them here.

"We can shelter under the boat!" Hawk says, desperate to get them all out of this rain. The temperature has dropped significantly and he can feel Sam shivering.

"Give me the oar!" says Wren and Hawk feels her pull something away from Sam, then hears splashing as his aunt makes her way back in the direction of the boat.

Hawk and Sam follow her, wading through the shallows until they're standing on damp sand. Sam's skin is far too sensitive to have stayed in that water for another moment.

Hawk pauses to press his cheek to the top of Sam's damp head. Her hair might be soaked through, but somehow, she still smells like his past, his present and his future all wrapped up in the most beautiful package he's ever seen.

Yep. He's got it bad.

"Come on," he says, taking her hand and urging her further along the sandbank. "Let's get you to shelter."

"In a moment," she says, her feet planting firmly as she pulls him to a stop. "First, I need to say sorry."

"For what?" He frowns as he returns his arms around her. "For getting the oar when I told you to stay back?"

"No." Her arms slip around his waist and she squeezes

tightly. "For telling you that kiss meant nothing to me when it meant the entire world."

"You don't have to say that." His heart leaps as he silently curses for trying to talk her out of saying the very words he's been so desperate to hear ever since she left the Newlands.

"But it's true." She pushes up on her toes and her face comes closer to his. "I love you, Hawk. In every way it's possible to love a person. Because you're my person."

Hawk lets out a sound that's a cross between a yelp and a moan, wasting no time in leaning down to reach Sam.

As the rain falls, cooling the temperature of their skin, he finds Sam's warm lips and at last he's losing himself in the kiss he'd dared to hope for all this time. The kiss that kept him going when everything else seemed lost.

Sam kisses him back without hesitation and he realizes he didn't say he loves her, too. But as her tongue darts forward, he knows he doesn't need to. This kiss is his declaration. Besides that, he's pretty sure his every action has been telling Sam he loves her since he was about five years old. And he told her how he feels back in the Newlands.

Her shivering intensifies and he knows he has to get her to shelter.

"Come on," he says, dragging his lips off Sam's. "You need to dry off."

There's a flash then a loud boom of thunder as if the gods are agreeing with him and Sam slips her hand into Hawk's as they run for the boat.

The lightning strikes again just as they get there and Hawk sees that Wren's used the oar to prop up the overturned vessel like a roof, and he wonders why they didn't do that when they first arrived in the Newlands. How naïve they'd been back then.

They climb in beside her, the relief from being out of the rain instant. Hawk sits in the middle, tucking Sam to his side and reaching for Wren.

"I'm fine." Wren shuffles away just a little, as independent as ever. She'd probably choose to freeze to death over accepting his offer of comfort.

He smiles in the dark, his heart swelling with love for his feisty aunt.

"Thanks for coming to get me," he says.

"I thought I was getting my daughter," she says back.

He laughs, knowing her well enough to know she means no offence by this. "Sorry for being the booby prize."

Wren sighs loudly. "I'm glad you're okay, Hawk."

"Me, too," says Sam.

"Me, three." Hawk laughs.

"That was a close call out there." Sam's voice is shaking but her trembling seems to be improving. "If this sandbank wasn't here, we'd have been a leatherskin's dinner by now."

"What is with this sandbank anyway?" Hawk asks. "Is it new?"

"The oceans are receding," says Sam. "Haven't you noticed our beach in Askala is growing in size? That's how the Newlands were formed. I'll bet this sandbank will become the next Newlands in years to come."

Wren snorts. "It seems Hawk and I have a habit of finding new land masses together."

"And it seems I have a habit of almost dying on them," he adds.

"Are you sure Mercy's okay?" Wren asks, her voice taking a serious tone.

"She's with Luca," says Sam, answering for him. "She's fine."

"She's better than fine." Hawk wishes Wren could see his face to see that he means it. "She's...happy."

"I know that Mercy's in love with Luca," says Wren, plainly.

Hawk and Sam freeze, not knowing what to say. This feels like something Mercy needs to talk to her mother about.

"Mother's intuition?" Sam asks.

"No," says Wren. "Ekon told me."

Hawk smiles. That wasn't what he'd been expecting. "And how do you feel about it?"

"I couldn't care less who she's in love with, just as long as she comes back to me alive," huffs Wren. "At least I know Luca's a decent human."

"But she was so worried about what you'd think," says Hawk. "With Luca being her cousin and all that."

Wren snorts. "Hardly! They're not blood related. And even if they were, they'd only be half second cousins. That's not exactly going to play havoc with any genetics."

"They grew up like cousins," says Sam. "I think that's what she was worried about."

"Kian and Nova grew up together, too," says Wren. "Does that make your parents' love wrong?"

"Of course not," says Sam quickly.

"Or you two," adds Wren. "I didn't need to be able to see in the dark just now to know that you were kissing over there. It seems like you were all very busy over in the Newlands."

"I love Hawk." Sam nestles into his side. "Always have. Always will. I just needed to become a Seeker to see it."

"I love you, too," says Hawk, taking the chance this time to say it in return.

"Okay," says Wren. "I think I might throw up now, which is going to make this little shelter a little uncomfortable."

Sam giggles. "My mom told me that you and Dex were pretty loved up when you first got together."

"All lies," says Wren, not very convincingly.

"It's funny but my dad said the same thing." Hawk grins as he squeezes Sam.

"It's a conspiracy," Wren grumbles. "They're trying to ruin my reputation."

"Did you know that Gust was scared of you?" asks Hawk,

remembering the conversation they'd had when they were locked in the Round House.

"He was a smart guy," Wren retorts. "No wonder he passed his Proving."

"I'm sad he's gone." Sam rests her head on Hawk's shoulder. "Although, I hate to say it, but he was a bit annoying as a Seeker."

"Not always." Hawk tries to keep his tone calm. "We just didn't understand him. Gust was a good guy. He became a friend once it was just the two of us. I wouldn't be alive without the way he took care of me."

"I'm so sorry I left you!" Sam cries. "I thought you had Mercy and Luca there to look after you. I would never have left you if I knew."

"It's okay," says Hawk, biting his tongue. He hadn't meant for Sam to take that personally. "I understand why you left. You were trying to keep us all safe."

"That didn't turn out so well, did it?" The defeated tone in Sam's voice tears at Hawk's heart.

"Apart from losing Gust, it turned out just fine." Hawk drops a kiss on Sam's hair. "We're both here now, aren't we?"

"I guess so." Sam snuggles in closer and he notices her shivering is subsiding now that they're out of the rain. "Hawk, there's something else I need to tell you."

His heart pounds as he waits to hear what she's talking about.

"Seb died." Her voice breaks with the agony at having to say these words out loud and tears spring to Hawk's eyes.

"No," he says, shaking his head as his mind whirls. They knew he was sick, but surely not *that* sick. "Not Seb."

"I think…" Sam sighs. "I think he was poisoned. There are so many people unwell. Zali died, along with a number of others. And my mom is very weak. The infirmary's full."

"But who would do that?" Hawk fights back tears. Surely,

this can't be happening now right when they need their people to be strong.

"Charity," says Sam. "Wren and I are both certain of it."

"That can't be right!" Hawk remembers how weak and vulnerable Charity had seemed. A girl like that doesn't seem capable of murder.

"It's true," says Wren. "We found the note you sent hidden in her bed. And Sam saw her picking deadly nightshade in the forest. We just need to catch her in the act so we can prove it."

Hawk tries to take all this in. Charity is Grace's daughter. Does that mean Grace knows about this? Had she put her up to it? He'd been sure he could trust Grace! That she had a hard life being married to the Commander. Is it possible he had that all wrong?

"I'm so sorry, Sam," he says. "I know how close you were with Seb."

"Thanks," Sam sniffs. "I loved him a lot."

"So, what's our plan?" Hawk asks, directing his question at Wren. His aunt will have a plan. She always does. "If what you both suspect is true, we need to get back home as soon as possible."

Wren shifts on the sand beside him and Hawk knows she wishes she could pace while she thinks. It's one of her trademark moves.

"We wait until morning, put this boat back in the water, and get the hell out of here," she says.

"I like that plan." Sam straightens up. "That's a very good plan."

Wren yawns loudly. "But first, let's try to get some sleep. We'll need our energy."

"Should one of us keep watch?" Sam asks.

"Unless leatherskins have learned how to walk, I think we'll be okay," Wren says, sleepily.

There's the rustle of fabric and Hawk assumes Wren just laid down. It's even darker underneath the boat than it had been outside.

Hawk settles down on his back, frowning at how damp and cold the sand is.

"Lie on top of me to keep dry," he says to Sam, not wanting her shivering to start up again.

Wren coughs. "I'm right here, you know."

"Don't worry, we know," smiles Hawk. "You're not easy to forget."

"He's right, though," says Wren. "You'll be warmer if you're off the sand, Sam. Just no funny business, okay?"

Sam crawls on top of Hawk and he winces as her elbow sticks into his ribs. He seals his lips, not wanting her to know she's hurting him in case she chooses to sleep on the wet sand.

She settles into a position that's thankfully tolerable for Hawk and he closes his eyes, drinking in her closeness as he reminds himself of what Wren just said.

No funny business.

There definitely won't be any of that. Just the blissful torture of having Sam pressed against him and knowing he can't do a thing about it except hold her tight.

It's not long until Sam's breathing deepens and she drifts off to sleep. Hawk manages to doze a little. At least, he thinks he does. The need to keep Sam safe overpowers the need to fall into a deep sleep. He won't sleep well again until he's back in his bed in Askala with Dove jabbing her pointy feet into his lower back.

Maybe one day he'll get to share a bed with Sam in a hut all of their own. Have some children with red hair and a thirst for learning useful facts about the world. Because now that Sam's told him she loves him, he can dare to dream such dreams. His future has been set on a new shared path.

If only they can keep Askala safe...

When the morning arrives, sending rays of delicate light

filtering into the boat, Hawk decides that no matter how uncomfortable he'd been, it was the best night of his life. Even better than the nights he'd shared with Sam in the Newlands because this night had been the first time he'd known for certain her heart was his.

Wren's no longer under the boat, having climbed out the moment the rain had stopped. Hawk's not sure if her inability to keep still is one of her greatest flaws or strengths.

"Sam," he whispers. "It's time to wake up. We need to go home."

"Home," says Sam, opening her eyes and smiling up at Hawk. At least one of them got a good sleep.

"Good." Wren sticks her head into the boat. "You're awake. Tide's coming in. We need to get moving. This sandbank's about to get swallowed up."

Wren disappears again and Sam climbs off Hawk.

"Thanks for keeping me warm," she says, leaning over to give him a quick kiss.

"Anytime." He grins at her. "Let's do it without my aunt around next time."

"I heard that," says Wren from outside the boat.

Hawk chuckles as he steps out into the morning sun. "Sorry, Wren."

She rolls her eyes and shakes her head, not letting him off that easily.

Hawk looks around, seeing how much closer the water has crept up the sandbank. Wren's right. They really do need to get moving.

Sam emerges from underneath the boat, the golden flecks of her hair catching in the sunlight. She's as beautiful as ever despite the drenching they got last night. And he knows he's not sorry at all. He really does want to spend the night with her without his aunt around.

Wren takes one end of the boat and nods at Hawk. Together, they flip it the right way up.

"Climb in," says Hawk. "I'll push it out. No point in more than one of us getting our feet wet."

"Pass me the oar," says Wren, getting in.

Hawk lifts Sam in then goes back for the oar, grateful Sam had the courage to save it for them. Without it, they'd have had no choice but to float around aimlessly and hope that someone from Askala came looking for them eventually.

With the water lapping at his feet, Hawk pushes the boat into the ocean and climbs in.

"I'll row," says Wren, refusing to hand over the oar. "I slept better than you. Besides, I know how sore broken ribs can be."

"How did you know they're broken?" he asks, certain he'd hidden his pain well enough.

"Experience," she says, dipping the oar in the water and dragging it through. "And Sam told me."

"Are you still in pain?" Sam asks, looking guilty. "You should have told me! I wouldn't have slept on top of you."

He raises a brow at her and waits for her to think about what she just said. That was exactly why he hadn't told her.

"Oh," she says, slapping him gently on the thigh. "You really need to stop being so selfless, Hawk."

"I'll try." He smiles, having no intention of doing any such thing when it comes to Sam.

Wren rows with strength that seems impossible for someone of her small stature, Sam using the position of the sun to help navigate. It seems they weren't as far off course as they'd feared, and before long, Askala comes into view.

Hawk lets out a sigh. Home. He's actually going home. How could he have been so foolish to think his future lay anywhere else? Soon he'll see his parents and his sisters and all the other familiar faces he grew up surrounded by.

Except for Seb.

It's hard to believe he won't be seeing Sam's curious little brother around anymore. What an absolute tragedy. It just makes it even more important they get home before anyone else suffers the same fate.

"Let me row for a bit," he offers, anxious to keep this boat moving as fast as it can.

"Or me," says Sam, quickly.

"I'm fine." Wren keeps focused on her task. "We're nearly there now."

Hawk turns his eyes back to Askala, willing them to get there sooner, even though Wren's rowing with impressive speed.

Sam lets out a gasp and points when she sees something that Hawk had just been blinking at, wondering if he'd been imagining it.

"What's wrong?" Wren pauses her rowing and follows their gaze.

"Fire." Hawk blinks as if he can clear the worrying sight before them. There's a large plume of dark black smoke trailing into the air and it's unmistakably coming from the part of the island where their huts are built. "Askala is on fire."

SAM

The tower of smoke becomes darker and thicker the closer they get to Askala. It billows up in thick waves, staining the sky with the same ashen shades as the Outlands.

Sam finds herself leaning forward, wanting to go faster even though Wren's rowing the hardest she's ever seen. She grips Hawk's hand hard as they try to identify where the fire is.

Try to figure out how big it is.

How much it's destroyed.

Hawk leaps out of the boat the moment they're in the shallows, hauling it up to the sand. Sam and Wren are out before it's stopped, splashing through the ankle-deep water. They run, instantly registering that the smoke is coming from the center of the village.

It has to be coming from a hut. Or several huts.

People are running frantically past them, carrying buckets and tubs, their faces flushed as they continue to the village.

"No," Wren moans, and Sam sees why.

A hut is ablaze ahead, little more than a timber frame being held together by flames. Wren and Dex's hut.

"Dex!" she screams. "Dex!"

261

Sam's heart stutters in her chest as she scans the crowd ahead. There are people everywhere, some throwing water on the flames, some standing back, shielding their faces from the heat. They're all people Sam recognizes, but she can't see Dex anywhere.

No...

But then the crowd parts as someone pushes past. "Wren?" Dex calls, as if he can't believe he just heard her voice.

Wren rushes at him, launching herself into his arms. Dex catches her and they hold each other for long moments, heads tucked in close.

Sam comes to a stop, Hawk beside her. Their hands instinctively twine together and she wonders if his throat is as tight as hers. The love between Wren and Dex feels more powerful than the raging fire they're standing beside, a pocket of calm and connection beside an explosion of carnage and destruction.

They pull apart and the world starts rushing at Sam again. The heat hits her like a wall and Hawk pulls her behind him as more people run past, their buckets full.

Sam sees her father away to the left, covered in soot and sweat as he calls out instructions. "Keep back! Pour the water there, we don't want the fire spreading! Keep an eye out for spot fires!"

"They've kept it localized," Hawk observes.

He's right. Sam registers that the people with the buckets are throwing the water on the adjacent huts, not on the one ablaze. Now that adrenaline doesn't have her heart thundering so hard, she notes the way people are moving quickly, but they aren't panicked.

They join Wren and Dex, who are now standing back a little, their arms still tightly holding the other.

"I'm fine. The hut was empty," Dex is saying to Wren. "No one was hurt."

Dex's eyes widen when he sees Sam and Hawk and his gaze shoots to Wren. "Mercy?" he asks in a pained whisper.

Wren presses her hand to his chest. "She's in the Outlands with Luca. Our girl is probably doing what she can to protect Askala."

Dex's brow contracts as he processes this. But then he smiles despite the pale tension that's drawn his face tight. "Good to have you back, Hawk."

Hawk nods. "It feels good to be here. Is there anything we can do to help?"

Shaking his head, Dex glances at his hut. "There's nothing to be done. Although our hut is lost, we've kept the fire under control."

"Hawk?" Felicia, Hawk's mother, is running at him, her hand over her mouth. "Hawk!"

Before she's reached him, the squeals of Hawk's flock of sisters pierce the air. Sam steps back as he's engulfed in love. He winces as his mother barrels into his arms, followed by Dove and the others. Phoenix stops beside them, pulling in deep breaths as his eyes glow with pride.

Their boy is back.

Sam retreats, giving Hawk a reassuring smile when he notices her moving away. This is his moment with his family, where he realizes how loved he is. How much Askala is his home.

Plus, the sooner they get their welcomes out of the way, the sooner they can be alone.

Deciding to go tell her father she's back, Sam sees him scanning the people milling around, his lips moving. He's doing a headcount, making sure everyone is accounted for. Even beneath the streaks of ash on his face, his exhaustion is apparent.

Sam quickly starts doing her own inventory of the people of Askala, wanting to help her father. Hawk's family have contracted around him like the flower of an *Osteospermum* closing at night. Dex and Wren are holding each other as they watch their home collapse into a pile of embers. The leaders and people are there, ready with their buckets of water or comforting each other as they try to comprehend another tragedy. Everyone seems accounted for.

Sam frowns. Except for Charity.

Doing a slow spin, Sam scans for the fair-haired girl. Dex said no one was hurt in the fire, so she must be here, somewhere. Except, even when Sam slows her search and studies each face, she can't find her.

Something in Sam's stomach tingles, and she wonders if this is what Wren was talking about when she spoke of gut instinct. Brows scrunched low, Sam lets it guide her, finding herself heading to the kitchens.

The path is quiet and empty, with everyone now at the fire. Sam hurries through the trees, not sure she likes this unsettled feeling that's churning through her abdomen.

She's probably just hungry, she tells herself. The last time she ate was yesterday sometime, after all.

The door to the kitchens is open, the smell of the soup they've made each day since people started getting sick wafting through. Sam slows, hesitating as she comes closer, unsure what she's looking for.

What she's hoping to find.

Peeking through the open doors, Sam finds the kitchens like they always are. A large, open space, with a hearth at one end for the small amount of cooking they do, two rows of benches dividing the room, one stacked high with fresh produce. A pot bubbles over the embers in the hearth, tendrils of steam coiling up.

Sam lets out a slow breath. The kitchen's empty.

Relaxing a little, she steps further in, the scent of fresh fennel and celeriac, a hint of tomato, tickling her nose. She hopes they've been adding the reishi she suggested.

Bang. The sound of the door slamming behind her has Sam spinning around.

Charity leans back against it. "What are you doing here, Sam?"

Sam steps back, and the tingling sensation in her stomach has her skirting around one of the benches until it's between them. "Hi, Charity. I was just checking where you were."

"And you thought I'd be in the kitchens."

Instantly, Sam realizes her error. It looks like she's suspicious of Charity, and although that's exactly what she was, she doesn't want Charity thinking that.

Not with the cold way she's looking at Sam.

"Well, you spend so much time in here…"

The icy fire in Charity's eyes flares and Sam snaps her mouth shut. The tingly feeling in her gut is now a full blown electrical storm.

Charity takes a step forward. "You noticed that too, huh?"

The need to keep as much distance between them is strong, meaning Sam instinctively takes another step back. She bumps into the bench behind her, a knife clattering on the timber surface. The green, tangy scent of tomatoes hits her again. Charity's eyes darts to whatever's behind Sam, and Sam's gaze follows her.

The first thing she sees is the large, serrated knife that just tumbled off a chopping board. Her heart lodges in her throat so hard and fast she feels nauseous. But then she sees what the knife had been dicing.

Small, tomato-like fruit.

"Deadly nightshade," Sam whispers.

The pot simmers only a few feet away, and Sam can see more innocuous looking pieces bobbing on the surface.

Her gaze flies to Charity. "The fire was a distraction. You needed to get Dex off your back."

Another cold, calculating step and Charity's beside the first bench. "You told him to stay close to me, didn't you? Because you suspected something."

Sam doesn't answer. The panicky feeling powering through her body is no longer helping. It's making it hard to think.

A few stealthy steps and Charity's on the other side of the bench. "I should've killed you in the forest. But it was too risky, too hard to make it look like an accident." She angles her head to the side. "Or a deliberate act on your part."

"Zali," Sam gasps.

The Askalan elder didn't commit suicide. She was murdered.

And Charity's hard features are full of the promise that Sam is next.

Sam knows she needs a plan. She doesn't have the skill to fight, but she can run. She just needs to get to the doors.

Doing some quick calculations, she notes the distance is shorter to go right, but Charity is probably thinking the same. Which means getting ready to dart left the moment Charity moves.

Except Charity doesn't move left or right. In a flash, she leaps onto the bench, knocking the knife away as she lands in a crouch. Sam goes to run, but she doesn't stand a chance against Outlander reflexes. Charity jumps, landing on Sam and knocking her to the ground.

Sam fights, desperately and frantically, but Charity's too fast. Her hands wrap around Sam's wrists, slamming them into the ground as she straddles her. Panting, Sam tries to push her off, knowing that being trapped means death.

But despite Charity's slight size, Sam finds herself pinned, staring up at a face twisted with hate. "My mother thought your smarts would be useful," spits Charity. "But your brains won't save you now."

Sam stops fighting, knowing it's useless. Despite what Charity says, right now, her intelligence is all she has left.

Realization stabs her in the chest. She promised Seb she'd do what he couldn't–what Charity took from him. Live.

And she might not have strength, but she has a whole colony who care for her. She has Hawk.

Which means keeping Charity talking for as long as she can. Until someone comes looking for her. Sam glares up at Charity. "Think this through, Charity. There's no way you'll get away with this."

"I'm just as smart as any of you fools," snarls Charity. "Probably smarter. I never would've let the Commander's daughter set foot here, let alone welcomed her."

"We gave you a home," Sam says quietly. "You have everything you need."

"So I should thank you? For throwing me your leftovers? When my family, my people, fight to survive on the other side of the ocean?"

"They could come, too—"

"We deserve more than to beg! Than to wait to be deemed worthy!"

"No, that's not—" Sam stops, seeing that she's only making Charity angrier. "You kill me, and people will start asking questions."

"I know. I said I'm smart, remember?" Charity's eyes blaze with triumph. "Just like Zali, everyone will assume you died by your own hand."

"No one would believe I'd do that." Not when she's just found Hawk again.

"They will when you learn your mother's dead. That you couldn't save her."

Horror floods Sam, bringing another wave of nausea with it. "No, my mother's not dead." Unless that's why her father looked so tired and pale...

"Nova's weak, she won't be able to fight off a pillow on her face," Charity scoffs, unaware of the relief coursing through Sam. "And then the esteemed Kian will find the love of his life dead, his remaining child in a pool of blood beside her."

The relish in Charity's voice sickens Sam. So does the image she just painted.

It's vile.

And terrifying.

Charity moves, shimmying one leg up until her knee rests at the base of Sam's throat. Her face settles into determined lines. "I just need you unconscious…"

Charity pushes down and the pressure is instantaneous.

Sam's airway is cut off, her lungs spasming in her chest. Sam gasps, but there's no air to give her terror voice. She should've screamed while she had the chance. She should've called Hawk.

Hawk…

She only just got him back.

A black fog, as dark as death, closes in, narrowing Sam's vision. Her body goes limp without the necessary oxygen to fight, no matter how much she wants to. Even though she promised Seb… Surely Charity's face can't be the last one she'll see.

At least she told Hawk she loves him. At least he'll have that truth.

Please don't let him believe that she would choose to leave him, again.

Sam tries to tell herself that's enough, even as her mind rejects it as much as it rejects the fate that's inescapably engulfing her. Smothering her. Suffocating her.

Hawk…

Suddenly, the pressure's gone and her starving body is sucking air in great big gasps.

"Get off her!"

Hawk's voice, fueled by rage, reverberates through the kitchen.

Sam doesn't think she's ever heard anything more beautiful.

Charity's body flies through the air away from Sam. Then Hawk's holding Sam, lifting her up. She collapses into him, feeling sweet oxygen return life to her body. "I knew you'd come."

Hawk presses his lips to her forehead. "Always."

Sam yanks back. "Charity! We can't let her get away! She lit the fire so she could come and poison the soup again. And she killed Zali."

"She what?" Sam's father roars.

"Charity's not going anywhere," comes another voice—Dex —beside them.

Looking around Hawk's broad form, Sam sees it's not just Hawk who came to her rescue. Dex and Wren have Charity trapped between them, her father a few feet away. Others come rushing through the doorway, Avis and Thea, Diesel, Kozue.

Her father's fingers spear into his hair. "You killed Seb?" he asks Charity hoarsely. "You tried to kill Nova and Sam, too?"

Charity lifts her chin. "You sit back as the people of the Outlands die. How is that different?"

Sam's running before she realizes it. She slips between Charity and her father just as he reaches the girl, his face contorted with pain and anger. Sam presses her hand to his chest. "I'm fine, so is Mom."

Sam can feel the fury vibrating through her father's body as he breathes hard. "She...she almost..."

"But she didn't. And she's wrong. We're nothing like them." Sam holds his gaze. "We wouldn't choose to kill, no matter how much was taken from us."

Her father blinks, then blinks again before finally nodding. He turns away as if he can't bear the sight of Charity. "What will we do with her?" he asks tiredly.

"Put her in Zali's hut," suggests Dex. "We'll keep her under watch."

Wren nods. "She could be a goldmine of information."

Charity struggles against their grasp, quickly finding it's a waste of time. She turns her gaze to Sam, hatred once again flashing in their depths.

Sam instinctively takes a step back, finding herself coming up against a warm, strong body. She presses into Hawk, drawing strength from the knowledge she doesn't need to be physically strong. That she doesn't need to be everything.

Because she's not alone.

"You already know everything you need to." Charity sneers. "War is coming." Her lips tip up in a slow, cold smile. "And when the Commander arrives, we'll finish what I started. You'll all be dead."

MERCY

*M*idnight comes and goes, leaving Mercy with anxiety coursing through her veins. Tarquin is sleeping beside her in the boat. They'd retrieved it from its hiding place and dragged it down to the water, ready to go to Askala. They only need one more thing.

Luca.

Then they can go home. Mercy hadn't been sure she'd ever get the chance to go home again. She'd left as a Seeker with thoughts of saving the planet. And now she's returning with hopes of saving just their tiny slice of it. Because if they don't get there ahead of that fleet of boats they just saw, then everything will have been for nothing.

Askala will be gone. Overtaken by Outlanders who will pillage the island until only a wasteland remains. That thought breaks Mercy's heart almost as much as all the people perishing. Humans are on this Earth for such a short time. It's the legacy they leave behind that endures. It took Mercy becoming a Seeker to learn this reality that Sam innately seemed to know from the moment she was born.

Thoughts of Sam's grandfather, Magnus, plague Mercy. She's

heard the stories about how he tried to sacrifice his people to save the planet. She'd always been quietly horrified by this decision. But now...she wouldn't go so far to say she agrees with it, but she understands his actions so much more. Not everything in this world is made from black and white. There are a hundred shades in between. And in Askala's case, most of them are green.

Tarquin stirs, and Mercy weighs up her options.

She can wait here for as long as it takes. Which is going to be extremely risky when the sun comes up and their position is revealed.

Or she can go and find Luca to see what the problem is. Because there has to be a problem. There's no way he wouldn't keep his word to return by midnight, unless something had gone horribly wrong.

But going after him presents a new problem of its own. She can't risk Tarquin by bringing her along. But she also can't leave her here all on her own without explaining her plan. If she wakes up, she'll be terrified to think she's been abandoned.

"Tarquin!" Mercy jostles the little girl out of her sleep. "Wake up."

Tarquin sits and rubs at her eyes, moonbeams bouncing off the innocence of her face. "Is it time? Where's Luca?"

"I'm going to look for him," says Mercy. "I need you to stay here and mind the boat. It's a very important job."

Tarquin looks at her, blinks twice, then shakes her head. "That's not an important job. We can beach the boat on the sand. You made up that job because you don't want me to go with you."

Mercy lets out a sigh. One of the reasons she was so drawn to this small girl was her sharp mind. But one of the most frustrating things about her is...her sharp mind. It's impossible to get anything past her. "I really need you to stay here."

Tarquin crosses her arms. "And I really need to go with you."

Mercy shuffles about in their supply bag for her small knife, wishing she still had Fleur. Who knows what she's going to have to come up against. A flamethrower would be extremely handy right now.

"Are we going to sneak into the camp?" Tarquin asks.

"*I* am just going to get close and have a look around." Mercy presses her palm to her chest, then points at Tarquin. "And *you* are going to stay right here."

"You need a die cursion," says Tarquin, jiggling her legs.

Mercy frowns. "I need what?"

"A die cursion!" Tarquin throws out her hands. "You know, when someone makes a big noise so everyone doesn't see what's really happening somewhere else."

"Oh!" Mercy smiles. "You mean a diversion."

"That's what I said." Tarquin pouts.

"I tell you what," says Mercy, deciding it might be safer to keep Tarquin close. "You can come with me to see what's going on as long as you promise to stay back."

Tarquin makes a cross on her chest. "Cross my heart and hope...not to die."

"Nobody's going to die," says Mercy, hoping like Terra that Luca is still alive and breathing.

She pulls the boat a little further up onto the sand, tucking the bag of supplies into the bow, just in case an Outlander happens to take a midnight stroll on the beach. She'll move faster if she's not carrying anything. Tucking the knife in the back of her trousers, she reaches for Tarquin's hand and they set off in the direction of where they saw the boats being built.

She knew it was a bad idea for Luca to go and spy on them! They could have been halfway to Askala by now. He never listens to her, always thinking he's right. She's going to have to work on that. Prove to him that sometimes people who aren't the Falcon have ideas worth listening to. It's just as well he has that face she can't stop staring at or she'd whoop his stubborn ass.

Somehow, being angry with Luca pushes her on. She's afraid if she lets that feeling go, she's going to fall into a worried heap. What she needs right now is fire in her belly and courage deep in her soul. And maybe a visit from Lady Luck.

"I know a good die cursion," says Tarquin.

"No diversions, okay?" Mercy squeezes her hand. "I can handle this."

"But I really do know a good one." Tarquin keeps her steps fast to keep up with Mercy's pace.

"You promised," Mercy reminds her.

"Alyx said that sometimes in emergency situations it's okay to break a promise," says Tarquin.

Mercy bites down on her tongue to prevent her response. Alyx sold Luca out, which is just about the biggest breach of trust she can imagine. Of course, she'd say something like that. They wouldn't even be out here if it weren't for what Alyx did.

"Keeping your word is important," Mercy says instead. "You should always try to be honorable."

"You can't be honorable when you're dead," Tarquin retorts.

"You can be, actually," says Mercy. "At least, your memory can be. Don't you want people to remember you as a good person?"

"Fine then!" Tarquin grunts. "No diversions."

Mercy smiles, hoping Tarquin just learned a whole lot more than how to pronounce her words.

They fall into silence as the shadows of the boats loom in the distance. Luca had said this was where he was going. She can only hope that it's where he remains.

All is quiet at the camp aside from the murmur of voices. Mercy was sure she was going to find Luca mid-fight and she'd have to dive in and help him. Maybe he's being held inside one of the tents on the outskirts of the encampment?

She tugs on Tarquin's hand and they take a wide arc. There's a lone shrub, its straggly leaves glinting in the light of the stars and Mercy squats behind it.

"You stay here," she whispers to Tarquin. "I'm going to get a closer look."

Tarquin nods at her with wide eyes.

Slipping the knife from her waistband, Mercy grips it tightly. She crouches as she walks closer to the boats, careful to keep her footsteps light.

There are a group of men huddled around a small fire in the middle of the camp, despite the warmth in the air. She squats down behind a partially built boat, holding her breath as she listens.

"How long is it taking them?" a man with a deep voice grumbles. "I'm starving."

"They should've been back yesterday," another replies. "Maybe Gunnar found himself a woman in Fairbanks covered in mosquito bites."

"That sounds more like Vitron's type," the first man says. "He ain't fussy."

There's a round of hooting laughter and grunts.

Mercy scowls in the darkness to hear the way these Neanderthals talk about women. The only comfort is knowing that if they're waiting for Gunnar and Vitron then they're going to be waiting a heck of a long time.

As in, forever.

"Maybe we eat the Falcon," the man with the deep voice says. "I've heard people taste like chicken. But I've never had meself any chicken before to know."

"Falcons are birds. Chickens are birds," the other man says. "Same, same."

"He looked a bit scrawny when I tied him up," says a new voice.

Mercy's heart leaps to hear Luca is tied up somewhere here. And he's alive!

She leaves the men to their sinister laughter and creeps around the perimeter of the camp, eyes wide, looking for any sign of where Luca might be. She's not too keen on the idea of having to peer inside any of the tents.

Then she hears another voice. This one is whispering...

Squatting down, she cranes her neck, straining to make out the words.

"Over here!" the voice says. "By the boat!"

Mercy crawls forward toward the shadow of the boat in front of her, squinting as a cloud passes over the moon, briefly obscuring her vision.

Then she sees him. Lady Luck has paid her a visit after all! Now all she needs is the courage to back it up.

Luca is tied to the stern of a half-built boat by his wrists. She's certain it's him. She'd know his shape anywhere no matter how many shadows are being cast around him.

She edges closer and sees an Outlander asleep on the sand near him, not doing an especially good job of what she can only assume is his guard duty.

Her heart pounds so rapidly that for a moment she worries the sound will wake the guard. Trying to keep her breathing steady, she makes her approach.

When she gets close enough, she puts her hand to Luca's cheek, hardly daring to believe she's actually found him this easily.

"Shh," Luca hushes, like she was actually going to make a sound.

She runs her thumb across his lower cheek before taking her knife and severing the rope wrapped around his wrists.

Luca breathes a soft sigh and quickly presses his lips to Mercy's, before taking her hand and leading her directly away from the boat. The contact energizes her, and she grips his hand, drawing courage from his strength as joy winds its way through her veins.

She did it! She knew something was wrong, she used her smarts and she saved Luca. Tarquin is going to be so impressed! The Peregrine strikes again!

"Tarquin," she whispers, pointing to the shrub she left her behind. Luca nods as they walk as quietly as they can toward it, being sure to keep low.

But when they reach the shrub, Mercy's joy instantly evaporates as dread sinks in her gut.

Tarquin isn't there.

The whites of Luca's eyes flare in the darkness as they turn back toward the camp where there's the unmistakable sound of Tarquin's voice.

"Please misters, have you got any food?" she asks, her voice so loud she's almost shouting.

"Get away from here!" a man growls back. "You shouldn't be here."

"I'm hungry," Tarquin wails. "I'm all on my own with nothing to eat."

"We ain't got nothing to give you." There's no hint of softness in this harsh man's voice. "We ain't got nothing to even give ourselves."

"What is she doing?" Luca whispers urgently. "We have food in our bags!"

Mercy groans. "It's a diversion so I can rescue you."

"She's going to wake the guard," Luca hisses. "He'll see I've escaped!"

"I told her not to." Mercy shakes her head.

"I'm hungry!" Tarquin cries, letting her words dissolve into high-pitched sobs.

"Get out of here!" the man shouts back. "Scoot! Now!"

Tarquin turns and scampers back toward the shrub as Mercy grips hold of Luca's arm, unable to bear the tension another moment. Please, let her get back to them before the men discover they've lost their prisoner.

"He's gone!" a man shouts. "The Falcon's flown the coop!"

Luca stands and dashes toward Tarquin just as she increases her pace. Mercy rises, biting her lip so hard she draws blood. Luca reaches Tarquin and she jumps on his back.

Mercy runs, knowing Luca is faster than her and will easily catch up. She needs all the head start she can get.

"There he is!" comes a loud voice. "He's with the girl!"

And now Mercy's run becomes a full-blown gallop. She flies across the ground in the direction of the beach, hoping those men truly are as hungry and depleted as they claimed to be. Certainly, the sleeping guard seemed to indicate a distinct lack of energy.

Luca is beside Mercy in what feels like an instant and they push themselves faster, knowing there's no room for error here. Getting to that boat is their only hope.

Somehow, they manage to maintain their gap and when Mercy's feet hit soft sand, it's with sweet relief.

Luca gets to the boat first, throwing Tarquin aboard and pushing it into the water. Mercy tries to help but Luca won't hear of it.

"Get in!" he shouts. "Now, Mercy! Now!"

She clambers in, cursing once again how stubborn this man is as he shoves them out into the water.

Mercy readies one oar in the water, steeling herself.

"Tarquin! Get Luca's oar ready!" she calls.

Tarquin quickly does as she's told, seating herself beside Mercy with the second oar gripped in her small hands.

With one final shove of the boat, Luca launches himself aboard and takes over from Tarquin.

Together, Mercy and Luca row, heaving on the oars as the Outlanders run into the water after them. With arms burning in pain, Mercy focuses on the task.

All she has to do now is row. For their lives.

The boat tips and Mercy spins to see a man has grabbed hold of the gunwale and is trying to climb in. Fear climbs up her throat as she faces the reality that they might not be able to get away. Not every race can be won.

"Tarquin!" Luca shouts, shoving the oar in her direction as he leaps from his seat.

"Come on!" says Mercy, nodding at Tarquin's frightened face. "Fierce women know how to row!"

Tarquin looks instantly less afraid as she takes to the task and they surge the boat forward while Luca stomps on the man's hand, sending him flailing back into the waist-deep water.

"Row!" screams Mercy, willing Tarquin to find strength a girl her size can't possibly have. But anything is better than nothing right now. "Row!"

The boat tips wildly once more as Luca fights off another man but Mercy continues to row. That is her job right now and she's going to do it as best she can.

"There's a rip!" Tarquin calls out, pointing. "It'll drag us out."

Mercy jams her oar in the water and shifts their direction, heading where Tarquin's pointing. Her arms scream at her as she drives them forward, feeling an increasing surge of momentum as the rip takes hold of the boat, pulling them out to sea as if using an invisible chain.

"Keep rowing!" she shouts, not feeling safe just yet.

Luca takes the oar from Tarquin and they work their way further out.

It's not until they're a mile off the shoreline that Mercy lets out a long breath and slows her pace. The muscles in her arms are on fire. Her legs are like jelly. Not even a full body hug from Luca is going to be able to restore her energy this time. She's completely spent.

"We did it," says Tarquin. "We got away!"

"No thanks to you," grumbles Luca, reaching for Mercy's oar and insisting on taking the burden of rowing himself. "What were you thinking back there? You should have stayed behind the bush!"

"I was making a diversion," Tarquin says proudly. "And it worked! You got away!"

"Tarquin," Mercy says gently. "I'd already released Luca when you approached those men. You put us all in great danger by not doing what you were told."

"Oh." Tarquin's face crumbles and Mercy hates that her words were what did this to her. But she has to know how important it is to do as she's told. She almost got them all killed. This can't happen again. "I didn't…"

"You did good finding this rip," Mercy says. "That saved us."

"Alyx taught me about rips." Tarquin pulls back her shoulders as she stills her quivering lip. "She showed me how to spot them."

"And I'm glad she did," says Mercy, realizing that's the second time Tarquin's mentioned her big sister recently. She must be starting to miss her.

"You can thank her soon enough," says Luca.

"What do you mean?" Mercy tilts her head. "Alyx isn't in Askala."

"We're going to the Newlands," he says plainly, as if he hasn't just suggested the most ridiculous thing Mercy's ever heard in her entire life.

"Like hell we are!" Mercy stands in the boat and jams her hands on her hips. "They know you're the Falcon. They'll kill you the moment they see you."

"Sit down," he says. "Before you fall out."

"I'm actually not that hopeless." A wave hits the side of the boat, jolting her forward and Mercy plonks herself down before she proves herself wrong. "If you remember correctly, I was the one who saved you just now. You don't always know everything."

"I heard the men talking." Luca continues to row. "They said they were waiting on sap to coat the boats. Where do you think they'd get something like that? There aren't many mangrove pines around here."

"The sap trees!" Tarquin slaps a hand to her mouth. "I've seen them in the Newlands. Corbin's men have big urns that they've been filling with sap."

"Where are they?" Luca asks. "Where do they keep them?"

"In the Round House." Tarquin nods. "They're hidden underneath the seats. Loads and loads of them."

"Why didn't you mention this before?" Luca asks.

"I didn't know it was important!" Tarquin huffs. "And I just told you now."

"It doesn't change anything," says Mercy. "We're still not going back. It's far too dangerous."

"But Mercy, we have to!" Luca stops rowing to show her he means what he's saying. "If we can destroy the sap, we can stop them from taking the boats to Askala. Those boats will sink like stones if they're not coated in that stuff. The acid will tear them apart in no time."

"It's too dangerous!" she says again, wondering if Luca has a hearing problem along with his stubborn problem.

"And it's too dangerous not to," he says. "If we don't destroy the sap, everyone we've ever known is dead. Along with everything we've ever worked for. It's your duty as a Seeker, Mercy. You know it is."

Tears streak their way down Mercy's cheeks as she remembers how proud she'd been of her new understanding of the world. How important it is to do everything they can to protect this planet they call home.

"You're a Seeker, Mercy!" says Tarquin. "A fierce woman Seeker! You're the Peregrine!"

Mercy looks at Tarquin in the moonlight, then locks eyes with Luca. As annoying as it is, she knows he's right. Maybe that's what makes him so stubborn. Because the reality is that usually he knows exactly what he's talking about. Perhaps it's Mercy who needs to listen to Luca more often, not the other way around.

No. That's not right either. They're a team. The fact he's stopped rowing until he has her agreement is proof of that.

"Okay," she says, making the only decision she can, even if it fills her with dread. "We'll go to the Newlands. But as soon as we destroy that sap, we're going home."

LUCA

*L*uca can sense they're close to the Newlands. Despite being surrounded by dark night and black sea, he can almost smell the smoke.

Not long now.

Which means he needs to read the note.

He glances at Mercy, sitting on the bottom of the boat with her head and arms resting on the seat, asleep. Tarquin is curled up beside her, her head in Mercy's lap, also asleep. Luca's glad their exhausted bodies can get some rest before they arrive. The next few hours are going to be tough.

Life or death.

Quietly docking the oars, Luca slips his hand into his pocket, feeling the crumpled piece of paper. His heart thumps hard against his ribs. He wants to read it.

He wants to throw it into the sea and watch it dissolve in its acidic waters.

Mercy's words whisper through his mind. *You need to read it. You need answers.*

And she's right. There will be no more wondering, no more guessing.

Which is the problem. Once Luca knows, he can't unknow. He can't pretend his mother loved him. That she wanted him.

Yanking the note out of his pocket, Luca unwraps it. His breathing is harsh and his hands unsteady as he unfurls the last remaining folds. It was over two decades ago that these creases were made, that these words were written and hidden in the small wooden shell.

Will this be a history he'll be glad to learn?

The white paper unfolds, a pale strip of truth in the blackness that's swallowed Luca. Despite the night, the twinkling stars provide enough light to make out the scrawled words.

A single line.

A handful of sentences.

Luca sucks in a breath so sharp, it feels like daggers have lodged in his throat.

"No," he moans when he reads the last word.

"Luca?" Mercy sits up, frowning at him in the dark. "Is everything okay?"

He shoves the note back in his pocket, not sure his choked throat can utter the words he just read.

It can't be...

Mercy slips her legs out from under Tarquin and comes to sit next to him. "Luca? If you've changed your mind, we can still go back to Askala."

Luca shakes his head. "No," he says hoarsely and quickly clears his throat. They need to go to the Newlands more than ever. He grips her hand, anchoring himself to her warmth. "We have to do this."

Mercy shuffles closer. "Then what's wrong?"

Everything.

But Luca's not ready to say it aloud. For someone else to know what he just learned. Instead, he leans down and kisses her, his mouth seeking her heat. Her love.

And Mercy gives it to him. Generously. Unconditionally. Heart and soul.

Luca loses himself in everything good in his life, in proof that someone can love him and not leave him. It humbles him.

It has him falling another lifetime in love with her.

He pulls back, pressing his forehead against hers. "I'll tell you later, okay?"

Mercy hesitates and he wonders if she's guessed it has to do with the note. "Okay," she says quietly.

Relieved he can push away the knowledge that just tipped his world upside down, Luca presses another quick kiss against her lips. "Thank you. We need to stay focused right now."

Tarquin stirs and Mercy pulls back. "What's the plan?"

Straightening, Luca grabs the oars and starts rowing again. "Tarquin said the sap is in clay jars in the Round House. We need to get in, empty them, and get out, all without being seen or heard."

"Sounds easy," Mercy mutters, and Luca can just imagine the eyeroll.

"You two could stay in the boat, keeping it ready for a quick getaway," he offers.

"Nice try," she huffs. "But the quicker we take that sap out of the equation, the better."

Of course she's right.

And if they can stop the Outlanders' impending attack on Askala, then they have to try.

Tarquin shuffles then sits up. "We're almost there. I can smell it."

Luca's not surprised she picked it up, too. Any child in the Outlands who has survived as long as Tarquin has, did so because their senses are permanently on high alert.

"We need to be quiet and fast," Luca instructs. "Okay?"

The two agreements that reach him in the dark are solemn.

Luca wishes he could give them some reassurance, some sense that this isn't as dangerous as it sounds. But he can't.

Being caught will mean certain death for Luca.

He refuses to consider it might be for them, too.

They're almost at the Newlands before they see it. The dark hulking mass becomes visible only a few moments before the bottom of their boat scrapes over sand.

They're here.

No one speaks as Luca silently slips into the water and drags the boat up the beach. He listens with everything he's got, trying to hear whether there's anyone patrolling the shore. Whether they've been seen.

But there's only the muted crash of the waves as he follows them up the sand. The boat crunches as he draws it up so the bow is out of the water and Luca freezes.

Still nothing.

Mercy and Tarquin move in close as they creep toward the tree line.

When Tarquin gasps, Luca's by her side in a second, shoving her behind him. Every cell in his being is ready to fight.

"Tarquin?" asks a quiet voice, achingly filled with hope.

Tarquin darts around Luca and is in Alyx's arms before he can blink. Mercy moves closer to him as the sound of Alyx's stifled tears reach them.

"Are you angry with me?" Tarquin whispers.

"I was, and I probably will be, but right now I'm too happy," replies Alyx, her hushed voice full of emotion. "I'm so glad you came back, Tarquin."

"Me, too," says Tarquin. Luca feels her hand grab his and he realizes she's back by his side. "But we're here for the sap."

Luca imagines Alyx's large blue eyes are darting between the three of them and he wonders what she's thinking. How does she feel that Tarquin just called the three of them 'we'? That she's back by Luca's side?

He stills. Does she think they told Tarquin that Alyx betrayed Luca?

"I see," she says, even quieter than before. "You need to know the other Seekers are gone. Gust died, and Hawk has returned to Askala."

Luca blinks. It's sad to hear the Gust didn't survive, but at least Hawk and Sam returned home.

"We need to try and stop this," he states flatly.

There's a pause and Mercy shifts closer to Luca. He wonders if she's aware of her unconscious show of support.

"I'll help you," Alyx says resolutely.

Luca doesn't respond, unsure of how he feels about having her on their side, especially with the other Seekers gone. Alyx betrayed him once before. And although he can understand that she was desperate, he'll never trust her again.

He tightens his grip on Mercy's hand. "Let's do this."

They make their way through the forest as silently as possible, pausing often to stop and listen. The canopy above them blocks out what little light the stars provided, leaving Luca wired and tense. A Newlander could be standing only a few feet away and they wouldn't know.

They reach the edge of the clearing that circles the village. Stopping once again, Luca waits and watches. There's no movement. No noise. Not even a breeze.

Frowning, he waits a few more seconds. A breeze would've been good. Wind, even some rain, would have covered up the sounds of their movements.

"Silent and fast," Luca breathes to the others before stepping into the clearing.

He barely allows his feet to touch the ground as he runs, crouched, to the Round House. He can hear the panting breaths and muffled footsteps of the others. With each faint sound, his heart jerks.

Reaching the central hut, Luca presses himself against the

rough wall, watching the outlines of the others as they do the same. More strained seconds of listening.

Nothing.

He slips into the Round House like a shadow, quickly scanning the hut. The dying fire in the center of the room gives him enough light to see that it's empty apart from the silver statue of Ronan.

"Clear," he whispers.

Mercy, Tarquin and Alyx enter behind him, eyes all wide with a mixture of fear and resolve. Tarquin ducks to the closest wall, bending down to look under the bench seat. She pauses, then waves her hand underneath. It doesn't connect with an urn.

She scoots right, repeating the movement and finding more emptiness and air.

Mercy rushes forward, scanning under the benches on the other side. She turns around to look at Luca, her eyes heavy with dread.

Luca's stomach sinks so hard and fast the painful jolt has him gritting his teeth. The jars of sap aren't there.

Sweet Terra, they're too late!

Alyx walks to the center of the hut, stopping at the edge of the fire. "That's why they were all so quiet today."

Luca looks up, seeing what she sees. A large, metal barrel is sitting on a tripod over the fire.

"They're preparing it," he breathes.

Before the sap of the mangrove pine is painted onto boats, it's boiled and reduced to a thick tar.

"Yes!" Mercy whispers in excitement.

Which means they're not too late.

What's more, all they need to do is tip over the barrel and the entire supply of sap will be ruined.

Luca reaches forward, extending his arm over the fire only

to hiss when his hand touches the metal. He draws back, his fingers scalded.

Mercy presses a hand to his arm but he shakes his head. They don't have time to tend to a minor burn. Luca looks around, trying to figure out how they can get to the barrel. A moment later, a plank of wood waves before his face.

He looks down to find Tarquin grinning up at him. "Push," she says simply.

Luca ruffles her hair in response as he grins right back. That's exactly what they need to do.

He takes the piece of wood, swinging it so one end is pointing at the barrel. He glances over his shoulder at Mercy, communicating without words what they need to do.

Tip it. Ruin the sap.

Run.

She nods resolutely, grabbing the other end as Alyx and Tarquin do the same.

Luca shoves the tip in between the barrel and the metal stand it's sitting on. The timber jams in, but not much. Jaw tight, Luca quickly finds another, shorter piece of wood. He looks back at the others. "I'll lift it a little," he whispers urgently. This is taking too much time. "You slot it in."

Three heads nod in the flickering light. Luca jams the wood under the lip of the barrel. He pushes up, expecting it to be heavy.

It doesn't move.

Stepping in closer, sweat instantly beading on his brow as the heat from the embers rises around him, Luca presses his shoulder against the barrel. The smell of burnt cloth hits his nostrils as his shirt singes, but he ignores it. Pressing his feet down, he pushes up again.

This time, the barrel lifts an inch and Mercy and the others quickly slip the length of timber in.

Luca steps back, patting at his shoulder, glad the tendrils of smoke rising up are from his shirt and not his skin. He grabs the wooden plank, the sense of urgency multiplying.

Tip it. Ruin the sap.

Run.

He nods at the others. "Pull down."

Tarquin leaps up, gripping it and dangling off the end, using what little weight she has. Mercy and Alyx wrap their arms around, drawing down, too.

Luca moves closer to the fire, combining the power of his muscles with his own weight.

The barrel lifts an inch. Then another.

"It's working!" Tarquin hisses with excitement.

They just have to get the barrel to the point of no return and then gravity will do the rest for them. Another pull on the lever. Another inch higher.

Pushing the plank further under the barrel, they heave again and it rises a little more. Now at an angle, Luca wonders if the sap is getting close to the lip. He almost reaches out and pushes the barrel himself. They're so close.

Crack. The plank snaps, twisting and slipping to the side, almost yanking all three of them off balance.

But the *clang* that reverberates through the hut has them all freezing. Luca spins around to see the statue teetering—the other end of the length of wood must've hit it. He rushes forward but the gravity that was supposed to tip the barrel has already grabbed hold of Ronan, yanking the heavy effigy down.

The statue *bangs* against the wall of the hut, then crashes through the timber seat before slamming to the floor.

Luca's heart feels like it's stalled. Stopped. Hung in suspended animation as he tries to grasp how desperately they've failed.

Three sets of terrified eyes stare at him in the half-light.

"Run!" he whispers hoarsely.

Dropping the wood, Luca's at the door in a few strides.

Maybe if they're quick enough, maybe if the Newlanders don't realize what's happening, they'll be able to get back to the boat.

He'll go first, make sure the way is clear, then let Mercy and others out. Once they're out of the village, he can come up behind.

One step out the door is all he's afforded. The strike to the side of Luca's head is a hammer of pain. He drops to the ground, barely managing to break his fall with his hands. He gasps, blinks, tries to claw his way out of the agony.

But it's reverberating through his head, detonating along every nerve. Darkness beckons him with the promise of oblivion.

He holds onto consciousness with one word. Mercy.

And then another.

Tarquin.

Even Alyx's name slips through his mind.

If he's knocked out, they're all dead.

"Bring his body inside," growls a voice.

And then Luca's moving, his body shifting and feet dragging. A moment later, he's collapsed on the ground again, his mind a whirlpool of darkness. The current's too hard to fight.

The pain's winning.

"Luca," Mercy moans.

The agony in her voice has Luca pushing himself up.

What he knows…it can save them.

"He's alive," whispers Alyx.

"Not for long," someone snaps.

Luca looks up, having already recognized the hate-filled voice. Corbin stands above him, eyes alive with anticipation as he draws back a foot and ploughs it into Luca's chest.

Luca groans as he crumples into the dirt, a fresh wave of agony crashing over the first.

"No!" Mercy screams. "You leave him—"

"Shut up, bitch."

The sound of a slap has Luca rolling over, his mouth working. But his collapsed lungs are still fighting for air. Mercy's face has snapped to the side, a trickle of blood appearing at the corner of her mouth.

"You thought you could stop this?" Corbin sneers. "So much for you people being smart."

Through slitted eyes, Luca sees several Newlanders are now in the Round House. Each one holds a spear. Each one has the desire to kill stamped on their face.

His gaze flicks past Corbin and Raiden. There's only one person who can save them.

Luca watches as Grace appears beside her husband, placing a hand on his arm. She always had a calming, controlling presence around him. It's exactly what they need right now.

She shakes her head sadly as she takes them in. "You shouldn't have come back." She lifts her chin. "You can't stop something that started over two decades ago."

"They need to die." Corbin's face lights up. "They need to burn, just like the others will."

Mercy raises her chin, brave even in the face of death. "Askala is stronger than you think."

"Nor will they give up their riches without a fight," Grace agrees. "Which is why you must die. We cannot have them warned."

Mercy's face twists with desperation. "What you're doing is wrong—"

Raiden's eyes flash a warning. "The Commander has spoken."

For some reason those words have Alyx's head dropping. Is it with resignation?

Or...guilt?

Mercy glares at Corbin, but it's Grace who steps forward.

"My son is right, I have spoken."

Sweet Terra. Grace is the Commander.

Suddenly, it all makes sense. Corbin never seemed smart enough to coordinate a war that's far more deadly than Askala could ever imagine. He's too blood-thirsty. Too impulsive.

But that means…

Luca blinks, trying to clear his pain-filled mind. Suddenly, his plan isn't so foolproof. If Grace is the Commander, she's been working toward destroying Askala for a long time.

She's already learned death and loss are necessary sacrifices.

But it's the only chance they have.

Luca pushes up so he's kneeling. Corbin instantly raises a foot, but Luca speaks before the blow is born.

"You won't kill us."

Corbin pauses, confused. It's all Luca needs. He removes the note from his pocket, the words on there already branded in his mind.

I'm sorry. Had to leave you. I hope you find me one day. My name is Grace.

He looks to the woman who's his mother, noting the way her eyes widen at the sight of the crumpled slip of paper. "Because I'm your son."

THE END
Ready for the next installment in The Thaw Chronicles?
Check out Book 8, EXPOSE, now!
http://mybook.to/ExposeThaw

BOOK EIGHT - EXPOSE

BEYOND THE THAW

Only the chosen shall seek.

Sam, Hawk, Luca and Mercy.

They were meant to bring Askala to the world. Now the war is coming to Askala.

Sam, Hawk, Luca and Mercy must return home to protect the society they were bred to champion. But how do they defend peace loving Askala from the greatest threat yet?

As secrets are revealed and loyalties are tested, everyone will be forced to question who is friend and who is foe. The Commander is far more dangerous than anyone realized. The Outlanders are divided about whose side they're really on. And Askala is unprepared for an attack.

In the ocean separating the two worlds, the final battle will decide the future of not only Askala, but who will control the Newlands. Sam, Hawk, Luca and Mercy will have to accomplish the impossible—unity.

Lovers of Divergent and The Hunger Games will be blown away by the breathtaking conclusion to Beyond the Thaw from USA Today best-selling author Tamar Sloan and award-winning author Heidi Catherine.

Grab your copy now!
http://mybook.to/ExposeThaw

WANT TO STAY IN TOUCH?

If you'd like to be the first for to hear all the news from Tamar and Heidi, be sure to sign up to our newsletter. Subscribers receive bonus content, early cover reveals and sneaky snippets of upcoming books. We'd love you to join us!

SIGN UP HERE:

https://sendfox.com/tamarandheidi

ABOUT THE AUTHORS

Tamar Sloan hasn't decided whether she's a psychologist who loves writing, or a writer with a lifelong fascination with psychology. She must have been someone pretty awesome in a previous life (past life regression indicated a Care Bear), because she gets to do both. When not reading, writing or working with teens, Tamar can be found with her husband and two children enjoying country life in their small slice of the Australian bush.

Heidi Catherine loves the way her books give her the opportunity to escape into worlds vastly different to her own life in the burbs. While she quite enjoys killing her characters (especially the awful ones), she promises she's far better behaved in real life. Other than writing and reading, Heidi's current obsessions include watching far too much reality TV with the excuse that it's research for her books.

MORE SERIES TO FALL IN LOVE WITH...

ALSO BY TAMAR SLOAN AND HEIDI CATHERINE

The Sovereign Code

Elemental Games

ALSO BY TAMAR SLOAN

Keepers of the Grail

Keepers of the Light

Keepers of the Chalice

Keepers of Excalibur

Zodiac Guardians

Descendants of the Gods

Prime Prophecy

ALSO BY HEIDI CATHERINE

The Kingdoms of Evernow

The Soulweaver

www.ingramcontent.com/pod-product-compliance
Lightning Source LLC
Chambersburg PA
CBHW031555240626
47153CB00002B/515